CW01662359

This novel is pure fiction and it has been written to entertain - nothing more. Prisons are a far more serious business and the grave challenges of self-harm and violence are tackled every day by staff and by prisoners who are trained by the Samaritans to work as Listeners. The content of this book is in no way designed to demean the impressive and essential daily achievements of either of these groups. In fact, I hope it highlights the immense challenges they face every single day.

Trouble on the Wing is my first novel and I'm fantastically grateful for the support and advice I received from my learned ex-colleagues and friends. You know who you are ...

The front cover has been created by the absurdly talented Rupert Smissen (www.rupertsmissen.co.uk).

Chapter 1

It's not yet eight o'clock and most of the inhabitants of B Wing, HMP Hatcham, are still locked up. Probably still asleep. What life there is right now consists of a dozen or so prisoners queuing for the Medication room - near where B Wing meets the prison's impressive central atrium - and, forty yards down the other end, a handful more out and about working as cleaners. Some are in the Servery, sound like frustrated percussionists the way they crash, bang, wallop the oversized trays and pans. Another wields an ancient-looking buffer to polish the lino floor, make the cigarette burns shine.

A prison officer starts climbing the steel stairs that zig-zag upwards. Stumbles as she picks her way through Wet Floor signs. She is young, the officer, but looks unhealthy - her neat features, trim figure undone by lank-looking hair and a sallow, almost yellow complexion. She is also on the skinny side. Lacks the curves to test the seams of her black, white uniform.

Up to the fourth floor she trudges. There, starts leafing through a bright orange document before shutting the thing and strolling along the B4 landing. She unlocks the door of a cell.

"Good morning gents," she says. Then, to an overweight man on the bottom bunk: "How are you getting on?"

The man looks up but does not speak.

"Any problems, let me know, alright? I'm on here all day today. We'll be getting you out for showers and phone calls, hopefully. Just waiting for Meds to finish."

Without waiting for an answer, she shuts the door with a mighty clunk and, leaning on the balustrade that runs around the landing, begins writing in the orange file. But hardly has her biro begun moving when something stops her. Convulses her like a jolt of electricity. Letting out a gasp, she drops the document onto the floor and turns her head towards a cell two doors away. Flinches as words - more rasping words - penetrate the steel barrier.

"That's right, Jenny. It's me. I've come back for you. Next time you open this door Officer Hughes … I want my welcome present."

Panic on her face, the woman bends down, scrambles stupidly to pick up the file.

"Yeah, you practise on your knees for me, you little slut. Make my time here nice and easy. Because if you don't ... well, we both know what will happen. Don't we Jenny?"

The voice turns into a deep snigger. And as it does, the officer has to use the railing to pull herself up. Staggers like a drunkard towards the gated area at the end of the landing. Reaching the gate, she puts in the wrong key at first, has to try another. Shakes so much, the thing actually rattles inside the keyhole. Finally she makes it in. Manages to turn the lock. Almost throws herself onto a plastic chair.

For minutes, she does not move. Just sits there, forehead on the school-type table. Only when another officer arrives at the top of the stairs does she finally look up. Peers at him with puffy eyes.

"You alright?" he says, letting himself in.

"Yeah, I'm OK. Just feeling a bit rough, that's all."

"Who was that laughing? I was on the threes and thought I heard..."

"Oh ... oh, him! Just some nutter, I expect. You know what they're like."

He knits his brow.

"Listen. I've got a nicking this morning. Got to be down the Seg at half nine."

Jenny Hughes looks at her watch.

"You're on an Early as well, aren't you? That means I'm on my own here this afternoon ... OK, well let's get them out now, give them showers, phone calls. Stop them going mad."

He gets out his keys, is about to unlock the landing when she calls out after him.

"Like I said, I'm feeling quite rough. So, er ... I'm going to stay in this gated bit for now. Make some entries in the prisoners' files and this ACCT," she says, holding up the orange file. "That kind of thing. Any trouble, I'm right here."

Association passes uneventfully. The prisoners on the B Wing fours mill around seeming more than their forty-two number. They have showers, they argue over the PIN phones, they lean over the steel railing to take in the godforsaken view. The male officer stands half-way down the landing where a mini-bridge joins the two galleries, spends most of the hour fielding questions from frustrated prisoners. Why has my mail not arrived? Why won't they give me a job? Why is the money my nan sent in not in my prison account? Usual stuff.

Jenny Hughes stays in the gated area. Busies herself with the files whenever her colleague looks her way. Most of the time, though, seems more interested in the table, as if lost somewhere within its grey laminate surface. Rarely looks up. One time she does, she jumps a mile. Grabs a pen as if it was a sword, makes her knuckles go white. It's when a heavyset Hispanic-looking prisoner - veins bulging out of his neck like worms, a huge eagle tattooed across his back - appears just beyond the wall of bars. He smirks when she flinches. Then kisses the air before lazily pulling the towel from around his neck, ambling heavily into the showers.

At lunch, between half twelve and half one, when all the prisoners are locked up and the other fours officer has gone home, rejoined the world, Jenny Hughes joins her colleagues in the staffroom at the bottom of the stairs. Asks, between chews of her sandwich, if someone will swap with her in the afternoon, let her work another landing. But they laugh, her fellow officers. Joke that of course she wants to swap, everyone hates the fours. It's so far away! No-one seems to notice the desperation in her eyes, the quivering in her voice.

Staffing is tight in the afternoon. So tight that B Wing's Supervising Officer says he only wants the bare bones: ACCT checks, cell fabric checks, emergencies.

"Let's just get through it, guys."

The staff could not agree more. Exchange reassuring nods as they disperse. Jenny Hughes nods too, begins climbing back up to the fours. On the way, pats the bulky radio on her belt and feels for her whistle. Hesitates when she gets to the top. Finally walking along the landing to check the prisoner on suicide watch, she again leans on the railing while she makes an entry in his ACCT. No voice this time.

Depositing the document back in the gated area, she returns to the landing. Starts carrying out cell fabric checks. Goes into the first cell, makes sure everything in it works, from the taps to the emergency call button. Then checks the window bars have not been sawn through, or tunnels dug. Moves onto the second cell. After that, the third.

Half-way around the landing, she checks the cell of a first-timer who came in a day or two ago. He looks unremarkable, the man - average height, normal build. Even has a bland face unless you count the scar down his right temple, the light tan of his skin that speaks of sunnier climes somewhere down the line. Age-wise, must be mid-thirties. More, maybe, going by the stone-hard eyes, the widow's peak.

She asks him if anything is not working then, without ceremony, starts taking down pages of topless women stuck with toothpaste onto the wall.

"My cellmate's," the prisoner mumbles, sounding every inch a Londoner.

"Of course they are, Mr Djemil. Well tell your cellmate he can have the breast, not the nipple. It's Prison Rules."

As she goes to leave the cell, the prisoner swings his legs off the bed.

"Just a sec, Miss. I've got an appointment down Healthcare at half two. Will you come back, let me out?"

She looks at her watch. Tells him it's coming up to quarter past now, she'll still be doing cell checks. So what she'll do is leave his door unlocked. He can let himself out, go down to the ones himself.

"Only shut your door, mind," she adds, before walking out, leaving it ajar.

She spins out the process of checking the next cell. Trades small talk with its two meek, mild foreign occupants. Lingers while she checks the taps and taps the bars. Eventually, though, leaves their cell as well. Shutting the door, returns to the deserted landing. Stands there, eyes fastened on the gated area at the end. She looks apprehensive. A couple of times blows out her cheeks.

"Right, then," she whispers.

She approaches the next cell. Seems mesmerised as she contemplates the card outside: Lopez - High Risk, SINGLE CELL. Checking her radio again, she peers through the inspection flap before shutting it.

And goes in.

The Hispanic-looking prisoner who blew her a kiss in the morning is sprawled on the lower bunk. He does not react when she says: "Just doing a fabric check." Nor when she starts turning on the taps, checking for holes in the wall and tries the cell bell. Even so, she looks jumpy. At one point, as she thudding the window bars with the heel of her hand, she wheels around for no apparent reason. Catches the eye of the hulking figure. Immediately starts to leave the tiny room.

But half-way to the door, a strong hand grabs her knee and stronger arms get her in a bear-like grip. Jumping off the bunk, the prisoner pins Jenny Hughes against the wall opposite. At the same time jabs the door with his foot so it is almost shut. Shut enough to hide what he will do next.

"Give me my welcome present, you little slut," he says, yanking her by the hair and pushing her down. The angle, the force put her on the floor in a second. With his free hand, Lopez pulls down his tracksuit bottoms.

"Do it now, or I will fucking slice you, you little slut."

Jenny Hughes's mouth does open. But not in the way the prisoner wants. Instead she lets out a muffled cry. It travels only a dozen yards.

But it is enough.

The door slams wide and the new prisoner, Djemil, is suddenly in the cell. Lopez reacts immediately. Shoving Jenny Hughes out of the way, he bludgeons the intruder with a headbutt to the face. Lands a thundering right to his body. Or at least, he tries to. But Djemil is too quick. The headbutt, he dodges with a dart sideways. The punch, he lets fly into empty air by the door. Now it's his turn. And he is fabulously fast. So fast, the bigger man doesn't even start to react. Djemil fells him with two lightning-quick moves - a two-finger jab, then a punch to the chin. Jab! Punch!! Within a second, Lopez is a bloody-nosed heap on the floor.

Eerily, Djemil calms down as quickly. Feeling the beaten man's pulse, he seems to decide he will live, then moves to the window where Jenny Hughes is cowering. Reaching under her shoulders, he gently pulls her up. Half-ushers, half-drags her out of the cell. As the heavy door slams behind them, the prison officer bursts into tears. Collapses, sobbing, onto the ground.

"I hope you're OK, Miss," says the new prisoner, looking awkward as he stands over the officer.

It takes a while for Jenny Hughes to recover her composure. When she finally does, Djemil accompanies her down the stairs. Watches as she lets herself into the B Wing staffroom. Then walks quietly away.

* * * * * * * * *

In the middle of a tarmac yard just to the right of a drain cover with its raised concentric squares, lips pucker, blow out a perfect halo of smoke. But the man beneath the halo is no saint. He is Governor Tony McKenzie, Hatcham's Head of Security. Tall - six four on a good day - he has a shaved head, even fiercer-looking face. Cuts an imposing figure as he stands there alone and splays his shiny shoes.

Up close, though, the impression is more mixed. Because despite the fierce physiognomy, there is a distinct look of hardship in the long haggard face. Furrows criss-cross his brow while bags hang heavy below the eyes, suggest a non-stop onslaught of nightmare shifts. As for the eyes themselves, they shine out defiance. Suggest an expectation of adversity - at the same time, a ready resistance to it. A punctured beach ball with a rock inside comes to mind.

The view around McKenzie is spectacularly bleak. Behind him, five metres twenty of the greyest concrete in London rises up, massive and unyielding, adamant that life's pleasures do not exist. Never have done. In front, things are not much better. Because there, grand and monstrous as the British empire, stands one of Hatcham's four giant wings, with its endless rows of cell windows, its millions of bricks looking like they've been battling weather, fumes, pretty much everything since they were laid over a century and a half ago. But at least the speckled brickwork creates a bit of visual interest. The odd human shape through the bars, a hint of life.

The Rothmans cigarette arcs back up to the ashen lips. Taking one last drag, McKenzie flicks the butt onto the ground, immediately gets out another. Sucks in hard on this second cigarette, hollowing out his cheeks. As he does, there is a clunk to his right - the sound of hefty keys turning a high-quality lock. He turns, McKenzie. Looks in the direction of a wiry, fairly short figure emerging from the Reception building. Seconds later Governor Chris Jenkins - Hatcham's Head of Residential - has come to a standstill alongside, is rummaging around the inside of his shiny suit jacket. Finally producing a pack of superking menthols, he lights one, then shuts his Zippo with a teenage flourish.

He's a bit older-looking, this second governor - nudging fifty, you'd guess - but markedly less worn. As if life does not get to him the same way, or burdens find a way of sliding off his narrower shoulders. His movements are sharper too, his eyes altogether beadier, brighter.

For a while the two prison governors stand side by side in silence. Seem happy just to get their nicotine fix. Conduct their 'security check', as they put it.

But then Jenkins speaks.

"Well well well. Who'd have thought it? Our top dog Senor Lopez cut down to size!"

He lisps the 'Lopez' when he says this, draws an imaginary cape across his chest. But McKenzie does not smile. Instead takes another drag. Sounds thoughtful when he answers.

"This Djemil guy, Chris. Have you met him?"

"The one who clumped Lopez?"

"Yeah."

"Not met him, Tony. Why?"

Another halo.

"I was talking to Jenny Hughes about it. Bumped into her in the Gate last night, on the way out. She was saying the way he came in and dealt with Lopez was - how did she put it again? - 'like a fucking ninja', that was it."

"Well you don't hit someone on the head in slow motion. Tends not to work very well."

"Ha ha. You're a funny man, you know that? But what I think she was getting at, Jenny Hughes ... she said her brother's a boxer. Handy middleweight, by all accounts. And the way Djemil came in, dodged whatever Lopez threw at him, used his jab ... well, he was just like her brother, she said."

"So there you go, Tony. Djemil's obviously of a pugilistic persuasion himself. In here trying to keep his head down, sees something happen, feels obliged to intervene. But if you're curious, why not do a bit of digging? See what come's up."

"Have done. The guy's got no previous offences, and there's nothing on the Police National Computer either. I got our Police Liaison Officer to run a check. And I even went to speak to Djemil myself. Yesterday, doing my rounds as duty dog. Told him I was checking he was alright, all that crap."

"And?"

"And he was polite, but gave nothing away. Smooth surfaces all round."

"Did you ask him where he learnt to fight like that?"

"I did, as it goes. 'On the road' - that's all he said."

"That's helpful," says Jenkins, looking at his watch. "Come on. Time to get our arses kicked."

A final drag, followed by a rotation of polished size nines, size twelves on sodden tarmac. Turning to go in, they walk in single file across the yard. As Jenkins draws his keys to open the door of Reception, McKenzie is still muttering on behind him.

"The question is, what road?"

* * * * * * * * *

Reeking of smoke, the two governors are among the last to arrive for the eight-thirty Morning Meeting in the prison's Boardroom. Join the assortment of fifteen or so managers seated around a long beech table - some of them in uniform, most in civvies. One woman dressed as a nurse draws doodles on a sheet of paper in front of her. Another, wearing a tracksuit, has her eyes fixed firmly on the door. A third person, a man in a dog collar, doesn't stop laughing as he talks to the young woman at his side. McKenzie, bits of paper in hand, nods here and there as he finds his seat, jangling his key chain as he sits down. Jenkins takes a place opposite. Straight away begins nattering to the tracksuited woman to his right.

For a minute or so, muted chat fills the room. Then, suddenly, the faces look up, posteriors shuffle and the murmur fades. A middle-aged man is walking into the Boardroom. With his slender frame and side parting, and wearing a grey suit, dark blue tie and snazzy metal-framed glasses, he looks more like a senior civil servant than a prison governor. Allowing someone else to shut the door, he approaches the head of the table. Shows no sign of haste as, with two skinny arms, he pulls out a chair before lowering himself down and shuffling the thing forwards. Thus ensconced, he produces an expensive-looking pen. Beams out white teeth - indiscriminate as a lighthouse. Left, right, left.

"Good morning everyone," says John Simmering, Hatcham's Governing Governor. "What a lovely gentle drizzle for a Tuesday morning! Right. Who was duty governor yesterday?"

The top man's question gets no response at first. Only a sad little chirrup from a couple of radios and empty stares back. But then a broad hand waves halfway down the long table. Eyes swivel towards the large angular head belonging to Tony McKenzie.

"That was me, Governor," he says, the hand now stroking his crew cut. "Not too bad a day overall. Right ..."

He coughs, McKenzie, then scrunches up his eyes while he looks down at his Duty Governor's daily report. The room falls quiet and fainter noises find voice: a key unlocking the battered wooden door right outside the Boardroom; two prisoners holding a conversation through cell windows which, judging by the shrieks, must be twenty yards apart; a whispered "Sorry!" as a late arrival to the meeting opens the door onto a colleague's legs. The sonic mosaic caresses cochleae. Lets McKenzie gather his thoughts.

"Unlocked at eleven thirty-four, had eighty-two discharges, eighty-four admissions, locked up at eleven thirty-six. Two new staff off sick, making a total of four sick for the day. Forty-three prisoners on suicide watch, three of them new, and we've got eight ACCT reviews due today. Twelve prisoners on anti-bullying, and there are eighteen adjudications, twelve of them new. Issues yesterday ..."

His eyes work through the summary sheet which he filled in, shattered, late last night.

"A fairly quiet morning. Nothing, in fact, till fourteen twenty-six hours when we had what could have been a really serious incident. Officer Jenny Hughes on B Wing was grabbed and pinned against the wall by prisoner Carl Lopez HA1477. It happened in his cell on the fours and she was alone. Mr Lopez was making demands of a sexual nature apparently. Understandably Jenny Hughes panicked. Didn't raise the alarm. Couldn't think straight, she said."

McKenzie does not see - he's busy reading - but Simmering has gone ashen.

"Fortunately she was saved by a prisoner. A new guy called Yusuf Djemil HA2684. When she screamed, it seems Mr Djemil came to her aid.

As we know ..." - McKenzie nods at Jenkins over the table, a been-there-done-that kind of nod - "... Mr Lopez can be a handful. But somehow Mr Djemil managed to get him, er ... under control. Very quickly, by all accounts."

"It sounds like he mullered him," says Simmering, relief in his voice.

"I was trying to be more PC, Governor. But you're right. Mr Lopez was out for the count. In fact the nurse was worried about him for a while. But he came to. He's OK."

Simmering taps the table top.

"Mr Lopez ... Are we talking about the same one? Came here from the Scrubs last year? Spent most of the time down the CSU?"

"That's him, Governor. Last time we had Mr Lopez, he was a six-man unlock, a real control problem. So Jenny Hughes is incredibly lucky this Mr Djemil character was there. Whoever he is."

"Where's he now, Mr Lopez?"

"Down the Seg - sorry, the CSU. Jenny Hughes was adamant she didn't want it referred to the police, for some reason. Wasn't even going to place Mr Lopez on report at first."

He reports on a few more incidents, McKenzie. A fight down the gym - "just handbags, Governor" - an act of self-harm on B Wing. Finally an intelligence-led cell search on another B Wing prisoner. A mobile phone and some tablets were found.

"And, er ... that was it, Governor."

"Thank you, Tony," says Simmering, tapping the table a few more times. He turns to the Head of Residential. "There seems to be quite a bit happening on B Wing, Chris. It only takes up fifteen per cent of the prison, yet must account for about half our incidents these days. Think we need to shuffle a few people around?"

"We would if we could, Governor," Jenkins answers. "And you're absolutely right. B Wing's bubbling right now. We've got a few tricky customers on there like Lopez ..."

"Mr Lopez."

"Sorry, Mr Lopez. Problem is, most of the problem children can't go anywhere else because they've already been round the houses. So we're just going to have to manage them as best we can on B Wing. I've discussed it with Tony. We reckon these prisoners are the muscle for someone else. Throwing their weight around for a Mr Big who's controlling all the drugs that are coming in."

Simmering leans back as if he needs a rest.

"Well it's something we need to find out," he says. "B Wing is jeopardising the stability of the whole establishment at the moment."

He clasps his hands, looks sternly down the table.

"I don't need to remind everyone that we continue to be in a vicious circle of violence and self-harm in the prison, and the victims are not just prisoners but staff as well. And unfortunately, now that we find ourselves in that cycle, it's going to be very difficult to get out of it. Especially as staff sickness has increased and - correct me if I'm wrong, Chris - the staff on the wings are getting a bit less sure of themselves. Becoming a bit reluctant to enforce the rules."

A couple of nods along the table.

"Carry on like this, and things will only get harder," continues Simmering, unclasping his hands and sitting up. "The good news is there is one thing at the root of it all and that is the number of drugs coming into the prison. If we find out how to put a stop to that, we'll be able to stop the rot. But to do that, we need the intelligence. And that means all of us need to be helping the Security team. We need to be giving them our eyes and ears from all over the prison. So please, after this meeting, make sure you reinforce this message to your staff. And please remind them of the importance of Security Intelligence Reports. Passing on any snippet of information they come across, however small or insignificant it might appear."

The lighthouse beam switches on again. Pointing it McKenzie's way, Simmering asks in a voice suddenly full of sweetness and light: "Anything else, Tony?"

"Er, just the Security meeting, Governor. Today, two o'clock. Here, in the Boardroom."

"Good!" Simmering booms. "I look forward to some better news on the Mandatory Drug Rate! I know the Security team have been pulling out all the stops."

McKenzie does not answer. Does not even smile. Instead, as Simmering begins the ritual of going round the room, asking all the other managers, one by one, if they have any issues to raise, the Head of Security kicks the beady-eyed man sitting opposite. Holds a gun-shaped hand to his temple. Pulls the trigger.

* * * * * * * * *

The B Wing fours are out on association and the top floor hums to the comfortable rhythm of routine. Slamming cell doors, orders shouted out by confident-sounding staff, the backdrop chitter-chatter of prisoners - on the phones, to staff, among themselves. It is distinctive, their London street-talk. At the same time, strangely uniform, with its edgy worldliness, its scything cynicism. Defeat dressed as bravado.

Yusuf Djemil HA2684 leans on the railings outside his cell. Foot resting on the bar at the bottom, he looks more like a passenger on a ferry looking wistfully out to sea than a prisoner. Even when some muscle-bound giant walks past him, starts cussing, telling him he is dead meat - even then Djemil does not flinch. Just looks back at the giant with obvious disinterest. Almost as if he does not see him.

But then something does make Djemil look right - the approaching figure of Officer Jenny Hughes. She has a piece of paper in her hand. Stops right by him.

"You're on the Meds list, Mr Djemil. Another doctor's appointment. Be ready in five minutes." She points through the anti-suicide netting to the muster area three floors down on the ones. "There, by the lift. You see? Officer Siddle - he's on Meds again. Five minutes," she says again, as if used to short memories.

Djemil nods. But Jenny Hughes does not move. Instead she looks from side to side, then leans towards him. Says in a much lower voice: "Listen, yeah. I just want to say thank you for what you did. Er, stopping Lopez. It meant a hell of a lot. So, er ... well, that's it really."

"I'm just pleased you weren't harmed," he says, immediately looking away from her.

She smiles. Then brusquely moves towards another prisoner brandishing her list.

Minutes later, Djemil HA2684 accompanies Officer Siddle through the prison's Healthcare wing. They pass a bored-looking nurse keeping watch on a suicidal prisoner through a transparent cell door. Continue on to a consulting room at the far end. Instructing Djemil to wait outside, Siddle gives the door a polite knock and then sticks his head around the door. Checks with the neurological consultant: will she be OK alone with the prisoner?

Yes, the consultant replies, taking off tortoiseshell spectacles. Mr Djemil is OK. She has been treating this patient for months - well before he came to prison, in fact. With that, Djemil is allowed to enter and told to sit down opposite the woman. He complies. Does nothing to acknowledge her. Has no interest, it seems, in her smart practical trouser suit or her neat, if slightly boyish hair. Nor, it would appear, in her scuffed attaché case or the illegibly scrawled notes that lie, helter-skelter, on the table in front of her.

The consultant thanks the officer for delivering the patient and, with a whiff of haughtiness, gives him a curt nod as if to say, you can leave now. Then, putting her glasses back on, she picks up a pen and pulls some of her notes towards her.

The door closes. And the moment it does, Djemil puts his hands behind his head, stretches out his tracksuit-bottomed legs. Lets out a mighty sigh.

"We've got a problem," he says, looking round at the door. "I can't find him."

Chapter 2

Five minutes after the Security meeting that afternoon, John Simmering tells his PA not to put any more phone calls through, then shuts his office door. Now all McKenzie can do is sit there and wait. Wait like a ten-year-old for the bollocking.

He knows exactly how the gaffer will do it. Will start by putting on a silly voice, saying "Twenty per cent!" over and over again, as if he can't get his head round the Mandatory Drug Testing rate being so high. Then he will go through all the prisons he has worked in over the years, how he thought their rates were scandalous because they had gone over ten per cent. No doubt lob in some nasty little barb while he is at it, something like "Little did I know then!" Then will come back full circle. Squawk like a mynah bird: "Twenty per cent!", "Twenty per cent!"

McKenzie's predictions turn out to be bang on, and it is hardly surprising. He was here for a depressingly similar "chat" a month ago - same chair, same time - again, just after the Security Meeting. Only difference then, the MDT was eighteen per cent, not twenty. The month before that, it was sixteen per cent, up from fourteen. What will it be next month - twenty-two?

He barely registers, McKenzie, as Simmering gets into his stride - "the dressing down I got when the MDT passed eight, I tell you!" Instead the eyes in his tired face drift towards the window behind the gaffer's desk, to the slivers of blue between the thick square bars. And, crossing one of them, a jet plane - tiny from this distance - spinning out white vapour like some oversized aerial spider. He imagines excited people on board, bags packed, holiday-bound. Sea, sun ... sex. Has barely begun the fantasy - the sweltering heat as he steps off the plane onto baking tarmac - when he comes to. Hears the gaffer still jabbering away.

"So I hope you understand, Tony. In many ways, you're doing a good job. I wouldn't have given you Security if I didn't think you were up to it. And you did well on the audit. We're losing less time in Industries through tool losses, and finds of mobile phones are down. But this MDT ... For five months now - yes, five - you've been promising me things will improve, that we'll get down to our target of thirteen per cent. But they haven't. I even said I might have to shuffle around the Senior Management Team. And they still haven't."

Simmering shrugs.

"You say you're doing your best. Carrying out more cell searches, more staff searches, using the dogs more often. But whatever you're doing, Tony, it's not working. Drugs continue to pour into this prison. We've got the highest MDT rate in London - by far. I mean, twenty per cent! Twenty per cent!"

Simmering is by the window as he says this, looking out, so McKenzie cannot see his face. But the finality of the words alarms him. Has the gaffer decided to move him? Is he going to do what Jenkins predicted and give Security to Charlotte Rosesmith, the young graduate governor on the Prison Service fast-track? For a few seconds, McKenzie fears the worst. But then he reassures himself. Simmering might be a man under pressure, but if there's one thing he is good at, it's sharing that pressure. And McKenzie just cannot see him risking a key area like Security with Charlotte. She just ain't got the experience.

The second Simmering turns round, McKenzie sees he is right. The gaffer is going to keep him - at least for now.

The downside of this is the motivational number McKenzie has to endure, a pep talk so predictable, so patronising - "You show them, Tony!" - that he wants to grab the top man by the lapels and scream in his neat little face: "For Christ's sake, I'm not a fucking child!"

He doesn't, of course. Instead, as Simmering comes to sit back down, gives McKenzie a look of sympathy, the Head of Security just rubs the back of his head, smiles back weakly.

"So Tony. I want you to understand. You're getting it in the neck because I'm getting in the neck. If I don't sort out this MDT, I might be out of a job. And you know what that means."

McKenzie does know. Perfectly. But Simmering spells it out for him one more time.

* * * * * * * * *

Seeing the first few flaps of the graceful grey wings, the man releasing the pigeon freezes with fright for a second. The cargo's too heavy! The bird's going to fall! But he soon calms down. After heading downwards from the ninth floor of the 1960s housing block, straight for the forecourt of the garish pink SupaSuds car wash, the pigeon quickens its cadence, levels out its flight. Begins its commute from Waltham Forest to its destination seven or so miles away.

The usual route beckons. Over the graffiti-ridden cemetery, over the train tracks - locomotives climbing each metal strand like nits on hair - then the bottom bit of the artificial lake with its car park and, a fair bit later, across the busy dual carriageway. Not long after that, the pigeon reaches home. Its other home, where its other owner lives - in that mighty Victorian building.

No effort to hide the bird is made. Yet no-one notices it. The creature is so obvious, and pigeons flying around London, generally getting in the way, are so common, that hundreds, thousands of people see this one. Yet don't. The man deep in thought on his way over to the Security department, for example. Right in front of him the bird flies - and while his eyes see it, his brain does not. And as every undercover operative knows, it takes the two to tango.

The pigeon reaches its usual window ledge. Has hardly begun pecking at some seeds scattered along its top when two hands reach through some bars, cup around the bird's body. Slowly but firmly pull it inside. Placing the pigeon on a wooden chair, the hands appear to remove something from its legs. Quite what, the dim light stops us from making out. What we do see, though, is the velvet-glove handling of the bird - not unlike an auctioneer presenting a priceless artefact. This bird has value, no question.

* * * * * * * * *

The arguments, the risk assessments could be the envy of any executive boardroom. But this is a boardroom with a difference. For a start, there are bars over the window. And in the room - Cell B3-17, to be precise - the three men present sit around a tatty-looking Backgammon board. Do not play. Instead talk, nod, vigorously shake their heads.

They are striking, the men - two on account of their sheer size. One of them - the one who, just a few minutes ago, walked right past Djemil, told him he was dead meat - he must be six foot eight, this guy, could surely have done damage as a basketball player, even a rower, with his long levers, those mighty hands. The second man tottering on a chair opposite, he'd have made a better wrestler, prop forward. Has upper arms so thick they jut out at an angle. Make him look like a very strong penguin.

The third man strikes in a different way. Chubby, slightly balding and with goggly eyes, he wears a V-neck jumper, looks a good five years older than the other two. Early thirties, say. But the most noticeable thing about him is the confidence which pours from those bulging eyes. As if tilting his head forwards would fill any receptacle with certainty.

The basketball player is speaking. Thighs pointing up at the south-facing window, he jiggles them up and down, seems incredibly agitated.

"This new fucker - what's his name ..."

"Djemil."

"Yeah, yeah, yeah - Djemil. Who the fuck is he, man? I mean, who the fuck does he think he is?"

The question hangs heavy in the cell. Outside, through the window, a female voice is shouting at a prisoner to get off something in the exercise yard below.

"There is no way he is going to muscle in on our business. He wants a bit? Well let him try." The giant shakes his head. "Listen to me, yeah. He is trouble, man. So we hit back. We restore order. It. Is. That. Simple."

He pauses between each word, as if to show how simple it is, then places a cabbage-sized fist into a huge cupped hand.

The moment he does, the stockier man throws the dice, and all three of them lean towards the Backgammon board as if on a spring. The chubby one on the bunk slaps his knee for good measure, shouts "No way, man!" A second later, an officer passes the door. Glances in as he walks on by.

As the footsteps die away, the wrestler-type prisoner gathers up the dice.

"I'm with Shorty," he says. "We got to crush the shark egg while we can. This Djemil ..." He sucks through his teeth. "Even before he took out Lopez, I saw him. Said to myself, there's something not right about that guy. I mean, Lopez can look after himself ... And like Shorty said, times are good. We got to keep it that way."

Sitting back on his chair, he gives the tall one a slow nod.

And then silence. Silence as both men turn to the third figure in the room. Look deferential, the way they wait patiently for what he has to say. The chubby man takes his time. Finally announces his view with a shake of the fat head, a wheezy little cough.

"We are at a juncture, gentlemen. Do we or don't we?" he says with a guru's simplicity. "This guy Djemil is a worry. For sure. And Shorty is right. Man gotta hit back fast in times like this. Stop people getting ideas. And you Jarvis ..." He turns to the wrestler. "You're right too. Times are good so we got to keep it that way. But here's a few other ideas. We know what Lopez is like. How he thinks with his dick ..."

The chubby man snorts.

"But what neither of you have conjectured ..." - he lingers proudly over the word: con - jeck - churd - "... is that maybe our Lopez was out of order. Maybe this new guy - maybe he's just an old-fashioned gent. Just stepped in to preserve her innocence."

"Oh what!"

"Come on, man ..."

"Gentlemen, we don't know. That might be why. As for the way Djemil took Lopez out ... I mean, think about it. The spic's dick was probably so swelled up he had no blood for his fists, you get me?" Another wheezy chuckle. "And one more thing: we don't know shit about Djemil. Where he's from, who he knows. Word is, he's here for drink-driving. And we know what that means ..."

Blank looks back.

"It's what people say when they want to hide things. Means he's probably a rapist, kiddy fiddler, some shit like that. So he's hardly going to mess with us, is he? Either that, or he is here for drink driving and too big for the road. But we'd have heard of him then ..."

As the voice trails off, Jarvis, Shorty trade a glance. But the chubby one is quick to speak again.

"Gentlemen, the more I think about it, the more I see we've got to be cautious right now. Why hit back till we have to?" He chuckles at them both. "You tell me, how is this guy, how's any fucker going to compete with us? If he does, then OK, we will protect our interests, I swear to God." Menace invades his voice. Disappears as fast. "So yeah, we watch Djemil. We find out what this fucker's about. In the meantime ..." - again that wheezy chuckle - "... we carry on making hay."

The three men share a faint smile. Then Shorty leans forwards, speaks in almost a whisper.

"OK, Birdman. I get you. But what about our new best friend?"

"The shrimp?"

"Yeah. Think he'll squeal now he's off the wing?"

The chubby man tilts his head from side to side as if to slosh around some brain cells.

"Nah, I doubt it. He'll know he's coming back onto B Wing. Knows we'll be here waiting for him."

He chuckles again. Makes the point clear as day.

* * * * * * * * *

Snug in his lair, otherwise known as the Security department of HMP Hatcham, Governor Tony McKenzie settles his backside down on the swivel office chair, holds a pile of Security Information Reports between forefinger and thumb. Sixty odd, he guesses. Should take a steady hour. That will take him nicely to just gone eight, by which time only the last few straggler prisoners down Reception will need to be found beds for. Then, thank the lord, his physical presence will be needed no more. The sculpted seats of his Vauxhall Insignia 2.0 CDTi beckon like voluptuous velour-covered sirens.

He pushes himself back from the beaten up desk.

"Officer McKechnie!" he barks. "Where are you, you miserable lazy woman?"

A few seconds later, a tiny head appears round the door, its owner's cropped black hair, neat half-moon glasses hinting at efficiency, planning.

"Was that your lovely dulcet voice requesting my presence, Governor McKenzie? Go on then, give it here!"

She points to the mug on his desk proclaiming Everyone is Equal.

"You're an angel, Janet."

"And you're a slave-driver, Mr McKenzie."

As the door shuts, he hears her pad off to the kitchenette. Can't help smiling. Sets about crunching through the SIRs. The number being submitted has shot up recently, to the point where the sixty he has got today - give or take - is pretty much average. Staff finally seem to be getting the message that security is everyone's business, not just that tall bloke's in the tower. Mind you, sometimes McKenzie wishes they'd be a bit less conscientious. Like today, for example. England play Italy tonight.

He calls himself to order. Sternly tells himself the answer to his MDT crisis could be buried here among the SIRs. And indeed a quick flick through shows that quite a few do concern drugs. Not drug finds, per se. More circumstantial stuff. A group of prisoners huddled in a cell, a comment overheard that 'Friday's D-day', the dilated pupils of some prisoners over in Industries. There's even one report about a prisoner bragging that he's booked 'a cargo flight'. Why the reporting officer has ticked the 'Drugs' subject-matter box for that one, McKenzie's not got a scooby. Maybe it's about some sort of hallucinogenic substance that makes you think you can fly. Maybe the officer is on some himself.

He hears steps. Sees Janet coming through the door with a mug. A different one this time, informing him There's no "i" in Team.

"Who says the Scots are mean!"

"And you're a lucky man, Mr McKenzie. You've got two sugars in there. Heaped ones as well. Oh, and we're running out of milk. I'll bring some more in the morning. I'm in at seven."

Carefully placing the tea to his right, she has to move a stationery holder full of pens out of the way.

"Tell me how much I owe you, Janet. Now don't forget."

"Would I do that, Mr McKenzie?"

She doesn't wait for an answer. Instead pitter-patters away on child-size feet and shuts the door. That suits McKenzie fine. He needs to get on.

Opening the first SIR, he recognises the writing of Officer Damian Siddle off B Wing. Remembers he's the weird spotty one who joined last year. Would not stop asking questions when McKenzie was giving his usual security talk to the latest batch of officer recruits. Kept pointing his thick glasses McKenzie's way, demanding to know every last detail about everything. Bloody nightmare!

McKenzie reads:

Sir, at approximately 10.30 hours on 16 August, I was patrolling B3 landing during association and noticed three prisoners playing Backgammon in cell B3-17. The prisoners were Jarvis HA1690, Longman HA2213 and Samuels HA2214. On B Wing Mr Longman is known as Shorty, while Mr Samuels I have heard referred to as Birdman. I understand that up to three prisoners are allowed in a cell at one time according to prison rules, as long as the door is open. However I thought they might be gambling so I intended to break up the game.

I was about to enter when I heard them talking about prisoner Djemil HA2684, so I stayed out of sight just outside the door. Mr Djemil is a quiet polite prisoner who has only been on B Wing a few days. I was surprised to hear one of the prisoners (I think it was Mr Longman) say: "He's trouble, man." I believe he was referring to Mr Djemil. Then, a minute later, I heard another prisoner (Mr Jarvis, I think) say: "This Djemil ... there's something not right about that guy." I was shocked by this as it contradicts my perception of Mr Djemil. But I thought it might be of interest to Security. This concludes my report.

McKenzie lets out a sigh, stretches his arms, stares out at the orange-grey smudge of an overcast night sky in central London. A pretty useless SIR, this one. So some prisoners think this new guy Djemil is trouble. Bully for them. Not much he can do about it, is there? Not when half the cons in Hatcham are already jockeying for supremacy, trying to do each other in. Still, the fact that Longman, Jarvis are some of B Wing's top dogs, and even they are worried about this guy Djemil ... Yeah, maybe that does mean something.

He asks himself what clever 'action points' he can write down. Squints as he reads Janet's miniscule handwriting: "B Wing staff to observe

Mr Djemil closely, and check his Cell-Sharing Risk Assessment to ensure the safety of his cellmate. Staff also to keep an eye on Mr Jarvis, Mr Longman, Mr Samuels."

Lame stuff. But then, what else can you say? McKenzie's biro lands on the box below and, even more lamely, he writes: "Agreed. As above." Adding a big fancy signature to mask his lack of inspiration, he slams down Siddle's concerns to his left - the first of the 'Done' pile - takes a fresh SIR from his right. Opens it wide, then steals a look at his watch. Could still make the football.

Chapter 3

"Good afternoon, HMP Hatcham."

In a narrow windowless room where the only view is through the door, and then only of the walkthrough metal detector used for outside visitors to the prison, a pale and tired-looking woman in a black V-neck jumper answers the phone. Her forty-ninth call of the day. Above her, lights glare. Conjure up crevasses, lines, blotches in her washed-out face.

"Oh, hello," says a woman's voice at the other end. "Er, sorry ... didn't know you were going to answer so quick. What it is, yeah, I'm calling cos I'm worried about a friend who's, er, with you at the moment."

"Got his name and number?"

The operator speaks as if on auto-pilot. Picking up a chewed biro, she pulls an A4 pad towards her, gets ready to write.

"Yeah. Well, no. I've got his name. It's Matthew Schild. I haven't got his prison number. Do I need it?"

"Well, it does help," the first woman says. Then more gently: "Normally I can just punch the number in the computer. But it doesn't sound a common name. We might be OK. If you can spell it, I'll see how many of them we have. Can you do that for me?"

"Yeah. It's, er, Schild: S - C - H - I - L - D. He's only been with you a few days, and I'm really worried. He's not happy, he's ..."

"Just a sec. You said S - E ..."

"No. S - C for cat - H - I - L ..."

The operator scrolls down the screen of her PC, her hand on the white mouse showing a gaudy wedding ring.

"Here he is."

"Can I have his number? In case I need to call again?"

"We're not allowed to give that information. He'll have to give it you himself next time you're in contact."

"But that's my point ..."

The caller's voice cracks.

"I'm worried, see. Worried I'll never see him again. He might try and kill himself. It's his first time inside. He rang me this morning. Was crying, he was. Never heard him like that before. I mean he's been bad, but ..."

She pauses, as if having to breathe in deeply. Or sobbing, maybe.

"He's only been in a few days. Hardly spoke when he phoned. Just kept on crying. Wouldn't stop. Nothing I said did any good."

The phone operator's voice softens again. She repositions things on her desk. Speaks more closely into the receiver to counter noise from colleagues - one left, one right - also taking calls.

"Has Mr Schild ever self-harmed before?"

"Yeah, he has," comes the barely audible answer. "He just gets depressed. Can't cope. You don't know it's coming. Then bam!"

"OK. Well I'm glad you called us. I'll pass the information onto Charlotte Rosesmith, our Head of Safer Custody. And the wing where Mr Schild is located."

"Oh, I hope you do, thank you. He needs that. I don't know what staff are like on D Wing ..."

"B Wing," the operator corrects. "Although, hold on, I think he might be down the CSU at the moment."

"The CSU!"

"Nothing to worry about. Just a place away from main location. Quieter there. Sometimes they go down there for some time out. Away from the big wings. You know ..."

"Oh ... OK."

"Can I have your name, madam? In case our Safer Custody department need to get in touch."

A pause.

"Easier if I phone back, yeah. But thanks for your help. Keep him safe."

Receivers are replaced in two very different rooms.

That evening, when hundreds of TVs are chattering away across Hatcham prison, a tiny mobile phone is switched on in Djemil's cell. The prisoner is alone and he cups his hands around the device as he sits facing the window. It tells him he has had no calls and only a single text message since yesterday. He opens the Inbox and clicks on the envelope icon.

Four words flash up: "HE'S DOWN THE CSU."

* * * * * * * * *

"Mr Djemil, can you hear me?"

Cupping hands around the open inspection hatch of a cell door, the Custodial Manager squints as she peers into the darkness, speaks as loudly as she can without shouting. Grimacing as she adjusts her hands, she turns around and gives a shake of the head. Peers back into the cell.

"Can you hear me, Mr Djemil?"

Still nothing.

"Come on, what's this about, eh?"

The CM moves her feet and, as she does, a swirling noise makes her look down. Water is flowing under the cell door and out onto the B4 landing. Inside the cell, the sink has been ripped off the wall and smashed, the wooden table is in smithereens, and the square bedside cupboard has been squashed, somehow, made into a parallelogram. Along the floor lies a sodden mattress. And at the back of the cell stands the figure of a man, hands by his sides and head pointing straight at the door, as if he is in a kind of trance.

The CM will not give up. Forming her hands into a loudhailer shape, as if to coax her voice through the shallow hatch, she tells Djemil that one way or another, he is going down the CSU. He can cooperate, walk there, accompanied by staff. Or he can refuse. In which case the control and restraint team will come in, do the business. Carry him down if need be. Same result, different process.

It is no idle threat. Outside the cell, four staff are kitted up in the intimidating garb used by riot police. Look like they've just stepped out of a superhero movie, with their oversized helmets, padded limbs, thick gloves. The one nearest the cell, a couple of yards down the landing to the CM's left, carries a battered-looking plastic shield two-thirds his body length. Flanking him, either side, two others. Behind them, completing the diamond, a fourth, blond pony tail peeping out from under the huge helmet.

Right of the intervention team, an overweight middle-aged officer videos proceedings. Stops, every so often, to tinker with the controls of the small Canon device. A couple of paces further down the landing, an irate-looking man in a brown suit is leaning on the metal railings, his neat-featured face flitting between boredom and impatience. He keeps scratching his ear, then looking at his watch. The name badge on his lapel tells the world he is Chris Jenkins, Head of Residential.

Shoes shift, disturb the water. And then ... progress. The CM suddenly starts commanding Mr Djemil to put his hands on the rear wall of the cell and face the window. Turning around to her left, she exchanges nods with her Control and Restraint team before opening the door. Jumping aside to let them enter.

The shield man leads, eyes trained on the prisoner's hands. The officers at his side grab the prisoner's arms with chunky gloves, then pin them to the wall. But Djemil complies. He does accept to be handcuffed, does accept to be walked out of the cell, then down the sopping landing. Says not a word throughout the process. Nor do the staff - seven of them in all - who with a distinctly ceremonial air escort the prisoner down the three flights of stairs, along the deserted ones of B Wing, finally down to the underground CSU. Gates clang behind them the whole way, signal another stage passed.

In the CSU, the intervention team hand the prisoner over to three Seg officers. They strip-search the prisoner in a box cell - top half first, then the lower half - before flying through the rules of the CSU, walking him over to an empty cell. Only one cell is available: C0-03, quite near the staff office. There is another empty one, but it has shit smeared across its walls, awaits deep-cleaning by an outside company.

"Perk of the job, guys!" says Jenkins.

Following Djemil to the cell, the Head of Residential informs the prisoner he'll be put on a governor's report for damaging prison property and will have an adjudication tomorrow. Where he'll be after that will be for the adjudicating governor to decide.

Nodding at the officer to shut the door, Jenkins walks away. Steals another look at his watch.

A minute or so later, an elderly nurse with half-moon glasses enters Djemil's cell accompanied by one of the Seg officers. Her white shoes looking like slippers, she shuffles them in Djemil's direction so she can give him a quick once-over.

"Everything alright, Mr ..."

"Djemil," says a gaunt-looking officer at her side.

"No bones broken, Mr Jarmeel?"

"He walked, Edith."

"Ah!"

The old woman smiles, as if she knows something, then shuffles back through the cell door humming. The officer lingers a few seconds as if he is about to speak. But then he leaves too. Shuts the door as gently as its hefty mass allows.

* * * * * * * * *

Djemil HA2684 sleeps poorly that night. Spends a good part of it pacing his tiny cell or performing old-fashioned exercises like press-ups or sit-ups. Sometimes doing nothing more than touching his fist gently against the walls as if to check they are still there. The measured movements contrast with the senseless banging from a cell nearby. The din carries on almost till dawn.

When it does come, dawn, the birds perversely quieten down and Djemil finally stops tossing, turning on the narrow moulded slab of plastic and inch-thin mattress that serve as a bed. Two hours later, a clunk of keys. The cell door opens. Reveals a trolley and, behind it, a sprightly-looking officer and bleary-eyed prisoner. On top of the trolley, a hot water dispenser.

"Cup of tea, Djemil."

The prisoner walks over, quickly fills the tiny plastic mug.

"What's happening today, guv?"

"Got your nicking this morning. We'll see what the governor does with you after that."

The officer pauses.

"Did you hear me?"

But Djemil does not answer. His attention is clearly elsewhere. Over the officer's right shoulder, judging by his gaze. Over to where the elderly nurse from yesterday is talking to a prisoner in a cell directly across the landing. The door is only half open and the nurse is standing right in front of the prisoner. Obstructs everything apart from his long brown hair, his diminutive stature. But then the nurse moves. Reveals a rake of a man with small ears and - she moves some more - large sunken eyes bisected by a finely chiselled, remarkably thin nose.

"Mr Djemil, when I answer your question, at least pay me the courtesy of listening to me."

The officer sounds put out.

"Sorry, guv," says Djemil, looking back at him. "Bit all over place. Bad night's sleep. Tell me, do I get exercise down here?"

"As I've just told you, you'll get exercise today one way or another, whether it's down here or back on your wing. And again as I just explained, it depends on what ..."

"Yeah alright, guv, I get it."

And with that, the prisoner turns around, goes back to his bed clutching his lukewarm tea. And, behind him, the door slams.

Chapter 4

The little orange light keeps on blinking, adamant there's a paper jam. McKenzie knows there is not. He has spent the last forty minutes of his life doing everything the guy on the helpline advised in his broad Geordie accent, before going it alone, dismantling the flimsy printer with increasing belligerence. No joy. Not one tiny scrap of paper anywhere within its grey-plastic intestines. He dreams of finding the person who thought it was a good idea for all staff to fix their own IT issues, feeding him into a giant printer himself. Then, with some relief, sees it is coming up to nine. He is needed down the Seg.

Jacket on, McKenzie walks to the door of his office, stands quietly for a moment. Hears his three staff jabbering away next door in the main Security office. He pops his head round. Finds himself speaking to the petite one with cropped black hair.

"Off to do the nickings, Janet. We've got Worthington coming to pick up Lopez this morning. They've promised they're taking him. He should already be down Reception," he adds, looking at his chunky watch.

"Yes, I know all about Mr Lopez."

"Just make sure they do come, will you? If they're not here by ten, call their duty dog, check they're on their way. Any issues, get hold of me. Interrupt the nickings if you need to. It's all set up, there should be no problem. But you know what Worthington are like."

He leaves her scribbling on a dog-eared notepad. Savours the cool damp air as he makes the brief crossing under the sky from the Security department over to the prison proper. Quickens his pace the moment he enters the Admin corridor, goes past Simmering's office. Finally descends the steps to the CSU.

It's all go when he gets down there. By one of the cell doors, down the far end, two officers are having a set-to with a prisoner who is in his cell - something about him not getting his tobacco until he quietens down, behaves like a civilised human being. To McKenzie's right, towards the back of a cluttered-looking office - all files, metal cabinets and notice-boards - a strongly built woman is sitting behind a mound of paperwork. Keeps counting out loud and cursing as she shuffles, then reshuffles, the documents into some sort of order.

The only person who notices the Security governor's arrival, in fact, is an oldish-looking prisoner who is out mopping the landing. Immediately putting his task on hold, he doffs an imaginary cap. Follows this by offering a cup of tea. McKenzie accepts, muttering something about everyone being so obliging, and then saunters into the office.

A banging erupts the moment he crosses the threshold.

"Your customers don't sound too happy."

"Ugh!" says the Supervising Officer, at last looking up from behind the table. "That will be Smithy, the banging. Or Hammer Smith as we call him now. He's been like that all morning. Was at it all night as well, apparently. We need to get him psyched. Not sure he should be down here at all, to be honest. Not ideal when you've got vulnerable ones down here."

"Vulnerable? Like who?"

"Like, er ... well, Matthew Schild." She nods at a whiteboard on the wall showing which prisoner is in which cell. "Israeli guy, absolutely tiny. You must remember him. Found in possession of a mobile phone and some tablets. On B Wing, it was. He got seven days' CC two days ago. Has hardly said a word since he came down here, looks absolutely terrified. Not even eating. We opened an ACCT on him yesterday, and I've got one of Charlotte's Safer Custody team coming down as well now."

"I'm glad to hear it," says McKenzie, walking back to the door and taking his mug of tea from the old guy. "He shouldn't be down here at all, someone like that. Should be on normal location - especially if you've got banging going on, like you say. Better keep a close eye on him till Safer Custody get here. Between you and me, who was it who gave him the CC?"

"Governor Jenkins," says the SO with a little smile. "He's a bit old-school like that. What do you reckon, Governor?"

"I'm not saying a word."

There are twenty-two adjudications to get through, seven of them for prisoners who have failed Mandatory Drug Tests, and McKenzie zips through them as best he can. However the sheer number, plus the intricate defences put forward by Hatcham's more seasoned customers, mean that progress is slow. They take up pretty much the whole morning. By the time staff open up the cell of Djemil HA2684, lead the prisoner into the adjudication room, it's approaching twelve and McKenzie's mind is on other things. More specifically, the gym. He keeps seeing an image of

Jenkins hogging the dumbbells, doing bicep curls in front of the mirror, a sneaky smile around his thin ratty lips.

"Stand in front of the chair, give your name and number to the governor!" barks a Seg officer as the prisoner enters.

The adjudication for Djemil is brief. McKenzie asks him if he smashed up his cell on B Wing as per the charge. When the prisoner says that yes he did, McKenzie asks why. Djemil says: "I lost it, guv."

"You lost it," repeats McKenzie dead pan. Writes in the evidence box of the nicking sheet: "He said: 'I lost it, guv.'" Then asks Djemil if he often loses it. Whether he'd have done the same thing if he'd had to pay for all the damage himself. The prisoner's answers are polite but evasive: Yes, Governor. No, Governor. I'll do my best, Governor.

McKenzie takes a leisurely look at Djemil. Remembers this is the man who did such a neat job beating up one of B Wing's hard nuts, Carlos Lopez. He tries to imagine Djemil in full swing. Can't really. There is nothing out of the ordinary about the guy's appearance, and he's definitely not a monster like some of them. Not like that guy everyone calls Shorty, for example. Now he's a monster!

The comparison gives McKenzie an idea. Lopez used to hang around with Shorty. And Djemil beat up Lopez. So maybe - after the humiliation of Lopez - maybe Shorty began giving Djemil a hard time. Made him feel unsafe. So unsafe that he smashed up just to get off the wing. The theory strikes McKenzie as distinctly possible. No, more than that. A dead cert, now he thinks about it.

So he asks Djemil. Asks if he was having any trouble on B Wing. Gets the denial he is expecting. So immediately pushes it. Asks specifically if there was any fallout from the Lopez incident. Gets another no.

McKenzie shrugs. He has tried. Performed his duty of care, as Simmering would put it. Covered his arse, as Jenkins would say. He makes a note of his actions on the adjudication paperwork: "I asked Mr Djemil if he had any problems on B Wing, he assured me he did not.'"

Finally, with some words about the seriousness of damage to prison property and the vow that if they ever meet again under such circumstances he will throw the book at him, McKenzie hands down his award: fourteen days' loss of TV, twenty-eight days' loss of earnings at fifty per cent, fourteen days' loss of canteen, and fourteen days' cellular confinement, the last suspended for two months.

When Djemil asks what all that means, McKenzie explains that if he does the same thing again, he'll end up down the CSU.

"So I'm off back to B Wing?" asks Djemil. He seems disappointed.

"Yes, but you'll have lunch down here."

As he walks out of the adjudication room, McKenzie still can't decide whether he sees madness or badness in the man. But there is a nagging something. What the hell is it? He is still making up his mind when the SO sitting to his right looks up. Says out of the blue: "I tell you what, Governor. He's a bad'un, Mr Djemil. I can smell it."

So it's not just me, thinks McKenzie as he beckons towards the door. Waggles his mug at the old armed robber.

* * * * * * * * *

"What do you mean he won't go back?"

The distinctive gravel tones of Tony McKenzie fill the CSU staff office, fail to hide his irritation. It's early afternoon, and the Security governor has been called back down to sign some paperwork which, according to the same SO, he has overlooked. And, in the middle of all the signing, she has let him know that prisoner Djemil HA2684 is refusing to return to B Wing. Refusing normal location as a whole, in fact. There is nowhere she can send him.

The Seg staff grin as the tall man sounds off in the cramped space.

"OK, well we're not going to control and restrain him back up to B Wing, are we?" he says once he has calmed down a bit. "Although to be honest, we might be doing that with them soon. It's getting like Beirut up there."

"So what do we do?"

McKenzie blows through his lips, sounds like a horse.

"Get whoever gave him the direct order to move back to B Wing to nick him. Then make sure he only gets what he's entitled to down here. Absolute minimum, is that clear? We're stuffed to the gunnels right now."

A big hand waves at the whiteboard on the wall. “They're obviously seeing this CSU as a soft option, or trying to get down here because they're afraid. We've got to start making this a proper Seg.”

The SO could not agree more. Starts going on about the difficulties she has every day working out which prisoners can go out on exercise together. Seems to spend her entire life deciding who would be safe with who. Take Mr Djemil and Mr Schild, for example. What about them? Does Governor McKenzie think they would be OK together?

“Well what do you think? Mr Schild has just been put on an ACCT because you're worried he's suicidal, and about an hour and a half ago, you called Mr Djemil 'A bad'un'. Does that sound a safe combination to you?”

“But that’s my point," says the SO, breaking out into a grin. "We’re so pushed for time, we have to take some risks occasionally otherwise we'd never be able to give everyone exercise. And yeah, OK, so Mr Djemil is down here for smashing up his cell. But most of the other guests we've got have smashed up people’s faces.”

"Well there you go. Sounds like you've answered your own question. So do Djemil and Schild together. Just keep a close eye on them both. A puff of wind would make that Schild guy fall over. And besides, don't forget that Mr Djemil has smashed in someone's face as well - your old friend Mr Lopez. It's just not the reason he's down here now."

Ten minutes later, a Seg officer opens up the door of Djemil HA2684, asks him if he wants exercise. Tells him to put on his shoes when he says yes, then searches him, instructs to wait a minute outside his cell. The officer nods towards the open door of the cell opposite.

"Hurry up, Mr Schild," he shouts, "or we'll go without you."

Suddenly a man as small as a child appears in the painted brick doorway. He cannot be more than five foot three and, judging by his lack of heft, scrawny neck, must weigh under eight stone. Yet the amazing thing is, it is not his stature that strikes most, it's his ghoulishness: the heavy grey, almost black, semi-circles under his eyes, the pallor of his face which somehow claws its way through olive skin, turns it a light grey. He does not just look sleep-deprived, Schild. He looks other-worldly. Like some bioluminescent deep sea creature exiting its lair.

Banging shut his cell door, the officer searches the tiny man then, with a colleague, escorts the two prisoners through the rigmarole of doors, gates. As Schild and Djemil follow, neither man says a word or even looks at the other.

"Figures two prisoners on Charlie exercise yard," radios the officer as soon as they reach a forlorn circle of tarmac outside. The second officer locks the gate behind them, before strolling across to the opposite side and lighting up a cigarette.

It is a nippy overcast day but, despite this, the two prisoners blink after the gloom of the CSU. Appear disoriented by the real world. And then Schild suddenly looks up. Up at a seagull that is hovering overhead, constantly adjusting its slender wings in response to every whim of the wind. He looks incredibly vulnerable out on the yard, Schild. Not just because of his slightness, which shows in the way his tracksuit bottoms flap in the breeze, in the Adam's apple that protrudes alarmingly from the craned neck. Also in the way he carries himself - the arms weirdly straight by his sides, the tiny feet meekly together.

And as he stands there, transfixed, it would seem, by the bird, prisoners from C Wing shout out threats from their windows. Words like "Pussyboy", "Punk" dart over in the breeze. Must pierce the tiny Israeli like arrows, the way he flinches with each new volley. Yet still the seagull holds his gaze. Does so until it finally cedes to the sharp eastern wind, lets its feathery self be flung over the bleak prison walls.

"How long we got, guv?" Djemil asks one of the officers.

"Twenty-five minutes. Less if you both want to go in."

Schild must hear, because without warning he starts marching around the exercise yard, twiglet arms swinging wildly. He is half-way round a second lap when Djemil, too, starts walking around the yard's edge - anti to Schild's clockwise. Every half minute or so, the two prisoners come face to face. And each time they meet, Schild looks down at the ground like some wretched dog. Looks up again only when he is three, four paces past. The routine carries on for a good twenty laps, until the officer with the radio looks at his watch.

"Alright lads. Have you in!"

As the two prisoners re-enter the old building and walk down a gloomy corridor, one of the officers puts a hand on Schild's shoulder.

"You alright, sonny?" he asks.

Schild turns to look at him.

"Just checking. You look a bit down, that's all. Don't want you cutting up on me. Just had your cell painted."

Chuckling, the officer opens the wooden door back into the CSU. Stands there waiting for the prisoners to pass through. As Schild passes by, he looks at the member of staff through long camel eyelashes, disbelief on his narrow face.

"Don't worry about it," says Djemil, catching up with him. "It's the job. Turns them like that."

The Israeli does not reply. But as they come to a halt, wait while the same officer unlocks each of their cells, Djemil carries on in almost a whisper.

"Listen. Someone like you - you're never going to survive a place like this. You need someone ..."

He does not finish because, at that moment, the officer shouts at them to return to their cells. The two prisoners walk towards opposite sides of the landing. As they do, Djemil glances over his shoulder. Gives Matthew Schild a small nod. As if to say, I am that someone.

* * * * * * * * *

The heavy door of Cell C0-07 thuds shut and, the moment it does, the tiny figure of Matthew Schild edges forwards, pretty much collapses onto the plastic plinth that serves as a bed. He does not move, does not turn his head. Just lies there on his side, staring at the wall, the odd flicker of the cell light only emphasising his stone-like stillness.

But the appearance of the tiny Israeli is deceptive. Because behind that delicate nose and those deep-set eyes, and underneath that unruly long brown hair, the mind of Matthew Schild is racing. Frantically assessing his options. Who the hell is this guy who spoke to him just now? Is he one of them? Could they have found him already? And if they are that fast, why didn't he do it out there on the exercise yard? Is the guy just choosing his moment? Is that what they do?

He shudders. Starts shivering despite the stifling heat. Then leaps off the bed, rushes to the window, looks out at the metal fence around the yard all of two yards away. No escape. Not from the prison, not from his predicament, not from ... Like a madman, he begins headbutting the window bars. Gently, at first, then harder. Harder! Anything to blot out the panic. Sees quickly this is not a sustainable option. Makes himself sit back on the bed.

"Come on Matthew, stay calm. Think this through."

And yet his brain will not function. Blots out every thought with static. At the same time, feeds the panic. One minute he is on the bed, unable to move. The next, he is pacing the cell, door to window, window to door … The to-and-froing exhausts him. Only deepens the despair.

At about half past four, the food trolley comes. With it, a disinterested officer, a glowering prisoner. Eyes to the floor, Schild takes his meal, tepid tea. Jumps when the door slams shut, the starting gun for the next fifteen hours. Fifteen hours when he will be alone with just a rip-proof blanket, his own terror for company.

With no TV or radio, there is no escape from the nearby noises. No escape from the questions, incrementally more aggressive, from the prisoner in the cell next to him - "What are you, a fucking nonce?"; "Wait till I slice you up, you cunt!" No escape, either, from the lunatic howls, the banging of the deranged guy on the other side. Or the grim sounds late into the evening as a prisoner is brought down the stairs under restraint, fights staff every step of the way.

The night, though, is the worst. Hour after hour, Matthew Schild lies there on his bed, head turned towards the sliced diamond of orange hurled onto the wall by lights outside. Set within the diamond's centre, names, nicknames, scratched into the paintwork: STAX, AK-48, The GreEN CReW. Scrawls of a London underclass desperate for recognition. They alienate him, the names. Scare him. But then, strangely, he finds comfort in them. Works out why. The harshness of the cell - all moulded furniture, cool hard walls - it all seems designed to force people, individuals, to fit into a system. And somehow the names, the people who have scratched them somehow they hold up two fingers to that. Say no, actually, we come first. The system has got to fit around us.

Finally, dawn. And with it, voices from the dayshift, spiteful in their loudness. The chatter kickstarts Schild. He has to make a decision. Feet like lead, he moves for the hundredth time to the window bars. Thinks back to yesterday – to the prisoner who spoke to him. He is obviously a small-time criminal, the guy, judging by the surly way he spoke to the staff, the swagger - walking around the exercise yard as if he owned the place. And yet he offered to watch out for him. Why? What does he want in return? Repellent thoughts strafe Schild's conscious. Persuade him to steer clear.

But then that other thing - the horror he is running from - comes crashing into his conscious. Brings with it another wave of sweat, another spike in pulse. Cornered, Schild's mind clings onto the rational, however insane. OK, so the new prisoner is a risk. There is no doubt about that. But this other threat - the reason he is here in prison in the first place – that threat is definite, and far more terrifying. And although both options seem hideous at 07.00 hours in Cell C0-07 - right now one of them is slightly less hideous than the other. It leaves him no option. He must risk it with the stranger from the yard.

Chapter 5

"Come in, Matthew. Have a seat. I'm glad you've decided to give B Wing another go. Can't have you wasting away down the CSU with all the bad apples, can we? Right, we're just going to have a chat, see how you're getting on."

Governor Charlotte Rosesmith gives prisoner Matthew Schild a reassuring smile and gestures to an empty chair. The fresh-faced young woman has only been Head of Safer Custody for a month, to add to her existing remit, Head of Equality and Diversity. And yet to the amazement of some of her peers - not least a certain Chris Jenkins - she has grasped the role with genuine zeal, somehow juggling tasks and freeing up enough time to take a close interest in every vulnerable prisoner in the whole establishment. No wonder the self-harm stats are already showing a dip - and this is before Charlotte has even begun implementing his ambitious new plans ...

It was Charlotte, for example, who organised a multi-disciplinary team meeting down the CSU for Matthew Schild yesterday. Insisted on getting the rabbi down there. Decreed at the meeting's outset, "we must determine the care plan for this complex and sensitive prisoner going forward." It didn't take long before the young fast-track governor pronounced herself shocked by the Israeli's vulnerability. Could not believe, she said, that someone on an ACCT, in his very first month in prison, had been held down the CSU at all. Especially as a member of the public had apparently rung in, expressed concern. The top governor Simmering, also at the meeting, blandly agreed it was terrible. Gave Charlotte free rein to do as she saw fit.

"Right, then," she says now as Matthew Schild gingerly sits down. "You know everyone, I think?"

The tiny prisoner looks around the airless meeting room, made gloomy by the blue curtains drawn against the sun that, outside, shines brilliantly. Then at the three people ranged around him: Governor Rosesmith, the B Wing Supervising Officer and the landing officer Jenny Hughes. They wear earnest smiles, all of them. Flaunt open body language.

"So Matthew. How are you getting on?"

He does not answer, Schild. Just places hands under his drumstick thighs. Looks at the floor.

Charlotte tries again.

"We're here because of this thing which we opened up on you," she says, waving the orange document under his downcast eyes. "Do you know what it is? It's called an ACCT and it's something we use to monitor anyone we're worried might hurt themselves. And it seems that one of the officers in the CSU was worried about you, Matthew. Do you remember?"

Still silence. The SO coughs, crosses his legs. Then Jenny Hughes speaks.

"Matthew. Remember the chat we had in your cell down the CSU? When you told me you were thinking about ending it all."

This time, a barely discernible nod.

"So ... do you still think about ending it, Matthew?"

Another nod. Then, scarcely audible: "Yeah."

"How would you do it if you tried?"

"Dunno."

"What are you worried about?"

"Everything."

"What about your court case? Are you worried about that?"

No response. But the staff try valiantly to discuss his court case nonetheless: its timing, its likely outcome. How it is his first offence so he probably won't serve much time. Will probably get deported after a few months.

"Actually," says Charlotte, her voice lightening, "Hatcham might just be a nightmare you'll soon forget."

"When I die," says Schild.

They look at each other nervously. Start quizzing him about problems he might have had on B Wing. If he has had any visitors since entering the prison. Any contact with his family. If he goes out on exercise. Wants another chat with the rabbi. If he has ever self-harmed before. Tried to kill himself. The questions keep coming. Seem to go on for ever.

"What about your cell mate, Matthew?" asks Charlotte finally. "Do you two get on?"

Schild shrugs his shoulders, studies a rip in the brown carpet.

"Before I went to Seg?"

"The CSU. Yes."

"Not really."

"Why not?"

Schild says nothing. The staff exchange more glances.

"Is there anyone you'd prefer to be with, Matthew?"

The prisoner stays mute. Then an answer so quiet, neither Governor Rosesmith or the SO make it out. But Jenny Hughes does. Recognises the name immediately.

"Mr Djemil!" she says, reddening slightly. "He's on your landing, Matthew, isn't he? Came back from the CSU at the same time, I think."

Slight nod.

"Why him?" asks Charlotte, a hint of wariness in her voice.

"I trust him. We've been on out exercise a few times. Got talking. He seems alright."

The new Head of Safer Custody looks at the other two. Gets a shrug from the SO. Jenny Hughes, though, seems enthused. Tells Charlotte Rosesmith she knows Mr Djemil from working on the wing. Thinks he could be good for Matthew. Has him down as a "quietly confident character."

But Charlotte remains wary. Especially when the SO pipes up, reminds her that Djemil was the one who smashed up his cell a few days ago. On top of his fight with Lopez.

"Ooh, I don't like the sound of that," says Charlotte.

She is on the verge of dismissing the idea when Jenny Hughes argues for Djemil a second time. Says the Lopez thing was not a fight, but a rescue. Reminds them both that she was actually the one who Mr Djemil rescued. Saved her from a serious sexual assault. As for Mr Djemil smashing up, he was getting bullied on B Wing, she reckons. Throws in the fact that so does Governor McKenzie. She bumped into him in the Gate this morning and it turns out he had come up with the same theory. Besides, the Cell-Sharing Risk Assessment still has Mr Djemil down as a medium.

Jenny Hughes wins. Minutes later, the idea of Mr Schild sharing a cell with Mr Djemil is conscientiously written into the action plan of the ACCT document, alongside stipulations for one recorded interaction every hour, a visit from the rabbi, and a review in three days' time. Charlotte also tells Matthew Schild about prisoners called Listeners who he can talk things over with. Are available any time.

"They're like Samaritans," she explains gently. "They're there to help, Matthew. Here on B Wing, I believe the Listener is called Mr

Brannigan. He's been through it himself, and he understands how difficult things can get. So if things get too much for you, promise me you'll ask a member of a staff if you can speak to a Listener. Use your cell bell if you need to."

Minutes later, Djemil catches Schild in the queue for lunch.

"How did it go?"

"It worked," says Schild. "Like you said."

* * * * * * * * *

Charlotte Rosesmith and Jenny Hughes stay chatting in the consultation room. Do so after the Head of Safer Custody asks the B Wing officer to stay behind, says she has something important to say. Speaks to the uneasy-looking officer in the same gentle tones she used for Matthew Schild - caring, almost maternal, even though both women must be about the same age.

"You mentioned the incident with Mr Lopez just now," says Charlotte. "It might have seemed like I'd forgotten about it, but actually I hadn't at all. In fact that's why I want to talk to you now. So I can check you've received all the support you need. We think so much about prisoners getting depressed and self-harming, but not enough about staff, in my opinion. And between you and me, Jenny ..." - she gives the officer a conspiratorial look - "... I'm not convinced managers in this place always provide the care they should. Especially, dare I say it, the men. And ... well, I know traumatic events like the one with Mr Lopez can have a delayed effect."

Tears appear in Jenny Hughes's eyes. Amass quickly, start to roll down the young woman's cheeks. Seconds later become a heady stream. As the officer leans forwards, elbows on her knees, Charlotte puts her hand on her shoulder. Tells her it is all right. It is OK.

The crying finally stops. And when it does, Jenny Hughes looks up, starts apologising to the more senior member of staff.

"Don't be so silly!" says Charlotte. "I'm just really glad I asked you. You're obviously going through an incredibly difficult time. And you know what? I think you're really brave, the way you've come back into work, just soldiered on."

They talk on. Naturally, animatedly - like some ecdysis of the ranking structure. Free to be themselves, sisters looking out for each other in a chronically male environment. At the end of it all, Jenny Hughes cannot thank Charlotte enough. Finally someone who understands her!

She smiles, Charlotte. Is still smiling when she stands up, gathers up her stuff. Cannot stress enough that her door is always open. As they exit the room, the fast-track governor ushers the officer through first. Says not to worry, she will get the lights. Reaches over to the wall - and turns them out.

* * * * * * * * *

Charlotte Rosesmith is as good as her expansive signature. By mid-afternoon, prisoners Djemil, Schild are being moved to Cell B4-12. Officer Jenny Hughes sees to it herself.

"On the fours, I'm afraid," she says to Schild, taking him up there. "Not ideal if you're on an ACCT. Especially for the poor sods who have to keep checking on you. Still, best we can do right now."

Carrying his duvet and meagre possessions, the vulnerable-looking prisoner quickly installs himself in the top bunk, shuts the door. Djemil arrives ten minutes later. Immediately tells Schild to take the bottom bed.

"Safer mate, I promise."

Schild looks disbelievingly at him. But he moves.

They hardly speak at first. Instead eat their meal together in near silence - Schild sitting on the side of his bunk, mechanically munching his chips, the motion of his jaw oddly loud in the hard-surfaced cell, Djemil on a chair below the window, looking into the room, the little plastic tray across his thighs. He almost throws the food into his mouth. A grinder to keep busy.

After they have eaten, and the pale blue plastic plates, bowls are piled up on the floor by the door, Djemil lights a roll-up. Exhales as he stands up, looks out of the window. Over to where prisoners in A Wing, on the other side of the exercise yard, are swinging lines to each other, trading objects cell to cell on the ends of shredded sheets. Sometimes they need two or three goes to make their target. Sometimes more if the wind gets hold and the traded object is light.

He appears so engrossed by the action, the man from London, he does not seem to hear when Schild starts speaking. Asks, in a high-pitched voice, why Djemil wanted to share a cell with him. Why he has offered to protect him. Only after the third attempt does the Londoner finally turn around from the window, stare at Schild who is hunched over on the lower bunk.

"I'm not after a piece of your arse, if that's what you're worried about."

"That's not why I'm asking!" Schild sounds annoyed. "I'm asking because ... it just seems strange you'd go out of your way to help me out."

There's a pause before Djemil answers.

"Well ... it's like I told you. Prisons are tricky places and I know how they work. And I'm not being funny, but you stand out a mile in this place. You may as well have an arrow on your head saying 'Bully me'. And let's just say, I don't like seeing people getting bullied." He takes a puff of his rollie. "Anyway, if you don't trust my motives, why did you agree?"

Schild just stares at him.

"Listen," Djemil carries on. "When I said you look like a target for bullies, I didn't mean to offend you. I mean, you might not be. You might be OK here on your own."

A shake of the head from Schild.

"I'm not."

"How do you mean?"

"There are people after me."

"Go on," says Djemil, raising his eyebrows. "You won't tell me? OK, fine. But let me say this. The more you tell me, the more I'll be able to keep you safe."

Now Schild does look up, tears sparkling in the light.

"People are trying to kill me."

"Kill you?"

"Yes. Kill me."

Djemil looks thoughtful as he blows out smoke.

"Well, then, you need to tell me who they are. Like I said ..."

But Schild gives another vigorous shake of the head.

"There's no point. You wouldn't stand a chance against these guys. And besides ... you'd never believe me."

* * * * * * * * *

B Wing exercise is late that afternoon. Delayed at first due to inclement weather, it gets reinstated by the Supervising Officer on the grounds that, "You never know, might stop one of them topping themselves." Goes ahead around four. Even then, turnout is lowish - blame the blustery weather - and the queue to be rub-down searched quicker than normal. Moves at a lick thanks to Jenny Hughes and her colleague who seem to prefer going through motions rather than prisoners' pockets.

It means Djemil, Schild are outside in no time. Out with the sixty-odd other prisoners who walk around the circle of tarmac that nestles between the splayed residential spurs of A and B Wings. Follow centuries-old prison protocol by shuffling around anti-clockwise in tight-knit clumps, every one of them within a couple of yards of the high metal fence. Maximise freedom.

Even so, hierarchy looms large. Some of the B Wingers strut around ostentatiously, laugh loudly as they give high-fives, thump each other on the back. Others scamper around picking up fag ends or hover near the staff for protection. Most, though, blend into the hazy middle ground. Seem happy just to swap the stench of the wing for a bit of fresh air, some real light. A bit of chat.

Schild and Djemil are in this last group. With restrained body language and at regulation pace, they blend in. Exchange only the occasional word and, every so often, point furtively to things. Other prisoners, mostly. The only thing noticeable about them, in fact, and then barely, is the different way each man holds his head. Schild looks at his feet while he walks, hardly ever raises his eyes. Djemil, on the other hand, never stops looking around, his eyes on constant full alert.

Only a dozen or so laps get completed before the SO by the gate in the fence nearest the wing looks at his watch, starts rubbing his upper arms. A minute later, is calling time: "Have you off, lads!" The onset of rain hurries the exodus. Soon has the prisoners queuing for another rub-down search, this one even quicker than the last.

The huge figures of Jarvis, Longman lumber in and, as they do, other prisoners peel out of their way, like a zip undoing. Let the large men push in near the front of the queue. Seeing this, Djemil whispers to Schild to stay near the back, then also walks towards the front. Gets let in too.

* * * * * * * * *

Matthew Schild is one of the last to re-enter B Wing and, the moment he does, the relief from finally walking in the open air, from feeling slightly safer evaporates in seconds. Gets replaced by worry. Worry, specifically, about where the hell his new cellmate has got to. And the way other prisoners made way for him as he pushed into the front of the queue like that. As if everyone knows something ...

Jostled from behind, Schild begins walking back up to cell B4-12. Can't think what else to do. But when he makes the fours, sees Officer Siddle putting prisoners behind their doors the moment they go anywhere near their cell, he about-turns. Weaves through prisoners trudging up the stairs so he can get back down to the threes. Has no plan. Just wants more time to decide his next step. And, if he can, find out where Djemil has gone. What he is up to.

As the tiny Israeli gets to the end of the threes by the phones, prisoners on the landing are thinning rapidly as staff lock them up, one, two at a time. He starts walking back along the other side. Is still walking when something makes him look right - a stifled scream from a cell. The door is pulled to - a two-inch gap from the jamb. But through the gap Schild can see Djemil's face turned into a snarl and the Londoner drawing a finger across his neck. Then stabbing something with his finger.

Feeling sick, Schild shifts his gaze. Makes out the terrified face of a weedy-looking prisoner who was out on exercise with them, spent the whole session scouring the ground for fag ends. Now the weakling looks like he wants to cry. Putting up his hands, he turns, then opens the battery compartment of a crummy stereo behind him. From it, retrieves a mobile phone. Handing it over to Djemil, he submissively bows his head.

"Mr Schild! Get back on your landing. Up here now!"

Schild turns. Sees Siddle leaning over the bars of the fours. For a second, thinks about disobeying. Not going up. Or maybe going up and telling Siddle about his cellmate. Telling the officer he does not want to share a cell with Djemil any more. That he is scared. But as Schild mechanically obeys the command, walks towards the metal stairs, his mind rolodexes his options. Draws a blank. Or rather, reaches the same bleak conclusion he reached down the CSU. Djemil makes him nervous. He does not trust his motives and there is something not quite right about the Londoner. Something he cannot put his finger on. But there is still no certainty the guy will harm him. Whereas without him ...

Meekly climbing the stairs, Schild hurries along the fours landing, cops an earful from Siddle. Is on the lower bunk in B4-12 by the time Djemil returns a minute later.

The cell door thuds shut angrily.

"Who was that you were talking to?" Schild asks as Djemil goes for a piss behind the toilet screen.

Looking round, the Londoner seems surprised by the question. Answers mid-flow.

"I'm not going to tell you, Matthew. Because you'd never believe me."

And with a chuckle and a final spurt, he flushes the loo.

Chapter 6

Few places in the world can be more secure than the Reception yard of Hatcham prison. Not just because of the towering 5.2m-high walls which mark its perimeter, or the Dannert wire lolling along their top. Or even the impressive double gates which swing open to reveal a sterile area where prison staff - if they are having an unusually good day or if a security audit is in full swing - pore over a van's documents, scurry round with mirrors to check for prisoners clinging onto the vehicle's underside, make sure those really are staff in uniform, not prisoners in clothes 'borrowed' from poor sods they have hit on the head.

No, there is another reason for the yard's unparalleled security. It is because few other places are security-checked quite as frequently by two such experienced senior managers. And lo, here are Messieurs Jenkins and McKenzie at it again on a wet wonderfully scented Tuesday morning, weapon of choice in their respective right hands, yellow forefingers testament to their unstinting quest to ensure public safety, minimise the risk of prisoners escaping. Talk about committed!

McKenzie has adopted his customary stance - legs a yard or so apart, left arm loose by his side, sizeable shaven head staring ahead in apparent disregard of his colleague.

But if his look's intimidating, his chosen subject matter is softer altogether.

"That was a very fetching top Charlotte had on this morning."

"Oh yeah?"

"Don't pretend you didn't notice, Jenkins. You were so transfixed you couldn't even speak."

"Actually, I do remember seeing something rather inviting, now you mention it," the Head of Residential giggles. "And I have to say, I was quite touched by the way Charlotte let me pick up her hanky for her on the way out the Boardroom. Did you see how she blushed as she took it back?"

McKenzie scrunches up his nose.

"No I did not. But I'm glad her hanky brightened up your day, Chris. I could do with a bit of that."

"Brightening up, you mean? Why? No, wait, let me guess, Tony. The MDT rate. The way the gaffer was on at you again in the Morning

Meeting. Basically saying the prison is falling apart because you, our one and only Security Governor, can't find a way of stopping all the drugs pouring in. Must be that, no?"

"Thanks for putting it so delicately, Chris. But no, actually. I hardly notice that sort of thing these days, it's become so normal." He gives a bitter chuckle. "No, it's Matthew Schild I've been thinking about. You know, the little Israeli who was down the CSU. Remember last night I told you about the rumour of a bounty on his head?"

"Of course. And I told you prisons are full of rumours like that. They're part and a parcel of being a ..."

"Yeah, I know you did, Chris. But since then, I've had a long chat with my best informant. And he confirmed it, Lopez. No, come on, don't do your bullfighting bollocks again. Listen to what I'm saying. Lopez reckoned there really is a bounty on Schild's head. Told me it was for ... well, you guess how much."

"Fifty quid."

"A hundred grand."

"Jesus!" Jenkins pauses. "He's having you on, Tony. No prisoner's worth that much. Not in this place. And if they are, they need moving to Belmarsh. Besides, have you thought this through? I mean, why the fuck would Lopez tell you something like that?" He turns to the taller man. "What I'm saying is, if the bounty really did exist, he'd keep schtum, Lopez. Instead of telling you about it, he'd pretend he knew nothing so he could try and cash in with his mates."

"No, I know. Of course he would. And that's exactly why I made a deal with him. Packed him off to Worthington."

"You are joking me!"

Jenkins shakes his head.

"Your best intelligence source, and you get rid of him!"

"It was the only way he was going to speak," says McKenzie, suddenly sounding a bit unsure of himself. "So that was the deal me and the Police Liaison Officer made with him. Shoot your mouth off about the bounty, tell us about your Co-Ds - Jarvis and Longman, basically - and we'll drop the attempted rape charge on Jenny Hughes. Get you shipped out."

"Put it like that and I'm not surprised he went and bloody grabbed it."

"Yeah. But what he didn't know is that Jenny Hughes wasn't going to press charges anyway. So we got information without giving anything."

Another lull.

"Well, I still don't buy the hundred grand bit, Tony. And it makes me doubt the whole thing about the bounty, to be honest. No-one puts that kind of sum on someone unless they're a major player. And I mean major," Jenkins adds, lowering his voice to denote ultimate gangsterdom. "Did Lopez tell you why people are out to get a little Israeli guy who wouldn't hurt a fly?"

"The answer's no, since you ask. No-one has a clue what Schild's done to deserve it, apparently. Lopez made out all the other prisoners in the know were as gobsmacked as he was."

McKenzie rolls a stone underfoot, then kicks it so it hops, skips, finally thumps against the towering mesh fence.

"What's he in for, Schild?"

"Criminal damage. No previous convictions. And if you believe Lopez, no-one knows where the fuck the bounty's come from either."

"What about our resident copper? Any ideas?"

"Nada. Niente. But he did say the Met's undercover guys know nothing about it either. Nothing from the road, so to speak."

Jenkins has another puff. Shifts from foot to foot.

"How come you've not segged this Israeli guy, Tony? For his own protection. I mean, with a price like that on his head ..."

"Chris, I could not agree more. That's exactly the conversation I had with Charlotte. We had a right old ding-dong about it. I told her: 'This is the sort of situation that could bite you on the arse. If Schild gets injured or dies, God forbid, you won't have a leg to stand on. You'll be up there in a coroner's court ...'"

"And let me guess. She went and played the safer custody card."

"Pretty much. Started banging on about how Schild can't be on his own because he's on an ACCT, he's too vulnerable, blah-de-blah-de-blah. Said she only went ahead, kept him on B Wing, after a lot of - how did she put it again? - a lot of 'subtle judgement', that was it. Threatened to go to Simmering about it as well. So we compromised. Agreed to keep Schild banged up for his own protection. Got to say, it suited me in a way, keeping him there on B Wing. The CSU's completely rammed."

"Well, you'd better hope Djemil's not tempted by the hundred either," says Jenkins. "I mean - fuck - it's a lot of money."

"On Charlotte's head be it, that's all I can say."

The two men stare ahead, as if entranced by the dozens of torn turquoise sheets which, tied to cell window bars, flap furiously in the breeze, try to escape to the skies.

"I wonder ..." starts McKenzie. "I wonder if Schild could have double-crossed someone big time on the out. Or if he was into heavy shit in Israel. In fact ..." He pulls on his cigarette as he gets his thoughts in order. "Maybe, Chris, the bounty was issued from there."

"What, Israel? It's hardly a hotbed of organised crime, is it?"

"Well, for one, are you sure about that? Maybe it is, and we've just not come across it before. I mean, what do we know? Have you been to Jerusalem recently? No, I didn't think so. And two, maybe Schild's part of an international crime syndicate."

Jenkins considers the idea for a nanosecond.

"Bollocks, Tony. We don't get glamorous shit like that in Hatcham. Rapists, robbers from around London, that's what we've got. That's what pays the mortgage."

"Well I might still check it out. At least talk to Schild, see what he has to say. You never know ..."

"You do that."

A pigeon flies over the roof of A Wing, descends steeply, lands more or less in front of them. Waddling over to the cigarette end Jenkins has just flicked away, it pecks at it, then waddles on unimpressed.

"Obviously a non-smoker," says McKenzie. "You down the gym at lunch, Chris?"

"I reckon. I heard Charlotte's starting netball sessions. Thought I might give them a go ..."

* * * * * * * * *

The meeting chaired by Governor Charlotte Rosesmith that afternoon is notable for two things. The first is the alarmingly flushed face that sits atop

Chris Jenkins's neck. Looks like a beacon, the way it glows, emanates pinkness in the middle of the chapel. The second is that this is the first meeting in the history of Hatcham that combines Equality and Diversity with Safer Custody - a marriage of these crucial disciplines that Charlotte proposed little more than a month ago.

The two areas might seem different, she told fellow senior managers one day after a Morning Meeting, but only because people were used to treating them differently. There were, in fact, many similarities. In fact, she would go so far as to say they were complementary. Both disciplines were about equality of care and about quality of life. And both were fundamental to the overall performance of the prison.

Judging by his skyward eyebrows, the argument caught Simmering by surprise. The top governor fiddled furiously with his Parker pen for a few seconds, then appeared on the verge of saying something. But Charlotte did not appear to notice. Instead, tucking some hair behind a small ear, she serenely built upon her argument. Said that to distinguish Equality and Diversity from Safer Custody might even be considered racist by some people (although that would be a hardline view). Added that just as Equality Impact Assessments permeated the whole of prison life, so Safer Custody should pervade every activity too.

By this stage, Simmering was looking pummelled. And perhaps conscious that twenty-five pairs of eyes were trained upon him, waiting to see his response, he just nodded. Muttered something about racism of any sort not being tolerated. Added that Charlotte's argument sounded pretty convincing. Sounded pretty unconvinced.

Now, in today's meeting a month on, Charlotte is giving her first report on how well the combined approach is working and her delivery is decidedly upbeat. She starts by comparing stats from the last month with the previous three months. Points to the dramatic drop in self-harm incidents around the prison. Goes on to describe the dual roles performed by her team of prisoners - Listener Equality reps, as she calls them. Explains proudly that the new approach has helped share best practice across both disciplines. Waves willowy fingers in the prisoners' direction. Insists the increase in demand for Listeners from the prisoner population is to be welcomed.

"How do you make that out?" asks Simmering quietly. "Surely it could just mean we have more distressed prisoners."

Charlotte puckers her lips.

"Well, Governor. I believe it shows heightened awareness by my Listeners in spotting signs of distress, which probably reflects the extra training they received from The Samaritans recently. I also think it demonstrates the greater trust our more vulnerable prisoners are starting to have in our Listener team. Before implementing this dual approach, these kinds of prisoners may have stayed in their cell and silently cut up."

She shudders visibly as she says this.

"Now, though, they feel able to share their anxiety. They want to talk. Why? Well, I would argue that Safer Custody has lost some of its stigma and that, overall, Hatcham is becoming a more caring place. I can't overstate the importance of this, Governor. Especially in light of the very high drug rate we are suffering from at the moment."

She turns her gaze McKenzie's way. Lets it rest there a moment, like a magnifying glass lasering sun onto an ant.

"Actually, I suppose that does make sense," says Simmering, sounding cautiously impressed. "Just make sure you always consider the possibility of the opposite, Charlotte. That the stats have gone up simply because self-harm and things like bullying are getting worse."

The young woman nods meekly.

Towards the end of the two-hour session, Governor Charlotte Rosesmith thanks the prisoners in attendance for their valuable contributions. Introduces one of them in particular. Explains to the room that she would like to give Mr Brannigan, one of her most experienced and dedicated Listener Equality reps, the chance to explain first-hand some of the valuable work he carries out on a daily basis. In particular how his efforts, and those of his Listener Equality colleagues, contribute to the safety of prisoners and the performance of the prison overall. As a tall swarthy figure tentatively gets to his feet, Charlotte gives him a little nod of encouragement. And with a swish of her shiny brown hair, hands him the floor.

* * * * * * * * *

They are sitting down, both of them, but even so the man with the shaved head on the other side of the table towers over Matthew Schild. Introduces himself as Governor McKenzie, Head of Security. Says he needs a bit of a chat. Nothing to worry about. Should be done by tea.

He sounds slightly bored as he trots out stock questions. Where is Mr Schild from? Why has he been sent to prison? How is he coping?

Schild, in turn, provides stock answers. Israel, criminal damage, he is doing OK, thank you for asking.

The big face barely reacts. Just wrinkles up its nose, looks to the ceiling as if for inspiration. Shuffles the bits of paper in front of him.

"Do you feel safe?" McKenzie asks finally.

Schild shrugs.

"It's a prison."

"But every prisoner has a right to safety. That's our responsibility as staff. That's why I'm here now."

"OK ..." says Schild slowly. "So you think I might not be safe?"

McKenzie leans back.

"You were given seven days' CC last week. For holding a mobile phone and some Benzos. Now experience tells me ..." The voice drops an octave. "I've worked in a lot of prisons, Mr Schild. And experience tells me you were made to hold those things. That you were threatened with violence if you didn't hold them ... by prisoners who think they run the wing. Mr Jarvis or Mr Longman, for example. Am I right?"

Schild looks down at the table.

"You're right, Governor. I was getting bullied."

"Mr Jarvis?"

"It doesn't matter, because I'm OK now. I share a cell with someone who everyone's afraid of."

"Mr Djemil, you mean?" McKenzie's hand flies up to his chin. "You say everyone's afraid of him. Can you tell me why that is?"

Again the small man shrugs.

"No idea. It's like all the other prisoners know something about him."

"And, er ..." Another chin stroke. "Don't you want to know what they know, the other prisoners? After all, Mr Djemil is in your cell, not theirs. What I'm saying is, are you sure you feel safe with him?"

A nod. But then also a wince.

"You do know that Mr Djemil smashed up his cell recently?"

A second wince.

"While you've been with him, have you seen any signs of violence? Or temper? Have you seen that?"

"Governor. Djemil and me, we get on OK. And besides, I'm not getting bullied any more. So it's working. But thank you for your concern."

Schild glances at the door.

"Matthew, there's another reason I wanted to talk to you today. As Hatcham's Security governor, I receive a lot of information from multiple sources within the prison. Some of it is true, and a lot of it is not. Recently I received information that there is a bounty on your head. Now, as I said, I need to be able to ensure your safety. And to do this, I need to know whether you were aware of this bounty, or think there may be any truth in it."

Turning back, Schild grabs his hair. Runs a hand over his brow.

"A bounty?" he stammers.

"Yes. Now it might not be true, Matthew. In fact it most probably isn't. For a start, the information came from some other prisoners who claimed they were approached by someone outside the prison. Which I'm inclined to take with a pinch of salt as there's no way of proving this. And secondly, the figure they were talking about is not your normal-size figure. In fact it's so big, I have real trouble taking it seriously. But obviously I've still got to go through the motions, check everything out. So if you give me any indication it might be true, well ... I'll have to move you back to the CSU. For your own protection."

"How much am I worth, then?"

Schild's voice is shaking.

"A hundred thousand, Matthew. A hundred thousand pounds."

The Israeli puts his head in his hands.

"As I said, I need to examine all the possibilities. So ... let's just suppose, for argument's sake, this bounty does exist. It would mean you have some powerful enemies, Matthew. Very powerful indeed. So what can you tell me? Any ideas?"

* * * * * * * * *

One more time, spindly Israeli legs swing over the side of the lower bunk in cell B4-12 and size five feet land on the beige white-streaked lino floor. For a minute or two, they do not move, as if their owner is gripped by the earnest documentary on the television. It is about eagle owls and the threat some conservationists believe the majestic birds could pose if they begin breeding in the wild. A full-grown adult can carry a small piglet, apparently.

But then the feet do move. And in the flash, the flicker of light from the screen, a child-sized figure walks towards to the door. Is only half-way there when an exasperated voice brings him to a halt.

"Not again, Matthew! Come on."

The slight figure remains motionless for a second, then turns around, creeps back into the darkness.

"That would have been three times," says Djemil. "Take it from me, that door is shut. No-one will get into this cell."

"That doesn't mean they won't find a way."

Schild's voice is so quiet, so frightened, it is as if he can barely bring himself to speak.

"Who, Matthew? Who? You keep talking about 'they', but you won't tell me who you mean."

But Schild just looks at the ground.

"Listen, whoever they are ... they're not going to come and get you in this cell. For a start, we've got a big steel door protecting us. And if they are clever enough to get through thick steel doors, God knows how ... well, I'll deal with it. I'm quite good at that, as it goes. So get some sleep, and I'll watch the door. OK?"

Still no reply. Only the odd creak, rattle as fifty kilos turn from side to side, make the metal bed frame shake.

In hushed tones, the naturalist is explaining his admiration for eagle owls. They are quite small for their nine-kilo mass, he says - a wingspan of only six feet or so - but their talons, barrel-shaped build and hunting prowess make them feared predators. Most of the time, they hunt at night.

On the screen an eagle owl swoops down on a small mammal - mouse, rabbit, it is difficult to see - stretches out its mighty talons before snatching the poor thing, lumbering back up into the crepuscular sky. As the camera pans back, shows the little creature struggling to break free despite the rapid ascent - obviously wants to die on its own terms - pale blue floods the cell. Reveals, on the lower bunk, a face with hollow cheeks and a mad-eyed stare.

Djemil, in his customary windowside chair, does not seem to notice. Instead, nature programme finished, he mutes the volume. Lets quieter, more disparate sounds take over. The non-stop dubstep music of the Kavanagh brothers four doors away: dee-ba-ba-ba, dee-ba-ba-ba; the monkey-type screams of Hammer Smith who Governor Rosesmith wants to "try out on B Wing"; threats from other prisoners describing in gory detail what will happen to Hammer Smith if he does not shut the fuck up; the occasional sound of an inspection hatch slamming shut, as a night officer checks that prisoners on ACCTs still breathe.

Their own hatch opens. And as the lights flick on, the silhouette of a head, neck appears through the slit of window. Then the hatch shuts again, the lights go off, and the officer can be heard walking away. Seconds later, his footsteps reverberate on the metal staircase down, fall bizarrely into rhythm with the Kavanaghs' dubstep: dee-ba-ba-step, dee-ba-ba-step.

Djemil stays there by the window for a good hour. Until most of the noise has died down, and a snore rumbles out gently from the lower bunk. At last standing up, he stretches out his arms and, lighting a cigarette, peers through the bars at the full moon outside. Its position is perfect tonight - just above the prison wall, the silhouette of the Dannert wire against the mottled white disc becoming some thorny climbing rose.

Cigarette dead, Djemil glances at Schild before stealthily threading his hand through the narrow open window. Pulling on a bit of string tied to one of the window bars, he retrieves a small mobile phone. Cupping hand around screen, he switches the thing on. Sends a text: S SAFE, SHARING CELL, WILL STILL NOT ID. RUMOUR OF BOUNTY ON HEAD. CONNECTION?

A minute or so later, a return text. Djemil reads it, mutters "Stupid fuckers." Slowly shakes his head.

He rolls, then lights another cigarette. Stares once more through the bars at the floodlit exercise yard outside. Is soon sending another text. To a different number this time. I UNDERSTAND WHY BUT I'VE LEARNED. SECOND CHANCE?

He waits after sending this. Waits while eerie howls fill the silence. But to this text, there is no answer. Flicking away the end of his fag, Djemil rests his forehead against two window bars, looks through the gap in between. Then carefully returns the phone to its hiding place. As he does, Hammer Smith lets out another howl. And, far below, a gate clangs.

Chapter 7

"Alarm bell, B4 landing. I say again, alarm bell, B4 landing. Acknowledge Oscar 1."

"That's received, Oscar 1 over."

Over the radio net, a Custodial Manager acknowledges a new incident. Seconds later, shouts from staff ring out along four spurs of the prison, and up and down four levels: "Have you away lads!"; "Where do you live?" Are followed immediately by the random drum beat of slamming cell doors and, underneath, a deeper bass roll as staff across the prison sprint full pelt towards the bell. Doc Martens chirp as officers skid round corners, accelerate from gates.

"Where is it?"; "On B4!"; "Coming through!"

Charlotte Rosesmith emerges from the Admin corridor onto the Centre. Shouting after a racing officer to leave the gate open, she strides onto B Wing, her purposeful gait betrayed by the apprehension on her face, the radio that won't stop shaking in her tightly clenched hand. Past the Meds room, she goes, then through the second gate before turning left, immediately setting off up the stairs. The pace of her ascent does not waver. Means that twice, on the way up, she has to move aside, let officers race past.

Mayhem greets her at the top. Bodies are strewn in, out and around the shower area of the fours landing like a freeze-frame battle scene. Most are in various degrees of contortion and most of them, clad in black and white. Other members of staff stand around, hinder visibility like some corporeal cloud. And yet one thing is clear: there are four distinct clumps of humanity. In the middle of each clump, a prisoner.

One is on his haunches by the railings. Physique of a wrestler, he keeps retching and, every time he does, his entire torso convulses as if he is struggling to contain a monster within. By his side kneel two hefty officers. They keep a firm grip of the man's Popeye-like upper arms, his stout wrists, the massive hands. Nevertheless they look queasy, both of them. Try not to look at the gunky orangey mess that is pooled before them.

A second prisoner lies in the recovery position. Upper body in the showers but with legs poking out, he looks tall. Ridiculously so, going by the size of the spotless white trainers that point down the landing, seem to reach half-way along. A nurse in dark-blue trouser suit crouches by the giant's head, keeps checking his pulse against a silver analogue watch. Every so often, makes sure his airway is not blocked before looking back at the second hand, mouthing numbers. Someone offers the nurse a towel. He snatches it before tucking it under the large lolling head. Shouts out, voice verging on the panicked: "Can we get these people away?"

The CM reacts. Radioing Comms that the alarm is under control, he sets up a mini-exclusion zone around this second prisoner. Sends away the late-arriving staff who are on their feet, now just getting in the way. Charlotte Rosesmith gives the CM a tentative nod of assent. Whirls around when the wrestler-shaped prisoner gives his most violent retch yet.

The two other prisoners at the scene are more visible. One is on a black plastic chair just outside the gated area, looks bizarrely out of place. Weedy, bookish and wearing nothing apart from a towel around his waist, he leans forwards with his head in his hands, sounds like he is in a violent struggle for breath. The two officers at his side keep only a loose grip on his stick-like arms and one of them keeps speaking to him. Or rather, she tries to. But the tiny figure won't respond - even with his eyes, which look blank, uncomprehending.

Flanked by two members of staff, the fourth prisoner shows no sign of resistance either. And yet the officers' grip on this man's arms is much more business-like. As if he represents a different proposition, somehow. No injuries are apparent, although the way the prisoner keeps opening, closing his right fist suggests something might not be quite right there. Otherwise he looks calm and alert. Stands quietly near the gated area, not far from the top of the stairs.

"Right. Seg him first," says the gruff-sounding CM, pointing to this last prisoner by the stairs, "followed by him ..." - he points to the vomiting wrestler-type - "... then him, if he turns out OK." He nods towards the skinny man on the chair. "This other one ..." Now he gestures to the giant on the floor. "Keep him here for the moment, let the nurse decide if we need an ambulance." A pause, then a glance to his right. "If that's OK with you, Governor?"

"Yes, yes ..."

Charlotte Rosesmith gives a succession of rapid nods, awkward little coughs.

"G4DP from Oscar 1," drawls the CM without further ado. "Three prisoners en route to the CSU, Oscar 1 over."

"That's received, Oscar 1. Acknowledge Kilo 1."

"That's received, Kilo 1 over."

On the CM's cue, two staff begin walking the fourth prisoner down the stairs. He complies, the man. Nevertheless they walk three abreast on their way down. As they reach the half-way platform on the first flight of stairs, between the fours and the threes, staff and prisoner turn a hundred and eighty degrees like some gargantuan six-legged beetle. And as they do, the prisoner looks up. Catches the eye of the weedy-looking one hunched over on the chair. Gives him a wink. Then carries on down.

* * * * * * * * *

Compliance pays. Prisoner Djemil stays down the CSU over lunch, has a larger than normal portion of toad in the hole and chips, and, due to population pressures and Charlotte Rosesmith's sympathy for his argument ("Only trying to protect my cellmate, Miss"), is on his way back to cell B4-12 by two o'clock.

When Djemil enters the cell, he speaks to the motionless figure on his lower bunk. Gets no response. So taking his usual seat by the window, unrolls the fresh newspaper he arrived with - the one he suggested to Charlotte "might brighten up Matthew's day, Miss." Flicks through its pages noisily. After a minute, turns around, leans over Schild. Speaks, almost shouts.

"Are you OK?" he asks for the second time.

Still no answer.

"Right. If you won't speak, I will. That attack was not a coincidence, Matthew. It was planned." He pauses. "And you were right. You do have people after you. I'm sorry, I didn't know whether to believe you before. Especially when you told me about the bounty. But now I do, Matthew. I do believe you. And what I know is, you must have crossed someone big time. Those guys ... what are their names again? Jarvis, Longman - they were obviously trying to get the hundred." Again he pauses. "The good news is I doubt they'll try again. Not after the pasting I gave them. And I doubt anyone else will, if I'm honest. But we still need to be careful. If the bounty still exists ..."

Suddenly Schild laughs. Kicks his feet up like a child.

"You haven't got a clue, have you!" he says, sitting up and giving Djemil an incredulous look. "Think you've sorted everything out because you hit two small-time criminals in the mouth? Think it won't happen again? Pah! I'm afraid the problem is not over, Mr Djemil. The problem is just beginning."

"How do you mean?"

A shrill chuckle from the lower bunk.

"Let's just say you made a big mistake when you promised to look out for me. And now that you have ... well, you are in over your head. Way over! It's not silly street criminals who are after me, it's ... it's professional killers who track you down wherever you are, whatever country you're in. And they don't stop until they've ..."

Djemil looks over for more information. But Schild's saucer-wide eyes are staring at nothing, and the bony little body is shivering violently. As if the threat is already with them, somehow. In the cell.

* * * * * * * * *

Matthew Schild has never felt terror like it. It is as if someone is punching him in the gut, then plunging him into ice-cold water, leaving him there gasping for breath, for sheer life, then yanking him out again only to start the punching again. It really does feel this physical. And yet, through the terror, a piercing awareness that the cause is hard undeniable evidence. Evidence they are after him. Evidence that backs up the tip-off from his old work colleague before he came to prison. Evidence that stamps, once and for all, on the delicate hope he had been nurturing quietly - the hope that they might not, after all, bother. Might just let him get on with his life. Forgive.

It was ridiculous, this hope. He knew that. And yet until the attack in the showers, until Longman's huge hands actually tightened around his throat, squeezed the breath from him like that - until that moment, there was always, in his mind, this pale green seedling edging upwards, vivid against the lead-grey sky of common sense.

Not now, though.

He wonders about talking to Djemil. Trying to share the terror. After all, his fear of his cellmate has been eclipsed by the new reality. But as he looks over, catches sight of the Londoner's brooding presence, can almost hear the cogs whirring around with painful slowness under that widow's peak of his, Schild immediately sees the futility of it. He just would not understand, Djemil.

Nor would Brannigan, for that matter - the prisoner who governor Charlotte Rosesmith suggested he should talk to if he gets really anxious. Schild has never met the guy, but he can imagine how useless he would be. After all, what is a common criminal going to know about the life of a fugitive?

And yet as Schild hunches over, does his best to blot out the world, the terror only grows. Plunges him back into the ice-cold water, delivers another punch to his solar plexus. Makes him panic. He has to do something. Anything.

He leaps out of his bunk. Hits the cell bell.

Djemil goes nuts when he realises. Rasps at Schild, why the fuck has he just done that? Starts going on about how the risk increases every time the door is opened. How a locked cell is the safest place to be. But Matthew Schild does not answer. Instead tells Officer Siddle, when he comes, that he desperately needs to speak to a Listener. It's all getting too much.

Ten minutes later, Siddle returns with the tall figure of Mr Brannigan IIA2022 in tow. Asks Djemil to accompany him down the landing to another cell, so that Mr Schild and Mr Brannigan can have some time alone.

Djemil does not comply at first. Just stares menacingly at the Listener. Even asks Officer Siddle if he can sit in with them. But the more he asks, the more adamant Siddle becomes. No, he repeats. They have to be alone. That is the whole point. Eventually Djemil relents. Allows Siddle to lock him up in a disused cell.

The officer collects him forty minutes later. Informs Djemil as they walk back up the deserted landing together that Mr Brannigan has already left, then ushers him back into cell B4-12. As the door clunks shut, Djemil looks at Schild who is lying on his bunk, appears transfixed, for some reason, by his toes that peep out from under the duvet. He initiates conversation a few times, Djemil. Tries different angles - Brannigan, Schild's childhood, the people who are coming after him. But he gets absolutely nowhere. Schild just keeps staring at his toes. Once, wiggles them. Shrieks in delight.

The Londoner gives up. Positioning his chair by the window, then sitting down, he lights up a rollie. Looks thoughtful as he smokes.

Chapter 8

Packed, today. So packed that McKenzie, uncharacteristically a minute or two late to the Morning Meeting due to a poorly timed phone call, has to stand behind the gaffer when he enters. Every seat is taken and the smattering of other late-comers are already standing, backs to the wall, around the snazzy beech table. The number of people, the rain outside, the tiny little windows give the Board Room a stale, slightly suffocating atmosphere. Glamorous, it is not.

Duty Governor yesterday was Charlotte Rosesmith, and the young woman is reading out her Daily Report. She reports on an alarm bell in the gym, where two prisoners squared up to each other over the weights. She reports on the pedestrian gate in the Gate Lodge that broke down yet again. ("We spend more time on that bloody thing than we do on prisoners," explodes Simmering.) And she reports on the fight that occurred last thing in the morning on the B Wing fours. Prisoners involved: Mr Schild HA2313 and Mr Djemil HA2684 versus Mr Jarvis HA1690 and Mr Longman HA2213. First two against the second two.

"It happened in the showers," says Governor Rosesmith, doing the hair-behind-the-ear thing. "Mr Schild was taking a shower, it seems, and you can see from the CCTV that Mr Jarvis and Mr Longman go in there fully clothed. Suddenly Mr Djemil, who's talking to an officer on the landing, runs away from her, goes into the shower area as well. The same officer then raises the alarm."

By the time staff entered the showers under a minute later, she continues, Mr Jarvis was unconscious, Mr Longman was throwing up and Mr Schild was crouched on the ground unable to breathe. The way the Israeli was holding his neck suggests one of the others, either Mr Longman or Mr Jarvis, tried to strangle him. That is what the nurse thought, anyway. Amazingly, though, despite the chaos, there were no visible injuries. Mr Longman was unconscious for some minutes but eventually came round. As for Mr Jarvis, he was throwing up on the scene. But again, no marks visible.

Unusually, Charlotte forsakes her usual laser focus on the facts. Lapses instead into her impressions of the scene. Describes it as strange, the way Mr Djemil was standing there, next to three men in various states of distress, looking like he was just waiting for a bus.

"Sounds like he was protecting his mate, and doing a fair job of it," says Simmering simply, before turning around. "Tony, have we got any background to all this?"

The Security governor's face turns crimson. Lifting his head and looking like a naughty schoolboy as he stands there by the door in his black suit, his striped tie, McKenzie tells Simmering of the hundred thousand on Schild's head. Keeps his gaze trained on the top man as he taps his fingers on the table, and others in the room shift in their seats, exchange glances.

"A hundred thousand," says Simmering finally, lingering over each syllable like he is collecting evidence. "One hundred thousand pounds on Mr Schild's head?"

Curled hand to mouth, McKenzie coughs awkwardly.

"That's correct, Governor."

He tries to steer the conversation onto Mr Djemil. Reminds the room that Mr Djemil is the same prisoner who intervened in the recent Officer Hughes incident. The one who, later on, went down the CSU for smashing up. Says that Mr Schild and Mr Djemil - "they've obviously both got their enemies" - but actually they both seemed to be doing pretty well on B Wing.

But Simmering won't be steered. Will not leave the hundred thousand.

"And did you know of this bounty, Tony?" he asks in a tone that smells a right cock-up. "Did you take precautions? Move Schild down the CSU, for example? Keep him behind his door?"

Straightening up as if to hide behind the majesty of his office, McKenzie stammers that yes, he did know of the bounty. But no, he did not take precautions. For a start, there was no corroboratory intel. Nothing of substance. Nothing he could really go on ...

"The sum involved was so big, and it was, er ... the first bit of info we had on Schild at all ... so, er, I wasn't inclined to believe it, Governor."

Jenkins shoots a look of gratitude to the man falling on his sword.

"And secondly, Governor, I discussed it with Charlotte. And, er ... together, we decided to take a holistic approach to Mr Schild's care. What I mean is ... balance any threat there might be to his safety, which as I say was unsubstantiated, against the benefits of sharing with someone he gets on with. But he's being kept behind his door now, Governor. Mr Schild, that is."

"And what about his cellmate? This Mr Djemil character. Do we trust him?"

McKenzie looks at Charlotte, inviting her to join the fray now that he has defended the position she took - even used the very word she kept inflicting on him: holistic. But the young woman has found a cuticle to tug. Seems not to notice.

"Well, er ... they do appear to get on well together, Governor," McKenzie carries on forlornly. "I believe it was Mr Schild who asked to share with Mr Djemil originally. And I checked with him yesterday myself. He insisted he felt safer sharing the cell with Mr Djemil than being on his own."

"Mmm," says Simmering. "Well I don't want a murder on my hands."

He tells Jenkins, McKenzie to make sure the two fighting parties are kept apart so they cannot knock seven bells out of each other. Says that, talking of bells, the names Mr Longman, Mr Jarvis seem to ring quite a few. Haven't they cropped up in morning meetings before?

"Quite a few times, Governor," Jenkins pipes up. "Both prisoners have been involved in a number of incidents recently. Are used to having things their way on the wing. Were on anti-bullying monitoring last time they were in."

"Sounds like we might need to put them back on it. I'm guessing they were all placed on report, Charlotte?"

Simmering's voice softens as he turns towards her.

"Yes, Governor. All on report, all the paperwork completed: Incident Report, Use of Force forms, Injury to Inmate forms ..."

"Great. OK, thank you. One thing that worries me - Mr Schild holding his throat like that. And the nurse saying that someone must have tried to throttle him. It's basically the same as trying to kill someone. Did we contact the police?"

Charlotte admits that "we" did not. Shakes her head in apology, explaining she did not think it was serious enough. Especially as there were no visible injuries. Vows to learn from her silly mistake.

"Well, it sounds like it's too late for any forensics," says Simmering, turning back to McKenzie. "But study the CCTV, Tony, see what you get."

As the tall man nods and the room falls silent, Simmering asks one final question. Who, he wants to know, was the officer who witnessed the incident? The one Mr Djemil was talking to when the whole thing kicked off.

This is one thing Charlotte does know. She looks up from her fingers, answers like an eager puppy.

"It was Officer Hughes," she says. "Officer Jenny Hughes, off B Wing."

* * * * * * * * *

Adjourned the previous day because Longman was out at court and CCTV evidence had yet to be gathered, the adjudication for the fight in the B4 showers takes place the next morning. Presiding over the event, a certain Tony McKenzie. The Security governor is not, it is fair to say, all sweetness and light by the time he reads out the charge: Prison Rule 51, Fights with any Person. The reason? He has just viewed the CCTV footage for the fours, B Wing, at 09.42 hours on 30 August. Noted its impressive clarity. Noted, too, the remarkable lack of prisoners under the camera's gaze. Nothing except some giant white trainers sticking out of the shower area.

Nevertheless he remains hopeful, McKenzie, as the accused prisoners are brought in one by one to answer the charge, give their side of the story. Quickly, though, optimism turns to frustration. All four defendants deny there was a fight of any kind. Longman claims he slipped in the shower area ("I've a good mind to sue the prison, Guv"), Jarvis that he walked into the push-on tap on the wall ("I was miles away, Governor McKenzie Sir!").

Djemil and Schild are no better. Remain adamant they saw nothing, had no idea what really happened. Mr Djemil, in particular, is circumspect. Tells McKenzie he thought he heard a cry coming from the shower area ("like someone slipped on the soap, it sounded like") so walked in to see if he could help. Saw, straight away, Longman, Jarvis, Schild all lying on the floor.

With blanket denials, everything rests on the reporting officer Jenny Hughes who has been sitting in the adjudication throughout. McKenzie turns to her. Asks very simply, what did she see happen? After all, she was the one who raised the alarm. Was the one actually talking to Djemil at the time. She seems to ponder the question for a while. Eventually answers with her eyes on the table. Tells McKenzie she can't be sure what she saw either. Only raised the alarm because she heard "a vague commotion." By the time she turned around, finished radioing Control, Djemil had disappeared and Longman, Jarvis and Schild were all on the ground. Maybe, she adds, hand in front of her mouth now, maybe the prisoners are telling the truth. Maybe it was a freak coincidence.

Voice shaking with anger, McKenzie asks if she seriously believes it possible that both Longman and Jarvis could have had simultaneous accidents like that. And what about Matthew Schild holding his neck and the nurse saying he might have been strangled? Did Schild have an accident too?

Jenny Hughes shrugs her shoulders. Can only say what she saw. Which was not much. Nothing, in fact. Fiddling with her watch strap, she looks back up. Apologises for not being a better witness. Suggests the attack by Lopez the other week may have had more of an effect than she realised. Speaks through tears.

In the absence of CCTV footage in the shower area to prove otherwise, and any visible injuries to corroborate the charge, McKenzie has to throw out the adjudication. Jarvis, Longman smile broadly when they are informed. Almost laugh in McKenzie's face - even when he tells them they will remain in the CSU on Good Order and Discipline. Djemil and Schild merely nod.

With the prisoners gone, McKenzie asks Jenny Hughes to hang on a sec. She nods, looking uneasy. Waits there silently while he completes the adjudication paperwork, presses down so hard with his pen, it's like he is trying to etch his comments on the wooden table underneath. But once he has ticked all the right boxes, signed at the bottom of the third page, he turns to her finally. Starts by saying how concerned he is, given her tears. Makes a half-hearted offer to contact Staff Care and Welfare. Moves swiftly on to the lack of evidence she gave in the adjudication. Says how surprised he is she did not see more.

The tears start up again. And it is as McKenzie mechanically whips out a tissue, hands it to the officer, watches her snivel, dab her eyes - it's then that he realises. Realises that not only was Jenny Hughes the member of staff talking to Djemil when the fight in the showers flared up. She was also the one who Djemil saved when he beat up Lopez. Could there be a link between the two incidents?

With Jenny Hughes blowing her nose now, McKenzie realises something else. And it is wonderful. He understands that the fight was not caused by the hundred-grand bounty on Matthew Schild. It must have been a revenge attack for Djemil battering Lopez - for the simple reason that Lopez used to work alongside Longman and Jarvis. That must explain why Jenny looks so awkward now. She knows she was the cause.

The realisation brings frustration and relief. Frustration because - McKenzie remembers so well now! - he predicted just such an attack when he adjudicated on Djemil down the Seg. Even asked him about it. Relief, because it means him - McKenzie - sitting on information about the bounty had nothing to do with it. Thank the Lord! He must find a way of letting Simmering know.

Immediately feeling happier about life, he reminds Jenny Hughes of the chat they had about Djemil smashing up to get off the wing. The one in the Gate that time. Says to her amiably, so they were right after all! Wonders, as an aside, did she know anything about the hundred grand? Slurps the last of his tea after putting the question to her. Knows exactly what she is going to say.

Except that she does not say it, the B Wing officer. Surprises McKenzie instead by vigorously shaking her young head, sputtering no, she doesn't know anything about the hundred grand. Why on earth would she? Doesn't even know Longman or Jarvis particularly. Never really talked to them. Never met them outside the prison either. Wouldn't pick them out in the street particularly. McKenzie lifts an eyebrow. Asks, who said anything about her knowing Longman or Jarvis outside? And what is it, exactly, that she's saying? Is she saying they knew about the price on Schild's head? Longman and Jarvis, he means.

At this, Jenny Hughes breaks down good and proper. Insists, though a steady stream of tears, that she didn't mean to say anything about knowing Longman or Jarvis. Certainly doesn't know anything about the bounty. In fact, the only thing she does know right now is she feels ill. Really ill. Like she's going to throw or something. McKenzie lets her go.

Stays sitting there once she has gone. Just paperwork, unsettling thoughts for company.

That afternoon, he spends two solid hours looking into Officer Jenny Hughes. Her Security record, her next of kin, any Security Information Reports with her name mentioned - even those submitted by her. Everything he can think of. He also gets the mighty Police Liaison Officer, once the behemoth is back from the gym, to have a rummage around the Police National Computer, see what he can dredge up. By five o'clock both men have drawn a blank. There is nothing on her.

McKenzie shrugs. What more can he do? Especially as he is covering Jenkins's duty governor shift this evening and the SIRs appear to be breeding on top of his desk. He has looked into Jenny Hughes, found no evidence to turn coincidence into misdeed, so that's that. Now he has got the small matter of a prison to run.

Only later that evening, as he stop-starts his sporty Vauxhall along the North Circular - nose to tail, must be another accident - only then does he think back to his detective efforts of the afternoon. And feels glad. At least if the shit does hit the fan, his arse is covered now. Getting streetwise in his old age.

Chapter 9

Why is it that, on the days when he is busiest - like today, for example, when there are so many adjudications, he cannot even think of making the gym - Governor Tony McKenzie gets a call from Simmering's PA asking if he can come in for a chat? Three o'clock do? The tall man grimaces as he puts down the phone in the cramped office of the CSU. Immediately feels like a man condemned. Knows full well the chat will be about be the MDT rate which, from what Jenkins was saying on the yard this morning, Simmering kept banging on about in the Safer Custody meeting.

"Completely went off on one, Tony."

Five hours later, the big man turns right into the PA's office, lets her know he is the three o'clock. And as he does, there is something sheepish about the way the civilian worker looks back at him. None of the banter or innuendo they usually trade. Just a strained smile, a sympathetic-sounding, "He's ready for you, Tony", followed by a speedy look back at her screen. Resumption of her inhumanly rapid typing.

The moment McKenzie swings open the gaffer's door, he sees why the PA was looking shifty. Because there, in one of two chairs opposite Simmering, sits Charlotte Rosesmith. The fast-track governor has her back to McKenzie as he walks in. Does not turn round. Instead gives a polite cough. Picks something invisible off her knee.

"Ah, there you are, Tony!" says Simmering from his chair, a shrine to faux leather padding and lumbar support. "We were just discussing this dreadful drug problem. How it's in danger of undoing everyone's good work, if we're not careful. And Charlotte was telling me all about her Security refresher course up at Newbold Revel. Thought some of what she learned up there might help us get on top of it. Eh, Charlotte?"

"Well, I certainly hope so, Governor. As I was telling John, Tony, the MDT affects all of us - in particular, the more vulnerable prisoners who often resort to drugs in times of stress. So it's up to all of us to try and get on top of it. Especially as you're having such a difficult time of it right now. So if I can be any help ..."

Silent and grim-faced, McKenzie pulls back the chair. Sits down. Fastens dull eyes on Simmering.

"That's right," says the top man. "I think it's important to understand, Tony, the world of Security keeps moving on. The basics remains the same. Of course they do. Keeping on top of prisoners' property, making sure they don't accumulate too much, conducting regular searching, using our intel properly. Passing on information especially. But as Charlotte was reminding me, if you do this day in day out, it can be easy to forget the basics sometimes. Even for those of us who are a bit more experienced. What was the word you used again, Charlotte? You put it very well."

"Complacent, Governor," she says, finding another speck on her knee.

"That's it! Complacent, Tony. You can become a bit complacent about the basics. And ... well, I'm not accusing you of anything like that. No, no, of course not! But as we've discussed a number of times, whatever you're doing about this drug problem is not working, I'm afraid. I mean, what are we now with the MDT? I know you told me ..."

McKenzie answers like an automaton. Has to. Any show of emotion and he would be shouting like a madman in Charlotte's face. Punching Simmering on the nose. Again and again and ...

"We're at twenty-two per cent, Governor."

McKenzie hears a sharp intake of breath beside him.

"I'm afraid that underlines my point, Tony. If we were doing the basics properly, there is no way we'd be that high. So what I'd like to do now is to go through - together, the three of us - to go through the basics. One by one. Make sure we're doing everything we can. Charlotte can remind us if we are missing anything. Can't you, Charlotte?"

"I'll certainly do my best, Governor. Like you said, it's a team effort."

* * * * * * * * *

In the sitting room of a high-rise flat in north-east London, torpor reigns. It has been a sweltering hot day but now, late afternoon, the heat has cooled and the open front door swings lazily in the breeze, its bobbly wire-threaded glass chucking light around the room like luminous confetti. Muted sounds add to the hypnotic effect: the gentle growls from diesel bus engines caught in traffic on the high street far below, the drone of a helicopter somewhere which must be flying out of the City, the odd shriek from children playing a game on a balcony a few floors down - together, they mix, merge, swirl softly around inside. Whisper as one: nothing doing.

A dark-blue leatherette sofa is positioned against the back wall. On it, sprawled, a painfully thin man in his twenties, his garish trainers resting on the low coffee table in front of him. Eyes glued to a widescreen television, he feels for a can of beer and, finding it, takes a swig before putting the thing back down, nudging some Rizlas, a cigarette lighter as he does so. Now he picks up the remote. Starts endless channel-hopping, as if the aim is not choosing where to stop, but to keep on moving, keep swimming like some kind of televisual shark.

When, finally, he has exhausted all corners of the sea, the skeletal figure sends the TV to sleep, leans back on the sofa. For minutes does not stir. Just lets gloom enter his sunken eyes, and summer sounds caress his ears. But then, a new sound: a fluttering of wings, a coo from the front door area. The man's eyes come to life. Heaving himself up, he pads over to the front door. At the threshold stops, then stoops to collect seeds from a plastic bag hanging just inside on the wall. Cautiously, in veneration almost, he crosses the doorstep onto the narrow walkway outside. There, gets down on his haunches and, palm upturned, offers seeds to a dowdy-looking pigeon that won't stop walking in circles, jerking its head in time with footsteps like a wind-up toy.

"Hello Stealth. Hello my beauty."

The bird approaches the outstretched hand, starts pecking at seeds in its middle. But not for long. With slow deliberate movements, the man scoops up the bird, gives the back of its head a brief stroke with a skinny finger before placing it inside a loft outside the door. He will let the creature rest. The next trip is not till gone eight. After bang-up.

* * * * * * * * *

Even citizens as upstanding as McKenzie, Jenkins find the lure of exclusivity difficult to resist. To restrict membership of their Reception yard chats, they have made their invitations to each other increasingly subtle. What started as a spoken "Cigarette outside?" became the euphemism "Security Check?" Then, one evolutionary cycle later, a silent mouthed form of the same words. And following that, a mere pat of the breast pocket in which the cigarettes were held. The latest invitation, made by Tony McKenzie at the end of today's Morning Meeting, must rank as the stealthiest yet. Fifth generation, if you will. Consists of nothing more than a raising, then lowering of his majestic eyebrows. Jenkins acknowledges the signal. Gives a slight nod.

Once out on the Reception yard, the two governors stand quietly at first, get in a few lungfuls. And then the taller man speaks.

"I told you about Jenny Hughes, didn't I? Her saying that maybe Longman did slip in the showers and Jarvis did walk into a hook."

"Tell me, Tony! You haven't stopped. Did you look into her like I told you?"

"I did. And not a dickie bird. There's even more on the priest, believe it or not - and that's saying something."

"Well, you've done all you can then. One to watch. If Jenny Hughes is a bad egg, you'll get her in the end. Because bad eggs ..."

"Stink. You've said that one before, Chris. What I didn't tell you is, I had to put Jarvis and Longman back on B Wing yesterday. No, come on, don't look at me like that. I was duty dog and, like I was saying in the meeting just now, the whole prison went completely mad - four fights, two cell fires, two smash-ups - no, hold on, one was a barricade - and that's before Hammer Smith decided it would be a good idea to start swallowing ten batteries or however many it was. So I had no choice. There was no space down the Seg and Jarvis and Longman were the ... what do you say again?" He looks into the distance. "The least worst option, that's it. Don't worry, they're still doing their CC, the two of them. Just doing it behind their door on B Wing."

"Well as long as that bone-idle SO on there doesn't let them out," says Jenkins. "I've got to say, it seems like every day is just about getting through it, these days. In fact you're lucky nothing did come up on Jenny Hughes. You've got enough on your plate with your MDT. How was your chat with Simmering, by the way?"

McKenzie starts shaking his head from side to side.

"You wouldn't believe it. Charlotte was there. She'd just been on her Security refresher course and Simmering made me go through with her all the steps I've been taking to get the MDT down. Even wanted Charlotte to decide whether I'd missed anything or could improve my approach. I mean, for fuck's sake. She's only been in the job five minutes."

He takes an angry puff.

"What I do know, because I'm not a complete fucking idiot, is that the gaffer's getting in the neck from the Area Manager, and he's not going to put up with it for much longer. Charlotte will have my job if I don't sort this thing out. I can tell. That's why yesterday, when I had to go and see him, I told him absolutely everything I've been doing: staff searches, prisoner searches, area searches, more police monitoring around the perimeter walls, you name it. Even went on about that time we borrowed extra dogs from the other London nicks, locked down all the wings. Nuked the prison's time-out-of-cell figures in the process. So he knows all that, the gaffer. Yet he keeps on at me - every fucking morning. MDT, MDT, MDT ..."

Jenkins looks at his beleaguered colleague. And as he does, the Head of Residential's face slowly changes. Crows' feet creep out of his eyes, as if drawn by the ratty lips that curl upwards in delight.

"What?"

"This is one of those situations you told me about, Tony. But the irony is, you can't see it yourself. The gaffer keeps on at you to sort out the drug problem. You tell him everything you've been doing, and he has no problem with any of it. In fact, you've probably done things he wouldn't have thought of."

"So?"

"So ... why do you think he keeps on at you?"

McKenzie looks genuinely lost for words.

"Because he wants you to do more than that."

"I don't get you."

"It's like you said, Tony. When you came into this job, you thought the rules of the Prison Service were what you followed. But then you wise up. You realise rules are what you say you've followed. Any investigation, any shit, you just whip out the rule book, point to what you've done, don't you? You cover your arse."

"So what's your point?"

McKenzie turns his big head, looks blankly at his colleague. A sad uncomprehending shire horse learning from a worldly rat.

"My point is, you're already doing everything legit. Every damn thing that's in the rule book. Which you said yourself, Simmering knows very well."

The horse blinks its big eyes.

"So can't you see?" An edge to Jenkins's voice now. "The gaffer wants you to go outside the rules. To use your initiative. Make the problem go away. That's part of our job too. To discreetly go beyond the call of duty when duty calls."

McKenzie nods thoughtfully.

"Cook the books, you mean? Like you told me to last time, when you got me to lie in all those meetings, stopped me sleeping for a month? Made me feel like a criminal? Never again, Chris."

"Well that's the traditional way, as you know, Tony. But you're obviously a bit sensitive for that sort of thing. Which is a good thing, I suppose. Besides, what with that investigation they've just had across the whole of London, you'll not get away with that kind of creativity now. Even the auditors are getting audited these days. It's gone completely mad." He shakes his head in disbelief. "No, this problem's different, Tony. This one, you're going to have to solve yourself."

McKenzie kicks at a pebble, as if to get rid of such a preposterous notion.

"How the fuck do I do that?"

"You tell me. You're the one with all the intel. But just from speaking to you, I know what I would do."

So Jenkins tells him. He mentions the man Djemil. The prisoner who McKenzie seems obsessed with but can pin nothing on. The prisoner who all the other prisoners seem wary of, especially after the latest Longman, Jarvis incident. The prisoner who Charlotte - the most risk-averse manager in the whole establishment - mysteriously lets share a cell with Schild, despite Djemil being a cell-smasher and Schild having a hundred thousand on his head.

"Had," says McKenzie. "From what I hear, it's been stood down now, the bounty."

"Fine, Tony. Whatever. But my point stands. Djemil is at the bottom of it all. Face it. That's why you got another big rise in your MDT the moment he came into the prison." He holds out a second cigarette, but McKenzie shakes his head. "So you see, it's all there in front of you. And yet ..."

"What?"

"And yet Djemil's not even one of the main guys on your Security radar."

"He is informally."

"Informally ..."

"Chris, I've got nothing on him! I think you're right. Djemil's probably up to his neck in it. But no-one, not even my new informer on B Wing, they won't breathe a word about the guy. In fact I've got about as much intel on Djemil as I do on ..." - McKenzie looks around the yard for a comparison - "... as I do on that pigeon over there."

"And that's exactly my point. Djemil rules the roost, but he appears clean as a whistle. There's your answer to the MDT problem right there, Tony. But to prove it, you're going to have to go outside the rules. Way outside."

Sucking in lustily, he watches while a prison van driver folds up the stairs of a 12-manner and shuts the door. As the lorry-sized vehicle begins a lavish seven-point turn, throwing around its human cargo with gusto, Jenkins turns to McKenzie. Asks in a voice so quiet, the tall man has to lean down to hear.

"Did I ever tell you about this spy shop I used to ..."

He finishes the question, Jenkins. Carries on speaking. But the gruff thrum of the van's engine, the falsetto of its squeaky brakes, drown out what the wily Head of Residential says next. And more to the point, how Tony McKenzie answers.

* * * * * * * * *

Perched on top of a tall slender metal pole, the CCTV camera gives an impressively clear view of the Regent's Park Road during the evening rush hour. The registrations of all the cars, taxis and buses in the traffic - provided the vehicles do not get in the way of each other, of course. And, thanks to its zoom, high-definition capabilities, the features, even the worry lines, of people's faces hundreds of yards away. Only rarely are these views enjoyed in real time. The camera's job is more a retrospective one. Images tend to be grazed by the Metropolitan Police only if a crime has been committed nearby - correction, is reported as having been committed - and further investigation is called for.

That is why no-one, in all likelihood, will ever watch footage of a bespoilered silver Vauxhall hatchback jerking forwards with each peristaltic movement of the constipated traffic twenty, thirty times, finally pull in left onto a double yellow line. Nor will they see the car's flashers go on, then a tall angular-faced man getting out, slamming shut the door. He must be over a hundred yards away, this man. Yet the camera, from its vantage point, makes out his rough-hewn face, the big ears all too easily. Close up, they look huge!

Somewhat shiftily, he looks up and down the road, the man, then at his hefty watch, before walking the dozen or so steps to a red-fronted shop emblazoned with the words The Spy And Surveillance Store. The gaudy exterior is matched by the technical wizardry of items in the window display. Bugs that look like plugs, cameras that masquerade as fountain pens, shirt buttons that are in fact microphones - it is all there. At the threshold the man hesitates, as if unsure whether the shop is open. But a push of its glass door shows it is. And in he skulks.

Despite his late entry, the staff of the shop leave at their usual time tonight. Because under ten minutes later, the same tall man emerges holding a small grey plastic bag. Again somewhat warily - in a way that would draw scorn if Governor Jenkins, say, were to witness the footage - the man edges furtively onto the pavement before looking up and down the Regent's Park Road. Then suddenly starts sprinting. Shouting. Waving his long arms. Repeating, from the looks of it, one mono-syllabic word in particular.

There follows a good minute's worth of remonstration with a lady in a uniform, peaked cap. She appears to be clutching a PDA and, ignoring the man's desperate pleas, stares intently at the registration of the car before typing something into the rugged-looking device. She can also be seen shaking her head, the vigour of her movement miraculously failing to dislodge her fierce-looking headgear.

Even when arms are flung towards the shop by the man, knees bent, hands clasped in supplication - even then the resolute woman refuses to give in. Thc tall figure, feared throughout one of London's toughest jails, can only watch, horrified, as she lifts up his car's right windscreen wiper, triumphantly slams down a plastic-covered document attesting to his transgression. Governor McKenzie, it would seem, has been nicked.

Little lip-reading prowess is necessary for a variety of hard-hitting (but for the lady, hardly novel) expletives to be divined, while the man's angry kick of one of the car's front tyres is more obvious still. As for the way the silver hatchback lurches dangerously into the queue of traffic without any warning or indication - well, a good twenty or so road users notice that!

Chapter 10

If Matthew Schild thinks his face gives nothing away as he approaches Table 23 in Hatcham's cavernous Visits Hall, he is so wrong. The moment the tiny Israeli emerges from the holding room in his demeaning red bib and locks eyes on the brown-haired young woman who is sitting at the far end of the room, fiddling with her hooped ear rings, he appears to lose any self-will. Glides towards her as if propelled by the laws of physics. Iron filing to magnet.

Other prisoners and their girlfriends smirk as he shuffles past their tables as if hypnotised. Crane round to see which table he is going to approach: "Who do you reckon will be the lucky girl?" Watch as he sits down on a fixed red plastic chair opposite a woman, mid twenties, her lack of make-up, grungy dress sense conspicuous in a room bursting with cleavages, bare midriffs.

Schild's visitor either does not notice or care. She leans forwards and kisses him on the lips.

"Hey ..."

"Farideh! It's so nice you came!"

His voice stutters, sounds weak. The young woman smiles. Dimples downy cheeks.

"Of course I'm going to come, you silly moose. I'd have come before if you'd asked me ..."

He offers no explanation.

"So are you OK?" she continues gently. "You don't seem too bad. A bit thin, maybe. And a bit grey - your face, I'm talking about. Oh, and you've missed a bit shaving ..."

She points to the underside of his chin. As she does, one of the officers patrolling the Visits Hall turns towards their table, has a careful look.

"Can't we touch?"

"No, we can. But you can't give me any drugs, phones or guns."

"Damn - and I've brought your Uzi!"

The smile fades.

"I've been worried about you. Why didn't you call?"

He looks away, his eyes filling with tears.

"It's difficult to explain. It's ... it's really hard in here."

"Oh come on, lovely! Don't be like that. You'll be OK. Just got to get through this little patch. Then ..."

She takes his hand, hands him a hankie. As she does, the same officer walks up to the table, demands to see it. Tells her no items can be handed over. If it happens again, the visit will be terminated.

"Wow, what a jobsworth! Fucking hell. Still, I'd better do what the man says. I don't want to get you arrested a second time." She giggles as she stuffs away the hankie, but her face quickly grows serious again. "So come on, tell me. Why is it so hard? Surely you thought about that when you put yourself here ..."

"It's not the prison," he says, more tears forming. "It's the prisoners. I thought I might be safe in here. Just live each day, do my own thing. But..."

"And can't you?"

He bows his head.

"Is someone getting at you? Have you told the staff?"

She looks round at the officer, as if she might beckon him over.

"No, don't! It's not anyone. It's ... that's just how prison is. You don't know till you get in here. Everyone trying to survive, everyone getting at everyone else. It's what you have to do. But I'm crap at it. Look at me," he adds, spreading open his arms to display his bony chest. "I didn't tell you, but I got attacked a few days ago. It was so frightening, I can't tell you. I was taking a shower and the two biggest guys on the wing ... One of them tried to strangle me. I could have died."

"Oh my God! So what happened?"

Schild tells her how Djemil intervened. Managed to fight off Longman and Jenkins. Maybe even saved his life.

"Your cellmate sounds amazing!" she says. "You're so lucky to have him, I reckon. Do you get on, the two of you?"

"I'm not sure ... He smashed up his cell soon after he got here so he's obviously got a temper. And some of the stuff he says, the way he acts ... also the way other prisoners are scared of him. That makes me nervous."

"Well, to me, he sounds like he might be OK," she says, triangling fingers and thumbs. "I mean, the fact he's got into trouble but has been OK with you ... maybe you're just lucky to have someone on your side. Someone strong. But promise me, if you feel afraid - even a tiny bit - go and tell someone. Get a cell move straight away or whatever it is they do. Do you promise?"

As Schild nods at her, the woman takes his hand. Starts asking him about his case. What's happening with it? Does he have a trial date? Has he got a solicitor? What length of sentence does he expect? But he seems distracted. Does not engage.

"Oh, that ..." he says. Fiddles distractedly with his red bib.

"What about your solicitor? Did you get the one Hector recommended?"

A cloud crosses Schild's face.

"How is Hector? You're not ..."

"I'm not with Hector. God, no! I've told you - I've known him for yonks. We had that one thing, but ages ago. We've been through this, lovely. Sometimes I feel I've spent half the summer reassuring ..."

"But are you still living with him?"

"In the squat? Of course. I'm not going to pay good money to parasite landlords, am I? We've been creating havoc over the last few weeks. I almost got locked up myself - you must have seen it on the news. The bank that got stormed ..."

Pulling away his hand, Schild sits back, plants bony elbows on the table.

"Why have you really come?"

"You're right," she says, sitting back as well. "There is something I need to tell you. Something serious. It's about Hector. But no, nothing like that." She shakes her head. "It's worse, Matthew. Far worse. Happened a week ago now. I didn't tell you because I wanted to tell you face to face." A deep breath. "Hector got beaten up. Was really badly hurt."

"What ... what happened?"

"It was weird. Really weird. Hector and Greg - remember him? Both of them came back to the squat one morning. And the moment they went through the front door, they got jumped by three blokes. Mona let them in. Was made to, it turns out. Anyway these guys - balaclavas on, all three of them - they wrestle Hector and Greg to the ground. Then one of them pulls out a blade, and the other two start smacking them around. No, I'm being serious. But wait, here's the weird bit. They weren't trying to take over the squat or rob us."

"No?"

"No. They only wanted one thing and that was to find out where you are."

"Where I am?"

Schild can barely get the question out. As he speaks, he bows forwards his skinny neck, oversized head, turns himself into a kind of human Anglepoise lamp from which, right now, only darkness shines.

"That's why I needed to tell you, lovely. I thought you should know."

"And so ... so what happened?"

"Well, at the beginning Hector tells them he hasn't got a clue. Says he's not your guardian, has no idea what you get up to. But then they start laying into him. Like, giving him a real pasting. And very quickly, apparently, Hector admits he does know you. Tells them what you told him, that you're a computer hacker. Swears blind he hasn't seen you for months. But then the guy with the knife pulls out a photo of you coming out of the squat. It was recent, Hector said, because there were yellow leaves on the trees. Anyway, the guy tells Hector he knows he's lying. Gets the other two to keep on punching him in the stomach. They broke his jaw in the end. Ruptured his spleen ..."

Schild has started rocking now, his skinny hands curled into fists on the laminate table top.

"Did they ..."

Farideh leans forward.

"Did they tell them where I was?"

"They had to," she says gently. "After all the injuries they were dishing out ... They even threatened to kill them both. So yeah, Hector told them you were in prison. Not which one, though. There's hundreds, apparently. And at least you'll be safe in here. You'll be out of their reach, whoever these guys are. And you've got your tough cellmate."

Her eyes follow the same officer walking past.

"You can imagine, all of us in the squat were really spooked by it. One couple have even moved out. We've got a new entry policy now as well. Anyway, we were racking our brains, all of us, thinking who the hell these guys might be. Hector was convinced they were from that bank you hacked into. You know, hitmen, private investigators, that kind of thing.

"But then I remembered all that crazy shit you told me about your time in Israel. I know I didn't believe you, lovely, but you can't blame me. It sounded so mad, all of it, I thought you were making fun of me. But now that this has happened ... well, who knows, maybe I was wrong. After all, it was only you they wanted, no-one else. And whoever they were, they seemed incredibly professional. Like hitmen, Hector said. So come on, lovely, tell me. Do you think these guys might have anything to do with your old job?"

While talking, Farideh has her head turned towards the drinks-dispenser machine on the other side of the Visits room, as if she is concentrating on her account of the event. But a retching noise makes her turn round. She looks back across the table. Back to where Matthew Schild is leaning sideways off his chair, throwing up all over the grey-pink lino floor.

* * * * * * * * *

"So the man who wants to die is back, is he? Tell me, Matthew, how would you like to leave this life? Would you like your throat slit, so the flesh gapes open and you can hear your own blood gurgling in your last few seconds? Or how about strangulation? Ooh yeah, that could be a nice one! In fact you know how that feels already, don't you? Gasping for air, less and less conscious by the second, but still able to wish the end would speed up. Or you could go for hanging, I suppose. People do a little jig at the end of the rope, apparently - if your neck doesn't snap, that is. Or ... what else? How about ..."

Djemil looks angrily at Schild who has just been let back into the cell, now stands by the basin brushing his teeth.

"I had a visit," says the Israeli, taking the toothbrush out of his mouth and speaking through the white bubbles around his lips. "Just like they recommended in my ACCT review. In fact the woman governor helped organise it for me."

"You had a visit. And you thought you'd just go off on this visit without any warning? Then just come back, expect me to carry on watching your back. Is that it?"

Schild spits into the sink.

"Pretty much. I can do what I want, can't I? I mean, I didn't ask you to protect me. No-one's telling you to. Anyway, it was just a girl I know."

Djemil sits down by the window.

"It's not the girl I care about. It's that I'm confused, Matthew. You said you reckon people are out to kill you. You keep on insisting they can get you any time, any place. Did it even cross your mind they might get you as you're walking through the prison? That you're a walking target? The man who's worth a hundred grand. Carry on like that and you will die, Matthew. And it's painful, dying. I've seen it many times ..."

"I really don't want to hear your dying stories. I won't do it again. Besides, I learnt bad news just now. This girl ... she lives in this squat in north London. Where I was before I came here. And she just told me ..."

As he speaks, a tremble enters Schild's voice. Takes over his whole body. He stretches out a scrawny arm to steady himself before shakily sitting down on the lower bunk.

"Two ... two of the guys she lives with got beaten up. Attacked by three guys in balaclavas."

Djemil looks up sharply.

"Kept asking where I was. And ... they told them I was in prison."

"Who do you think these people might be, Matthew?" He says this quietly, Djemil. As if the switch for emotion has just been flicked. And not on. "You must have some idea. Is it those people you said I wouldn't believe in? Look at me. Do you think it's them?"

A nod.

"And where are they from, these people?"

Schild flinches when Djemil asks the question. A split second later, jumps off the bed, rushes to the door. Starts thumping it with his tiny fist. When he turns round, he is struggling for breath. Stares at Djemil like a madman.

"They're coming!" he gasps. "They're here!"

Chapter 11

"We go back a long way, don't we Janet?"

The diminutive Scotswoman gazes lovingly at her boss. It is a look McKenzie knows well. One which normally makes him shudder but, right now, is exceedingly welcome. Because it will help him achieve his aim.

The two sit facing each other in his gloomy womb-like office at the far end of Security. Clutter and the gentle patina of well-used furniture create an intimate feel not unlike the staff office down the Seg. Similar, too, is the lofted window, the way it casts light downwards, gives the impression of being underground even though the room is two storeys up. The ideal venue for subterfuge, in other words. For hatching a plan.

"Go on, then," she says, sounding like an indulgent mother to a child. "What is it? As if I haven't got enough to do."

"Actually, this is important, Janet."

McKenzie motions for her to shut the door, take a seat.

"Is anyone about?"

"No, they've all gone. It's well past six."

"Oh right. Good." He strokes his chin. "Janet, I need you to do something for me. Something out of the ordinary. Something above and beyond the call of duty. Above and beyond any grade in this prison, in fact. Even the gaffer."

Curiosity whirls dervish-like across her neat features.

"And before you decide if you will take this task on, it's only fair that I make it clear to you - abundantly clear - that what I'm about to ask is not strictly legal. In fact, it will make you an accessory to unauthorised intrusive surveillance. Something the Home Office does not take lightly these days. Especially after all the hoo-ha over phone tapping, internet snooping and the like."

"Which means?"

"Which means that if you accept this mission, we'll both be in deep doo-doo if we get found out."

"What kind of doo-doo?"

"If they're nice to us, we could both lose our jobs. But if they really throw the book at us - and they probably would because we're civil servants - we could even get put away ourselves."

"Sent to prison!"

"Uh huh."

She knits her brow.

"Mr McKenzie, why on earth would you want to take risk like that? You of all people."

"Because if I don't, I could lose my job. This job," he adds, windmilling a long arm.

She still doesn't get it.

"Janet, it's the MDT rate. It's been going on too long. I've tried absolutely everything. But it's not working. It keeps getting worse. The gaffer's on my case, the Area Manager's on the gaffer's case. It can't go on. It has to stop. I'm convinced Djemil is the guy behind it all. Everything points to him. Every tiny little thing. But all of it is circumstantial. What I need is hard evidence. And the only way of getting that ..."

"But something illegal! Based only on a hunch."

"It's more than a hunch, Janet. It's ..."

"I suppose what I'm saying, Governor, is are you sure the likelihood of success justifies the risk? I mean, if this was one of those risk assessments that you like so much, what would it look like? Would it be the top left-hand corner - small risk, high chance of success? Or would we be down the bottom, somewhere on the right? Do you know?"

Janet's resistance is more spirited than McKenzie expected. More rational. And it is making him think. Making him remember the danger that Jenkins poses, with his corner-cutting plans, his Spanish practices - things he sometimes wonders whether Jenkins ever puts into action himself. Or if he just encourages mugs like him, McKenzie, to carry them out, so he can stand back, watch the fireworks ...

Janet saves him from the brooding.

"Come on, then, Governor. Tell me what to do."

Feeling an immediate sense of relief, the big man reaches down from his chair, yanks open the bottom drawer of his under-desk cabinet. From its nether regions, pulls out a small grey object, one inch square. Holds it out to her - forefinger, thumb - with an undeniable air of mystery.

"What the fuck do I do with that?" she asks, slightly ruining the moment.

"You do many things with this, Janet. Number one, you don't tell a soul about it. Not even your girlfriends in Security. Do you hear?"

She nods meekly.

"Two, you don't show it to anyone or lose it. Not because it cost me two hundred quid, and that's before you count the parking ticket I got when I bought it. But because if anyone else sees it ... well, we've already talked about what could happen. Got that?"

Meek nod number two.

"Three ..."

"Three?"

Her big eyes can barely contain her excitement.

"Three, this is what they call a wireless voice transmitter."

"A wireless voice transmitter!" she repeats, wonder in each word.

"Yes. Now all you have to do with this baby is put it into a cell. Somewhere where it won't get found, either by prisoners or staff. And you have to do it without anyone seeing. And I mean no-one."

"How the hell do I do that?"

McKenzie smiles. He asked Jenkins exactly the same thing.

"Here's how. You know how our Local Security Strategy says we have to search each cell every three months? Well, B Wing staff are way behind. Usual thing, the SO on there bleating on about staff sickness levels, all that crap. So they're playing catch-up. In fact, I gave him a bollocking about it the other day."

"Right ..."

"Right. Well ... they've got to finish all their cell searches by the end of the month. Where are we now?" He consults his watch. "Twenty-sixth. Plus the weekend. Which means they've got three days to get through them. So go and find out what cells they're doing when, then say I've sent you to do a quality check. Observing B Wing staff to make sure they're carrying out the searches properly, that kind of thing. But only go into the cell once they've finished searching it. That's important. If the officers hang around for any reason, you'll have to find a way of getting rid of them. And for God's sake, make sure they're still holding the prisoners somewhere else. You'll manage it," he adds, wondering how on earth he'd pull off such a feat.

Janet looks at him, mesmerised. Looks more serious than McKenzie has ever seen her. A good thing, in his book. Got a sense of the stakes.

"Now this ..." He holds out the grey square of plastic again. "Just peel this bit off - see here - and stick it somewhere clever. Don't choose any of the hiding places they normally use for their drugs: inside a bed leg, a mattress. It'll get found that way. Plus it will smother the sound and we need the microphone to work. So that when I ring into it ..."

He pulls out an iPhone from the inside of his jacket.

"You've got a mobile phone too!"

Janet is open-mouthed with astonishment - her boss flouting this most sacred of prison rules! "Only for things like this," he says, letting a smile break through. It does feel exciting, all of this. "So ... can you manage?"

"Don't you worry, Governor. I know just the place to put this thing. I'll find out straight away when they're doing the searches. What cell is it, by the way?"

He has to think for a second.

"B4-12. They haven't done it yet. I've checked."

She nods, slips the object into her shirt breast pocket.

"Not there," he says. "I can see it."

"You shouldn't be looking, Mr McKenzie!"

Chapter 12

Mid-afternoon the next day, Prisoner Djemil HA2684 has another appointment with his neurological consultant. Enters Healthcare Suite 2 where Liz Sherwyn is waiting for him, hands clasped loosely on the grey desk, the sleeves of her lambswool sweater ridden up, exposing a slender silver bracelet, feint veins.

"So how are you doing?" she asks as he sits down across the table from her.

Djemil does not answer. Just blows out his cheeks, puts a hand to the back of his head.

"Well, I'm glad to see you, at least," she continues with a nervous little laugh and pulling a file towards her. "I got your text, by the way."

He flinches.

"Ah, yeah ... sorry about that. A moment of weakness. It won't happen again."

"Rash, it's fine. Don't be silly. I can imagine how perspectives get skewed when you're in a place like this." She flicks opens the file. "Besides, I know you're not having the easiest time of it, what with the fight in the showers and ... well, I'm just glad you've come through it OK. I always forget what a tough nut you are. Between you and me, this is doing your rep no harm in the ivory tower. You're finally reminding the great and the good ..."

"It's not exactly the Yemen," he says with a snort. "Just some chancers trying to make a quick buck."

"No, sure. But you know how it works. It's not what you do, it's how visibly you do it. And a London prison - well, it's just up the road, so inevitably the grown-ups all take more notice."

"Yeah, whatever," he shrugs. "Listen, Liz. Things are starting to spiral in here. I can feel it. The bang-up, the close protection - they were in the job spec and that's fine. Eyes open and all that. But very soon ..."

"What do you mean spiral?"

"These three guys who turned up at Schild's squat ..."

"How do you ..." She coughs. "Actually, yes, it does sound like they had some visitors."

"Nice to know you were going to tell me."

"Rash, we're still looking into it."

"Still looking into it." The words coat the room like hoar frost. "It happened a week ago now, Liz. A week! I mean, come on, we both know that's more than enough time. This squat is in Islington, Schild says - it's bloody littered with CCTV round there. Including - and I know this for a fact - including those ones with iris scanners inside. So you just pull in this Hector numpty, get him to ID the three fellas, then do a trawl of the local cameras. See if any of them went walking under the iris scanners, and cross-ref it with our database. But Jesus! I don't know why I'm telling you this. You'll have done it already. Probably the same day. I bet you know who these guys are."

Sherwyn reaches down into the bag beside her. Has to pull it up onto her lap to find the thing she wants.

"Have a look at this photo."

She places a grainy image in front of Djemil. In it, a man of normal height is walking down a wide pavement bordering a busy London street. With a standard-type haircut, and wearing faded jeans, a grey zipped-up hoodie and dirty-looking white trainers, he could not stand out less.

"It's the Essex Road in Islington."

Djemil picks the thing up.

"Like you said," she continues, "it was taken by one of the nearby CCTV cameras. Got a strong reaction, not from Hector but from the guy he was with. He was adamant this was the ringleader. We reckon it was taken within five minutes of this guy leaving the squat."

"OK, so that's what he looks like. What do I do with it?"

"I just wanted you to see it."

"In case ..."

"Rash, you might not believe it but I'm trying to help here." She takes a deep breath. "I suggest you show it to Schild. See if he recognises the guy."

"What? In case it scares him shitless because he knows exactly who this guy works for? Be straight with me, Liz. If you knew these guys were professionals, would you tell me?"

She folds her arms. Looks at him intently.

"If we knew for certain. But as I said ..."

"For fuck's sake, I'm in the dark here. OK, so there are different things going on behind the scenes. Aren't there always? But what I'm saying to you is ..."

"Rash. We will tell you everything you need in order to achieve your objective. And in any case, Anne has given you the go-ahead. She wants you to make the offer."

"OK, good," says Djemil, his voice softening. "At least that's a step in the right direction. But what about my credibility? How will I convince him it's for real? Especially as I've been going off on one about my drink-driving conviction - which I told you at the start was a bad idea."

"It won't matter. You're offering him a way out. You're offering survival. It should be an easy sell."

"Survival? So there is a threat!"

No reply.

"And if he doesn't agree? Surely it would be better to hoik both of us out of here right now, give us ..." - he points to her, then himself - "... give us more time to prove who we are. Or at least give me reinforcements in here, stop me having to watch my back the whole time. It's got to be one of the two."

"It's not that simple."

"Go on."

"Listen," she says, unfolding her arms. "I'm only telling you this because it's you. This is the debate we've been having - Anne, Sir Jack, me. All of us recognise the risk of keeping you in prison. Me especially. But the counter-argument runs that if we pull Schild out too early, put too much pressure on him, he might dig his heels in. Even try something else."

"Like ..."

"Don't forget what the psych said about him in the briefing: how unstable he is, how stubborn he can become. Where Matthew Schild is now is where he put himself. So even though he's in prison, he still feels empowered to a certain extent. In control. Which is why Anne reckons - and I see her point - she's adamant we will never have as much influence over him as we do right now."

"Or as much power over me ..."

"I don't know what you mean." She starts zipping up her bag. "Just get him to agree, Rash. Then we'll get you out of here."

Djemil gets out of his chair, stalks furiously around the room.

"You're really not joking, are you?"

Sherwyn puts a finger to her lips.

"You should be OK in the short term ..."

"Liz, you can't really believe that. I mean, think about it. You got me in here without breaking a sweat. Police cooperation, a forged warrant. Think these guys won't find a way? I'm telling you, you need to get both of us out of here before it's too late. Cons I can handle. But not pros. I won't be able to keep him alive."

* * * * * * * * *

Consultant Liz Sherwyn is barely out of the prison gates when she pulls out a mobile phone, dials a number from memory.

"He knows, Anne," she says a few seconds later. "He didn't buy it for a second."

She is standing by a bus stop. Moves away as people come, huddle under the shelter. Begins shaking her head as she turns to face up Craven Road.

"No," she says. "And I've got to be honest, I am worried. I think we may have under-estimated how much talking two people in a cell are going to do every day. With the things Schild's been telling him, it might be difficult to keep to our plan ..."

She purses her lips as a packed bus pulls up alongside, releases a mother, two kids and a pram onto the pavement.

"No, but soon he will know exactly what he's up against ..." She has to jump out of the pram's path. "That's if he doesn't know already. What? No, he didn't. Well, not exactly. But what I'm saying is, if we did give him chapter and verse, then surely that would help him. It would allow him to force the issue. Get Schild to cooperate. Like I say, Anne, I know it's not my place ..."

As the bus pulls away, its windows displaying passengers still finding their seats, Liz Sherwyn starts kicking the space it has vacated.

"Alright, I'm sorry," she says, looking glum as two more double-deckers roll up. "I just thought I'd tell you my thoughts. I'm coming back now. See you in forty minutes."

* * * * * * * * *

Yusuf Djemil HA2684 has to wait twenty minutes before he can be escorted from Healthcare back to B Wing. Which means that at the same time as an uneasy-looking Liz Sherwyn walks onto the platform at a nearby tube station, the prisoner is following an officer through the maze of corridors, gates, doors that will take him back to cell B4-12. He knows the route. Stop-starts, stop-starts like some herded beast.

Not that he switches off, Djemil. The opposite, in fact. Starts furiously trying to piece together the elegant little plan that has obviously been dreamt up - Anne, Sir Jack at one end, him at the other and, pincered in the middle of it all, Liz. The planning, he has no problem with. He is used to plans. Used to being part of a bigger picture - it goes with the job. No, it is the way Liz was wriggling like a worm on a hook just now when he asked about the three men hunting down Schild. The fact that he, Djemil, obviously knows less than everyone else involved - Schild included. It makes him vulnerable.

As the officer unlocks the gate onto the Centre, a thought rips through Djemil like a bullet: they lied! Promised him - Anne, Sir Jack, even Liz, now he thinks about it - they distinctly promised him that he just had to turn up for his court case, get sent down. Spend "a few days" - those were the very words - a few days persuading Schild to work with them. Kept stressing how quickly the whole thing would be over, how minimal the danger would be. He even remembers Sir Jack lobbing in a matey, "Not like your usual missions, eh, Rash!" But throughout the briefing, no mention of the stakes at play or anyone else coming after Schild. No word breathed about just leaving him in Hatcham.

And now, as the officer opens the gate onto B Wing and ushers him through, another bullet: their selectiveness with the information they did share with him. All those hours with the psychologist going through Schild's profile, learning about the death of his brother in the Israeli army when he was thirteen; the portrayal of Schild's normal-enough childhood in Petah Tikva on the outskirts of Tel Aviv; the accounts of his self-harm as an adolescent. It struck Djemil as impressively thorough at the time. So there he just sat, nodding like an idiot. Agreeing to protect the little Israeli to prevent the diplomatic incident they said they feared - "Purely precautionary, old boy!" Failed to ask the blindingly obvious questions, like why Schild would chuck a brick through the window of a police car in the first place. Or why other Israeli prisoners in the UK did not merit the same attention.

God, he feels stupid.

The Healthcare officer opens the second set of gates onto B Wing, shouts "One on!" Is soon scuttling away as if Djemil was a disease. Leaves it to Siddle to do the escorting back up to the fours, open the cell. As the officer waits by B4-12, the keys in his hand, Djemil turns to him. Tells Siddle he just had some bad news about a brain scan. Feels low. Incredibly depressed, in fact. Like he doesn't trust himself. So can he talk to a Listener? The one who came to see Mr Schild, for example. Brannigan, wasn't it?

* * * * * * * * *

Prisoner Djemil HA2684 wakes up late the next morning. When he does eventually get out of bed, he performs none of his usual exercises. Instead just has a piss, takes his customary seat by the window. There starts peeling an orange before stuffing a segment into his mouth. Starts speaking while still chewing.

"These people you keep saying I've no idea who you're up against, Matthew. I remember exactly how you put it: people with long memories, even longer arms. Why don't you tell me who they are? Or what it is they're remembering?"

He waits like an anaesthetist who has just injected a patient, wants to see the reaction. But Schild avoids his gaze, says nothing.

"Who are they Matthew? Come on, tell me, for fuck's sake."

A second time, Schild refuses to answer. Won't stop staring at the floor.

Muttering under his breath, Djemil opens a dog-eared novel, pulls out the photo Liz Sherwyn gave him. Holds it ten inches in front of Schild's face.

"This guy. Have you seen him before?"

Schild squints as he studies the grainy image of the man in the bomber jacket. Then shakes his head. Looks warily at Djemil.

"Where did you get this?" he asks. "Who are you? Oh hold on. I'm starting to ... yeah, I get it now. You're not in for dangerous driving at all, are you? You're a spy!"

Djemil gives only a hint of a smile.

"I wish I was, Matthew. All those honey traps, I'd have a great time. But no, sorry to disappoint you, Matthew. I'm not a spy. But let's concentrate on you, shall we? Are you saying you don't know this guy? Never seen him before?"

Schild starts tapping his teeth.

"Tell me about the brick, then. The one you threw at a police car. Sounds to me like you wanted to get sent to prison because you were scared. In fact, you were shitting yourself. Am I right?"

A nod.

"OK, good. And now those three guys. You think they were Israeli, don't you? You think they're coming for you?"

But instead of answering, Schild just rolls on his side to face the wall. Djemil lets him. Chucking the last orange segment into his mouth, he gets out a Rizla. Takes his time rolling up a cigarette. Does it one-handed, standing up, looking at the yard outside. Lighting up, he smokes the cigarette absorbed in thought.

By the time the Londoner turns around, he is bathed in smoke. Sounds vaguely mocking when he speaks.

"You think they're the Mossad, Matthew. Don't you?"

No answer.

"Well let me put you out of your misery," says Djemil, a big smile spreading across his face. "There is no way they were the Mossad, Matthew. Professionals, yes. You can tell that from the way they got the information from your old mates in the squat. Fast. Efficient. Sound quite impressive, as it goes. And they're obviously on a serious mission to find you, whoever they are. You must have pissed someone off big time. But the Mossad?" He chuckles before taking another drag. "Not a chance. I mean, do you really think the security services in this country would just stand by while secret agents from Israel are running around London beating people up? It's just not going to happen, Matthew. What it might be, though, is some jokers pretending to be the Mossad so they can scare the shit out of you. And it seems like they've done a pretty good job on that front."

Still no answer.

"Matthew, do you hear what I'm saying? I'm talking to you."

"I hear you. But I'm ignoring you. Because you have no idea what you're on about."

"What do you mean?"

"I mean, because they were the Mossad."

Another broad smile. Followed by a shake of the head.

"You expect me to believe that you're so fucking important, you've got the whole of Israel focused on eliminating you? Matthew, I don't want to be mean, but I think you might be starting to lose it in this place. You've got some blokes coming after you, I give you that. And like I said, they're obviously pretty clued up. But Israeli secret agents trying to find you so they can break your knees or whatever their calling card is - give me a break!"

Hunching up in his bunk, Schild points a sneering face Djemil's way.

"You are so arrogant, you know that? You know nothing about me, you know nothing about my past. And yet you insist it can't be the Mossad who are after me. And that's despite the fact that you've obviously been sent in here to look after me by whoever it is you work for. No, don't look at me like that. I've worked it out. Of course I have. If you're not a spy, then you're obviously a bodyguard, something like that. No other way you'd have a photo like that. And yes, I can tell it's real because it's from around the corner where I used to live. Even though I never told you ..."

"So what are you saying?"

"I'm saying it is the Mossad who are after me and that I've got a major problem. OK, fine. Shake your head. Don't believe me."

Schild picks up his book, pretends to start reading. But the silence lasts only seconds.

"Well go on then. Tell me."

"Tell you what?"

"Tell me why the Mossad are after you. I mean, intelligence agencies tend to need a fairly good reason to go after people. Especially in other people's countries. Or so I've read ..."

Schild puts the book back down. Shuts his eyes, obviously deciding what to do. Then turns round to look at Djemil.

"The RQ-170 Sentinel. Ever heard of it?"

"A drone, isn't it?"

"Only the most expensive, sophisticated one in the US air force. Well ... one of them came down in Iran, near a city called Kashmar. Come on, Mr Djemil, you must have seen it on TV. It was a massive embarrassment for the Americans. The Iranians were claiming they'd brought the thing down and they put it on display - this big white mono-wing in what looked like a school hall - showed it to the world sitting there completely undamaged. Went crazy on the PR. Insisted they'd hacked into its guidance system, fed it false GPS data. Made it land in Iran instead of its home base in Afghanistan."

"Yeah, OK. I might remember something now," says Djemil, rowing the chair back with his legs. "And obviously it was all bollocks."

"It was half bollocks," says Schild coyly.

Djemil scrunches up his eyes.

"No way."

"You obviously find it difficult to believe anything I say, Mr Djemil."

"So is that what you're telling me you are, then? A hacker?"

But Schild ignores the question. Starts speaking as if he has just entered a dream world.

"I knew it was a matter of time before they traced it back to me. Not because I didn't cover my tracks. Of course I did. I haven't left a fingerprint on a server since I was a teenager. No, it was the Mossad that was the problem." He gives a sad smile. "They were following me. Had been for months. I knew that, of course. Stupidly thought I'd be OK hacking in from the Ichilov Hospital in Tel Aviv because I had an uncle who was a patient there. I used to go and visit him. Once a week, usually, sometimes more. There was an internet cafe at the back and, in it, behind this pillar, a seat away from any CCTV cameras. The last time I went, I spent six hours there. Typed in my code ..."

Djemil lets out a snort.

"So you're saying you brought down the RQ-170 from an internet cafe? You're as mad as a box of frogs, you know that?"

But Schild is somewhere else.

"I saw the Mossad tail the moment I came out. Sitting there like a moron in his beige Hyundai. Stood out a mile. Even then, though, I thought there'd be no problem. But they must have checked my uncle's discharge date. Found out it was the second of December. Whereas the RQ-170 came down on the fourth."

"And that's when you fled the country?" asks Djemil, the voice still laden with disbelief.

"The same night. Fled like a criminal, left a few red herrings along the way. Got a bus to Beirut. Flew from there to London. And now ... well, here I am." When Schild looks up, there are tears in his eyes. "So you see, Mr Djemil, your country wants me because I'm not like everyone else. I am the only person who can do this. The only one who can make any plane in the world come crashing down. Even planes with pilots. OK, fine, you're still sceptical, I can see it in your face. I knew you would be. But at least I've told you now. At least you know why you're risking your life."

* * * * * * * * *

Silence simmers after this, the men becoming islands in a sea of symbiosis - Djemil by the window, apart from the one time when he gets up, performs his routine of retro exercises like press-ups, sit-ups; Schild there on his bottom bunk, barely looking at the dog-eared novel in his delicate hands. He gets up for a dump once. Stinks the place.

And yet, despite the silence, the small room crackles with antipathy. Is full of tell-tale signs like darting looks away, retaliatory coughs, listening to the radio louder than normal. The silly games go on for a couple of hours.

Finally Djemil calls time.

"What gets me," he starts up suddenly, "is that here you are in a London prison, sharing a cell with me, behaving as if you just expect me to protect you. And all this time you've been afraid the Mossad are going be coming after you, and you didn't think to warn me or anything. Just thought you'd take me up on my offer to keep you safe without giving a toss about me or my safety? I mean, if I hadn't approached you down the Seg, offered to look out for you, then you'd probably be dead already. Or at least be in hospital somewhere with your skull caved in and a machine by your head - or what's left of it - going beep beep beep for the rest of your life."

He pulls his chair forwards, leans towards Schild's bunk.

"You knew you were putting both of us in serious danger, and you didn't seem to give a fuck."

"So you agree I'm in danger?"

There is terror in Schild's voice.

"Well let's think about for a moment, shall we?" Leaning back, Djemil crosses one leg over the other. Glowers at Schild. "You think you've got the Mossad coming after you and, I have to say, you've given a pretty convincing story about why they might be a bit upset with you, Matthew. Unfortunately for us, the Mossad also happen to have a bit of a track record at hunting down their targets.

"For example, remember that Holocaust guy - the Butcher of Riga, he was called - who they shot in the head in Argentina somewhere? Or the Canadian who was working on that Iraqi supergun - they finished him off in Brussels, I think it was. And - what was the guy's name again? Mahmoud Al-Mabhouh, I think it was. Twenty-six agents they put on that one, all on different passports. Happened two years ago. They ended up suffocating him in a Dubai hotel room. You must remember it, made a bit of a splash at the time. So yeah, Matthew. If the Mossad really are coming after you ... well, I think you're a dead man walking."

On the lower bunk, Schild has his tiny fists clenched by his sides. Djemil seems to contemplate the terror-stricken figure for a minute before getting up from the chair and going to stand by the window. There, he rolls himself a cigarette, lights it. Does not speak until he is half-way through.

"Matthew. I've been brutally honest, and I'm sorry if I've scared you. But it's really important you understand. You are not safe here in this prison. Somehow the Mossad are going to find a way to get you. Unless ..."

As a tiny head turns his way, Djemil takes another drag.

"Unless you accept this offer I've got for you. Do you want to hear it?"

Chapter 13

Janet pops her little head around McKenzie's door somewhere around mid-afternoon the next day, says she found the perfect place to hide the bug in Cell B4-12. Won't tell him where. He does not push it. As long as she has done as he asked, done it without being seen, he is happy. Grinning like a cat ("Janet, you need to be discreet!"), she spends the rest of the day fighting paperwork in Security. Goes home normal time.

At six, give or take, Tony McKenzie phones the Gate. Asks: is Janet McKechnie or anyone else from his Security team still in the establishment? No Sir, the voice promises. They've all gone.

Coast clear, he lights a fag, unlocks the bottom drawer of the wheeled cabinet under his desk, fetches out a small cardboard box. On it, a logo of a man in a coat, collar turned up, dark glasses over the eyes. Inside, an instruction manual. Turning the document over, he flips it around till he finds the section in English, then spreads it out before him. Feels nervous. Asks himself why. Realises the answer is obvious. He is playing with fire. Of course he is going to be nervous. But there is no going back. The bug is in the cell.

As he absorbs the blurb, nervousness gives way to excitement. It is actually pretty cool, this thing. Audio GSM bug, it is called. Stick it wherever you want - under a ledge, inside a light switch, sewn into a curtain - and the microphone will pick up whatever is going on in that room. Want to listen? Just phone in from anywhere in the world. It is that simple. He wonders whether he should make it a rule that he just phones in from home. Dismisses the idea. If the wife found out ... Better this way.

The nervousness returns. And as it does, McKenzie reminds himself why he let Jenkins talk him into it. Because he had no choice. The MDT is shooting up, his job is on the line, and everything about the sky-high drug rate points to Djemil. The way he took Lopez out. The way prisoners, even players like Samuels, Jarvis, Longman, leave the guy alone. How none of his informers - McKenzie's, that is - how none of them will breathe a word against him. Even Lopez, before he went. No, Jenkins is right. It stacks up, the whole thing. And now he, McKenzie, is about to get the proof.

Stubbing out the fag, he picks up the phone on his desk, squints at the sticker on the bug's packaging with its unique phone number. Pauses for a second, index finger on the '0'. What if the thing rings in the cell? Has to tell himself: of course it won't, you idiot Tony. It's a bug used by spies - so it's hardly going to make a noise and give the game away, is it? But then, another thought: what if he listens too long, runs up a big bill on the prison phone system? Might get flagged up, lead to questions.

Actually that is a point, he decides, putting down the desk phone and getting out his iPhone instead. He holds the thing in his hand, looking at it. Hesitates again as yet more questions crop up. Sees them for what they are: stalling mechanisms because he is scared. Scolds himself: "Don't be a woose, Tony!" Shuffles in his seat. Gives a last anxious look at the door.

Presses eleven buttons.

To begin with, the noises are an anti-climax. The vague sounds of two human beings in a confined space. The crackle of what McKenzie guesses is a crisp packet. The clicks, clacks of objects being picked up, rearranged, used. The fierce splashing of someone taking a piss. Fucking Shergar, thinks McKenzie, more of a tinkler himself.

He wonders where the hell Janet hid the thing. If it is not echoing he can hear, it is fuzz, static. But as he carries on listening, McKenzie, he starts getting used to being in the cell with them. Relaxes into the normality of it all. Sits back comfortably as he lights another fag, checks his watch. He will give it half an hour. Have another go in the morning. From the car, maybe, on his way in. Now there's a thought! Unlimited minutes on his mobile contract, plenty of time to kill in traffic. Yeah, that's the best place.

He carries on sitting there, savouring the omniscience of it all, for a good twenty minutes. Is just about to cut the call off when some words stop him. Words between Djemil and Schild. Wherever they are in the cell, they must be right near the bug because, despite the echo, the fuzz, McKenzie hears a good half of what is being said. The conversation starts innocuously enough. Spirals rapidly.

He is transparent at the best of times, Tony McKenzie. Cannot help wearing his heart on his sleeve. And to look at him now, you would say that whatever is entering his large ears must be pretty extraordinary. Because the Security governor grips the arms of his chair as if he is on a roller coaster. Opens his eyes so damn wide, they look like they might pop out of his head.

But the safest measure of McKenzie's astonishment is probably the three words he utters after putting down the phone, then leaning back, his big left palm over his eyes. He says these words quietly, slowly, as if hostage to doom-laden imaginings.

"Oh. My. God."

* * * * * * * * *

It's freezing the next morning. So cold, the countenances that grace Hatcham's Reception yard might be ice sculptures, the way they stare straight ahead, give nothing away. The two prison governors - Head of Residential, Head of Security - stand side by side, the shorter of them in a brown suit, the taller wearing a grey number nicely offset today by a white shirt, a silver tie. Behind them, the mighty edifice that is A Wing casts its shadow over half the yard, bisects it into a sunny side, a non-sunny side. McKenzie and Jenkins are in the non-sunny side. That is where their drain cover is.

Not that he notices missing out on the rays, McKenzie. A rather more serious matter dominates his attention: how to put the lid back on Pandora's box. Because, as he tells Jenkins in a succession of hoarse whispers, he thinks he may have stumbled on something way out of his league. An admission which, very quickly, leads to a fairly heated discussion. And remarkably soon after that, to various disclaimers from the Head of Residential. Things like: "I'm nothing to do with this, Tony"; "You're on your own, buddy." Disclaimers which, cumulatively, do appear to prick a ratty conscience after a minute or so. Make Jenkins admit that, OK, so maybe he does feel partly responsible, now he's "had a think about it."

"No, you're right, Tony," he continues, all magnanimous now. "I got you into this mess. I'll help you get out of it."

"Help us get out of it, Chris."

"Us. Yeah, yeah, of course. I mean, like I say, we're in this together..."

He tries hard to make his solidarity sound noble, Jenkins, but McKenzie knows better. Knows the real driver is self-interest. Because say he, McKenzie, were to lose his job over this, who's to say he wouldn't try to drag Jenkins down with him? People in crisis do desperate things. McKenzie is pretty sure he would not act like that. But that is what has been going on under Jenkins's balding pate, he can tell. Keep McKenzie onside, minimise the risk.

"So tell me again what it says, the tape."

McKenzie looks behind him. Spies might be anywhere!

"Not a tape, Chris. You phone in to hear."

"Oh right ..."

"It's like I said. You've got the English-sounding one, who's obviously Djemil, he's saying to Schild - it's difficult, because there's a lot of echo, I think Janet must of chosen probably the most echoey place in the whole cell, plus they're kind of whispering - but he's going on to Schild about offering him a safe house, twenty four-hour protection, a new identity. How the other lot are good, but not in the same league as the Brits. Then you've got Schild answering back, with his weird high-pitched voice, just laughing, taking the piss almost, telling Djemil that it's too late. That they'll find him wherever he goes. He is on their list."

"Fuck me!" says Jenkins, his size nines pawing the ground with excitement. "Er ... where's Schild from again? Iran, isn't it?"

"Israel, you plonker."

"Oh yeah, that's right. I knew it was an 'i'."

McKenzie looks at him with contempt. Rapidly softens his face when he remembers that he, too, needs an ally.

"So what do you reckon, Chris? About what I heard. You think Djemil's under-cover from MI6? Trying to get Schild - whoever the fuck he is - to spill his secrets about God knows what? Work with the UK government? And these guys Djemil says are not in the same league ... who are they? Mossad? Al-Qaeda?"

McKenzie cannot help looking sheepish when he says all this. Knows how silly it sounds. Like a schoolboy in the playground dying for a bit of excitement, telling his friend the chemistry teacher is an alien, the headmaster a spy.

"Tony. I don't want to be horrible, but I think you might have lost it. Djemil and Schild ..." - Jenkins's hands do a castanet-type movement till the right words appear - "... they're having you on, mate. Taking the piss. No way would under-cover agents be here. This is Hatcham, Tony. Hatcham, where the dregs of London wash up. You think Mossad are going to get on a plane over here, find their way into Reception, then kill the smallest guy in the whole jail?" He breaks into a snigger. "I can see it now: Schild, all eight stone of him, wrestling with Mossad agents, machine gun on his back, throwing grenades and shit."

He mimes chucking a grenade then cowering, hands over his ears.

"Alright, Chris. Calm down." McKenzie sounds hurt. "I know you find it funny. But I've heard of crazier shit. It's not just Boy's Own adventure stories, this stuff. It does happen."

"Well, I really doubt it's happening in Hatcham. And if MI6 or someone like that was here - and I don't for a moment think they are - there's no way they're going to be talking shop like that in a cell. Offering deals from her Majesty's government, talking about fucking Mossad! No way."

He laughs heartily. Sneers almost. Does it right in McKenzie's face. And far from being riled, the tall Security governor finds relief in it. So he was being a dickhead after all! He was letting his imagination run away with him. He can't blame himself, of course. After all, Djemil and Schild, they did say those things. But at least Jenkins, with his experience, his world-weary scepticism - at least he has reminded him how mundane Hatcham is. How shit that happens within its walls is only ever boring shit, not exciting James Bond-type shit. And right now, here on the Reception yard at eight o'clock on a miserable Tuesday morning - right now Tony McKenzie is happy about that. Really fucking happy. Happy to be bored. Happy not to be James Bond. Happy, even, to be Tony McKenzie. Now he can just get on with his job. Focus on being a Security governor. On getting the MDT down.

Feeling much better about life, he turns to go in. Pulls his keys from the leather pouch on his belt.

But then Jenkins spoils his day.

"Hang on, Tony. Just had a thought. You've got no doubts about what they were saying, those two. About the special forces, never lost one, all that shit."

"None," says McKenzie. "Why?"

"Well, think about it. Either their conversation was for real, and this prison's full of secret agents and spies. Which we decided is bollocks."

"Agreed."

"Or ..."

A cloud crosses Jenkins's face.

"Or what?"

"Or they were putting on a show. You know, play-acting."

"And?"

"So one possibility is they're trying to entertain the guys in the cell next door," says Jenkins, sounding like a primary school teacher all of a sudden - very clear, very simple. "But if they were whispering, like you say, they probably weren't trying to do that. So the only other possibility is they knew they were being listened to ..."

"You mean ..."

"I bloody do, Tony. They must know about the bug ... Jesus Christ! You've got to get it back. You are so fucked otherwise."

Chapter 14

When the door of cell B4-12 opens noisily at about eight o'clock, Djemil and Schild are still in bed trying to sleep. Barely have time to raise their heads before a clean-cut bespectacled officer marches into the cell, informs them both they are having a random Mandatory Drug Test. They need to get up now, follow him down to the MDT suite. Come on. He's got loads to get through today.

Schild jumps out of the bottom bunk, dutifully starts pulling on his tracksuit bottoms, then T-shirt, trainers. Djemil, though, does not move. Instead leans out of the bed, mumbles something about feeling sick, his stomach hurts. Doesn't think he'll be able to make it.

"I don't believe you," says the officer. "And you should be aware, Mr Djemil, that if you refuse to come with me now, you'll be charged under Rule 51, brackets 22, for disobeying a lawful order. Plus I'll add you to my Suss list," he adds, waving the A4 file in his hand. "You'll get piss-tested every fucking day after that, I promise you."

"And what if I can't piss now?" asks Djemil. "I've just had one. Emptied out, Guv. Didn't drink all night either. Felt too ill."

The officer absent-mindedly looks at his watch. Answers like he has heard it all before.

"What was that? Well, if you can't piss, you'll drink some water and stay in a room until you can. Right, you either both come now or I'm nicking you, Mr Djemil."

Cursing under his breath - "For fuck's sake!" - the Londoner climbs slowly down from the bunk, even more slowly starts putting on his clothes. Eventually joins the officer and Schild out on the landing. Follows them down to the MDT suite.

"Right, let's have you first, Mr Djemil. Need to give you a full search, then the piss test. In here."

He swings open a wooden door to a cramped and dirty little room. No window.

As the two officers stand by Djemil, one in front, one behind, they watch while he takes off his sweatshirt, then T-shirt, before quickly running through the offloaded garments with their blue latex gloves. Once done, they hand, almost throw them back in his direction. Repeat the process with his tracksuit bottoms. Let his boxer shorts stay on but demand that he gives them a shake, prove there is nothing in there. Seconds later one of the officers fills out some paperwork, opens an MDT testing kit. Hands the prisoner a collection cup.

"When you're ready," he smirks.

Folding their arms, the powder of the latex gloves leaving a whitish smear on their black pullovers, the MDT officers hover either side of Djemil waiting for him to urinate. Remain like that for a good minute.

"Come on, don't mess us around," says the one with glasses. "If you're positive, you may as well get it over with. And if you're not, well ... you've nothing to worry about, have you?"

One hand on the cup, the other on himself, Djemil carries on looking down.

"I can't go, Guv. You're both too near. Putting me off."

"Yeah, and I'll tell you why that is," says the same officer, an edge to his voice. "We're near because you tried to get out of it. And even now you're trying to get out of it. But I'll tell you something, Djemil: it won't work. We'll stand here all day if we have to. It's on the Security Governor's orders. Anyone who is reluctant to cooperate, tries to get out of it, we've got to watch especially closely, check they don't adulterate the sample. So you are going to have to piss."

The other officer looks a bit awkward at the strident tone. Says with an earnest expression, "Just imagine you're in the Gents down the pub, Mr Djemil. And you've got two blokes either side of you. No different from that."

"Weird fucking pub," says the prisoner.

Eventually Djemil does manage to go. Hands over a full steaming cup. As the first officer decants the dark yellow liquid into each of the two barcoded tubes, he handles them both as if they contain a vintage Scotch. Seals them before asking Djemil to initial the seal.

"Every positive test we get helps us help people like you," he says, now putting the tubes in a fridge. "We'll send the first sample off for testing. The second, we'll keep in case you dispute the results of the first one. Which something tells me you will, Mr Djemil. Oh, and just to let you know. If the result is positive, we will charge you within forty-eight hours of receiving the test result. So you never know, you could have a nicking by the end of the week."

* * * * * * * * *

They don't even know the fluorescent tube of the main light in their cell has gone, prisoners Djemil and Schild, until Jenny Hughes, their landing officer for the day, tells them as much when they return from the MDT test. She discovered it when she was carrying out her cell fabric checks, she says. Has already called Works to come, get it fixed.

"How's that for efficiency, gentlemen!"

Works should show up some time in the afternoon, she reckons. As long as there are no smash-ups around the prison. People playing silly buggers.

"You'll be lucky!" says a tall sinewy figure, turning round from the Equality and Diversity noticeboard where he is refilling Racist Incident Reporting Forms. "Works coming the day they're contacted? Unheard of, that is. Promise you, bruv."

He nods Djemil's way. But Jenny Hughes is having none of it.

"Mr Brannigan, how about you concentrate on replenishing them forms instead of eavesdropping on conversations that don't concern you? Or if you've finished with your forms, why don't you go round the wing, check on the more vulnerable prisoners we've got on here? Make sure they're happy."

"What, as happy as the rest of us, Miss?"

Brannigan gives a broad grin before ambling off.

Djemil cannot be bothered with the banter. Instead goes back into cell B4-12 to see if the light really is broken. Seems Officer Hughes is right. The thing does not work. Yet he could have sworn it did last night. They have not had the light on this morning because Schild - the delicate flower - was complaining about having a headache. Squealed whenever Djemil went to turn it on. Which means that if the tube has blown - and it seems like it has, because there is no denying the thing does not work - then it must have gone some time this morning. Even though it was off ...

The only explanation is it went while the officer was checking the cell. After Jenny Hughes switched it on.

Pushing the cell door to, Djemil stands on the edge of Schild's bed. Ignores the skinny man's scowls, his whinges about a headache. On his toes, has a good look at the plastic casing covering the tube itself. Makes out numerous holes burned in the plastic. Done using a cigarette lighter, looks like. Bored prisoners.

They do not interest him, the holes. They are in the plastic covering, have no bearing on the tube. What Djemil does find interesting, though, are the heads of the screws holding the covering in place. If he looks carefully, and it is difficult because of the gloom in the cell, he can make out tiny, shiny flakes around the head of each metal screw. As if someone has undone them. Not used quite the right tool.

He thinks about this, Djemil. Surely any maintenance guy - or Works, as Officer Hughes puts it - surely they would have the correct equipment. Would be doing up, undoing screws like this ten, twenty, a hundred times a day. He tries to turn the screw with his fingers, but it is done up too tightly. Been turned with some sort of implement, even if not the right one. Getting down from the bunk, he walks back out onto the landing. And the uneasy feeling grows. Something's up.

* * * * * * * * *

The knock on the door of Tony McKenzie's office is a small frightened one. So when, a second later, the larger-than-life Head of Works walks in, the Security governor is taken aback. The guy is no shrinking violet. Tends to knock doors down rather than on them like a mouse.

"What is it?" asks McKenzie, thinking: what's so bloody urgent that you walk all the way up to my office and disturb me? He's having another hectic day as duty dog: four alarm bells, two cuttings up, and Hammer Smith is on one again. And it's not even midday yet.

"Sorry to bother you, Tony. I thought I'd better come here before I murder Charlotte Rosesmith. I've got a problem."

"Oh yeah?"

"Yeah. You heard the gaffer giving me grief in the Morning Meeting? How we're behind getting all these maintenance jobs done?"

"I did, Bob. It was about getting those cell smash-ups back into action, wasn't it? And he's right, the gaffer. We need those beds. We've got no room at the inn."

"Yeah, I've got loads on. We both know that. And I'm doing everything I can. Even cancelled two of my guys' leave this month. Said it's an operational emergency."

"So what's your point?"

The Works head sighs. Explains he had four jobs lined up this afternoon for one of his new guys - including fixing a cell light for a suicidal prisoner. And now Charlotte Rosesmith has gone and torpedoed the idea. Told him, right at the last minute, that his new recruit has got to attend his Equality and Diversity training instead.

"This afternoon!" says the Works manager, incredulous. "So that's why I've come to you, Tony ... as Duty Governor."

McKenzie gently presses a clenched fist down on a pile of fresh SIRs.

"For fuck's sake, Bob. Twenty years in the job and you still can't stand up for yourself. I mean, why didn't you just tell Charlotte how urgent it is?"

"I did, Tony, I did. But she wasn't having it. Just pulled rank, said there could be no debate. But I'm going to get my butt kicked here. I've done everything I can to play catch-up, to get these cells back in action like Simmering wants. So what I don't need is some jumped-up little ..."

McKenzie holds up a hand. Bob is working himself up, and he, Duty Governor, he just ain't got the time.

"Let me see what I can do," he says, blowing out his cheeks. "Happy?"

"Thank you, Tony, I appreciate it."

Tony scribbles something on a Post-It, slaps it down on the desk.

"What's the name of this new guy?"

"It's the Greek geezer. The one you helped get security cleared the beginning of this week. Without him we'd be ..."

"Oh, him ..."

"Yeah, him. Never had one before. A Greek, I mean. Good worker."

"Right, well leave it with me. I'll get back to you."

The Head of Works has barely left the room when McKenzie lets loose a "Fucking unbelievable!" and stands up to make a cup of tea. Thinks better of it. Sitting down again to ring Charlotte, he gets through immediately. Has barely begun explaining Bob's position when she cuts him off. Insists she needs "absolutely everyone" whose name is down for the training. Reminds him there is an Equality and Diversity audit in a few weeks.

"We're meant to be past ninety per cent and yet half the staff have had no training whatsoever. They'll crucify us! Besides," she adds, in a calmer voice, "I've got full backing from John."

Charlotte is the only person McKenzie knows who calls Simmering "John" and it gives him the willies - something, he suspects, Simmering wouldn't mind giving her. What he does know for sure, though, is he is not going to win this one. In fact that is probably why Charlotte threw the John in - let him know, save them both time. So with a quick, "OK, thanks", he cuts her off. Asks Comms to get Whisky One to call his extension.

The phone rings.

"Sorry Bob. No can do. Simmering's behind it. Non-negotiable. You'll have to find another way."

Fruity phrases travel down the line. And as they do, McKenzie cannot help grinning. Bob versus Charlotte. The hilarity of it suddenly hits him. This crazy, addictive job!

"Hey, calm down mate," he says when the rant starts ebbing. "You haven't got your Greek, OK? Nothing you can do about it. No canny do. But listen, I've got a magic plan. What are you doing this afternoon?"

"I'm on an early shift," says the Works head warily.

"Well, there you go, then. Stay here the afternoon and do the jobs yourself. Lead your team like a lion, Bob. A lion! Rrrrrr!"

McKenzie puts down the receiver, creases up. He actually enjoyed that, in the end. Still grinning, he flips open an SIR, whips out a biro. Attacks the pile.

Over in the Works department, the Head of Works is a lot less happy. Slamming down the phone, he calls out for the new guy. Tells the young wiry man who appears at the door that he has to attend Equality and

Diversity training this afternoon. Is therefore relieved of his task sheet for the day.

He seems annoyed, the Greek. Insists he has got enough time to change the fluorescent light bulb in B4-12 before the training. Has the right tube, the tools, everything. The job will take him twenty minutes. The Head of Works looks at his watch, clearly impressed with the recruit's attitude. Reluctantly shakes his head. The prison might be in patrol state before then. Can't risk it, he says.

Bizarrely, the Greek does not back down. Starts getting narky. What about after the training, he asks. Couldn't he fix B4-12 then? Again, the Works head says no, a bit sharply this time. He will do it himself, and that's that. The young man stomps off without saying a word. Puzzled, the manager makes a note in his diary to speak to the hot-head first thing tomorrow.

He never will, though. The new recruit leaves the Works department - but not to attend his Equality and Diversity training. Instead he saunters onto B Wing which is already in patrol state. Half-way along the empty landing, gets down on his haunches, pulls an ISAK knife out of his tool bag. Seconds later leaves the fearsome-looking thing at the back of a cupboard marked Fire Hose Reel. Then, with a curt nod to the single officer who, at that moment, happens to emerge from the staff office, he walks off the wing. Down the Admin corridor. Moments later, through the prison's staff gate and onto a bustling Craven Road.

* * * * * * * * *

It is five o'clock, and prisoners Djemil, Schild are banged up for the night. Compelled to spend the next sixteen or so hours together, cooped up in a cell designed for one. They have been sharing the tiny space for three weeks now and, human beings being beings, have established a loose routine. Conversation for an hour or so after dinner, then some time reading a book or newspapers. Come nine o'clock - sometimes later, depending on the schedule - a bit of TV. The news, usually. Or, for Djemil, football whenever it is on.

Dinner had, Djemil stacks up the plastic plates and bowls by the door. Stuffs in his mouth a few of Schild's left-over chips in the process. Is still chewing when he takes his usual place under the window, lights up an after-dinner cigarette.

"Unfuckingbelievable!" he says between puffs. "Going to nick us for damaging prison property. Then saying the only reason he didn't was because he didn't know which of us did it."

Schild looks at him with his long eyelashes.

"At least the light works now."

"You can see how people lose it in this place. Feel stitched up. Maybe we should smash up, Matthew. What do you say?" He looks over. "Nah, calm down. I'm only messing. But I tell you what. Those wires the repairman said had been undone. Pulled out or whatever. They don't do that on their own, you know. Someone came in here while we were getting piss-tested and unscrewed them. You do know what that means. Don't you?"

Schild doesn't answer.

"It means they're coming for you, Matthew. Fuck, no. It means they must be here, inside the prison somehow." He pulls on the cigarette. "So what I'm saying to you is, it's now or never. You have to make your choice. You can still escape them. But only if you act now. If you refuse our offer, then I think you're probably right." He waits for Schild to turn his head. "You will die."

The Israeli visibly shrinks in the bunk.

"Matthew, I genuinely don't understand. You were the one going on about the Mossad, going on about how they can get you any time, any place. And now that it seems to be happening - no, is obviously happening - it's like you're putting your head in the sand. Can't bring yourself to admit it." Another drag of the cigarette. "In some ways I can see your point. It's difficult to admit you're about to die. Fuck, I should know ... But it's not helpful. Like I said, I want to look out for you. I am your only hope. So resisting me like this, coming up with silly explanations for what is obviously going on ... well, it's your choice, I guess. But it'd be a bad way to go, getting carried out of this place in a box."

Neither man says anything after this. Instead the only sounds in the cell - muffled, all of them - a TV game show which everyone on the wing must be watching, some mad throbbing music that, odds on, belongs to the Kavanagh brothers and, once, the single thud shut, then echo, of an exterior door outside somewhere. And then, puncturing it all, a question from Schild. A question so quiet, so sad, that Djemil has to lean forwards to hear.

"You really think it is them?"

"I really think it is them," says Djemil, his voice immediately softer. "I think they are inside the prison. So you need to understand: I won't be able to protect you. You've told me yourself how many resources they throw at these things, how carefully they execute them. What did I say again? Twenty-six agents to assassinate Mah ..."

"Mahmoud Al-Mabhouh."

"Hey, you remembered! I'm impressed. But listen, I want to be honest with you, I think it's madness we're still here. In Hatcham, I mean. If you'd just taken the solution I offered, both of us could have been out of here by now. They'd have put you in a safe house, given you twenty four-hour protection ..."

Schild leaps off the bed.

"You still don't get it, do you?"

"No," says Djemil, staring back at him. "I really don't. The way you're acting makes no sense whatsoever. But perhaps it will help if I tell you something, Matthew. Our Security services do this sort of thing the whole time. They scour the world for new technologies, then try and get the people behind them to switch sides, to work for the UK. You obviously think you're different, somehow. You think you're special. But believe me, you're not. You're just like so many others I've met. Weighing up your options, choosing which horse to back. Thinking you've still got time ..."

Again, Schild does not answer. Just turns back to face the grey-green towel hanging down at the end of his bed.

"Let me ask you this one question, Matthew. If, and I stress if, you were convinced that the offer from the UK government would provide a place that was genuinely safe for you, where you could live without fear, lead a decent quality of life, flourish professionally - if such a place existed, would you go there?"

Schild blinks at him slowly.

"Of course. Of course I would. But that place does not exist, Mr Djemil. It never will. And that is why I am staying in this prison. I'm safer here ..."

"And then what? You can't stay here for ever. You have to come out some time."

Schild just looks at him, panic in his big eyes, before pulling the duvet right over his head. A child in an adult world.

* * * * * * * * *

He struggles to sleep, Djemil, and this surprises him. After all, Schild bought the whole Mossad idea hook, line and sinker. Better than he ever imagined. So well, in fact, he is actually quite surprised the little Israeli has not already caved in, agreed to the offer. Let them both get out of this dump. He chuckles as he remembers the idea coming to him. Schild wittering on about his silly teenage fantasy, hacking into a drone's guidance system from a hospital in Tel Aviv, or wherever it was, and imagining the Mossad were tailing him. Then the moment he, Djemil, suddenly saw how the little nerd's dream world could be useful. All he had to do was run with it, stoke the fear. Let panic do the rest.

Why, then, does he still feel uneasy? Lying on the top bunk, Djemil conducts a rapid review of what he knows for certain. Starts with the fact that British intelligence want to protect Schild, want him to work for the Government. Moves on to the attack on Schild in the showers when there was a bounty on his head. There's no denying either of these things. What else? The three men in balaclavas who went looking for Schild at the squat in Islington where he used to live. Liz Sherwyn corroborated that one, so it has to be pretty reliable. Then the briefing Djemil received before they sent him into prison - the briefing in which Anne, Sir Jack chose to omit key parts of the story. No doubt about that happening either. The fact, too, that the light bulb in their cell suddenly stopped working - which may or may not be due to tampering.

Five dependable facts, then - none of which proves Schild's preposterous story. What worries Djemil, though, is they still don't rule it out either. It couldn't be true, could it? As the small Israeli turns noisily from one side to the other in his sleep, makes the bunk bed rattle and shake, Djemil realises he has not done everything he can to gather information. He has not been though Schild's belongings for days, for example.

Chiding himself for getting sloppy, he creeps down the three rungs from his bunk, pads in stocking feet over to the cabinet where the Israeli keeps his personal property. Stealthily opens the single rickety door. The bloody thing squeaks, makes Djemil freeze for a second. But Schild does not stir.

Precious little lies inside. Two books, some blank writing paper, a prison-issue razor. Taking out the books, Djemil studies the covers in the gloom: George Orwell's 1984 and If this is a Man by Primo Levi. The first book, he leafs through. Has a careful look in the centre of the pages near the binding. Decides Orwell is clean. Picks up the Levi, flicks through it as well. Immediately finds a piece of A5 paper, perforations down the side showing it has been torn from a jotter.

Taking it to the window, Djemil unfolds, then angles it for best light. Sees it's a letter.

Matthew, hello gorgeous.

How are you? OK, so it's a silly question. I know you'll be feeling pretty crap as long as they keep you in that place. But I hope you are as well as you can be. It's important you keep looking after yourself, and don't let things get to you. Easy for me to say, I know. But please - will you do that for me, angel?

Anyway, I didn't write to give you a lecture! I am writing to say I'm sorry about my visit and the way I scared you. Obviously I'm talking (well, writing!) about what happened to Hector. I never meant to frighten you like that and I probably shouldn't have told you. In fact I regretted it the moment I left the prison.

One thing your reaction has told me, though. It's made me convinced that the three guys coming after you is connected to your life in Israel somehow. What I'm saying is, I think I understand. I've joined the dots and I think I know why you reacted like that. I would have too.

I also wonder whether you have joined dots your end, Matthew. If you've made sense of my background and those stories I told you about my dad in the IRIAF, the people he became friends with. Maybe you haven't. Joined the dots, I mean. You certainly didn't give any indication during our visit. But if you have and you think I can help - well, you know where to find me. There is a good chance I might know people you want to reach. In fact I am sure of it.

One thing you told me which I was happy about: the cellmate you are sharing with. He sounds good news. Especially the way he can handle himself, beat everyone up! Stay with him, my angel. Keep yourself safe for me.

I'm not great at writing with a pen, so I will sign off now.

Loads of love, Farideh xxx

PS: Hector has almost recovered, although he still can't eat properly. Out of solidarity, we are having soup every day. It's getting boring!

Djemil holds the letter for a while, before refolding it and inserting it back into the book. Then he carefully replaces the book in the cupboard. Grimaces as he makes another squeak.

Sitting down on the chair, he rolls a cigarette. Lights up. A cloud of exhaled smoke catches the light from the spotlights outside, starts glowing in the cell like a thought bubble. And as it does, Djemil considers how the letter fits in with Schild's Mossad theory, the three men, the bounty, the deceit by Anne and Sir Jack. Feels himself start to shudder. Knows that, together, they represent a hell of a coincidence.

Sees, through the smoke, a red laser pinpointing the side of Matthew Schild's head.

* * * * * * * * *

Its gestation was rapid, but you would not know it from the intricacy of the plan. Its execution began that morning when a stranger in a suit, hard hat walked confidently up to a 1950s block of flats just around the corner from the tube station. Told the builders there he had come to inspect the scaffolding, conduct an on-the-spot Health and Safety inspection on behalf of the council. Met no resistance when he whipped out an ID card, waved his checklist. Quite the opposite. Seemed to instil fear. Was straight away allowed to clamber all over the metal frame, check the planks, the cross braces, the guardrails. Paid particular attention to the upper floors, the inspector. Even photographed the views they gave over the prison. Help with the report, he said.

They did help, the photos. Underpinned the briefing the commander gave his sniper team that afternoon, identifying the vantage points, how to access them, remain out of sight. Twelve hours later, within minutes of disabling the feeble alarm system protecting the scaffolding, two black-clad men sat crouched on the top planks. Could see into all the cells along one side of B Wing. An aspect that became even clearer when one of them swiftly, quietly assembled his rifle - a standard-issue IMI Galil Sniper SR-99 equipped with both night and red dot sights. Peered one-eyed through the cross-hairs.

The view was perfect.

As the second man kept watch, looked through binoculars this way, that, his sniper accomplice counted the cells, looked for his man. B4-12 was what he was after. He hit a hitch. In the briefing, the commander had said the cell numbers would be painted in white along the outside of the hundred and seventy-year-old walls, each number denoting the corresponding cell inside. But it looked like northerly winds and the squeezing of Hatcham's maintenance budget had taken their toll. The numbers had faded. Every one of them. To the point that, for all his hifalutin kit, the sniper could only make out a greyish smudge where each number should have been. Numerical clarity, it would appear, had not formed part of the Health and Safety inspection.

He thought about counting the cells, the sniper, beginning at number one on the left, working right. Realised he did not even know whether they started at number one, went up in single increments. Or if they went up in twos, odd numbers one side of the wing, even the other. Another deficiency of the inspection.

There was too much uncertainty. Too much to satisfy the 'Eliminate only if certain' rule. As the wind picked up, made hoarding advertising the building company strain at its scaffold tether, billow loudly, the sniper whispered hoarsely above the hoarding. Asked his look-out colleague what he reckoned. The accomplice trained his military-grade field-glasses on B Wing, was quiet for a good ten seconds. Then shook his head. Had to agree. The certainty was uncertain.

Lowering the binoculars, he motioned for them to descend. Escape while they could, leave no footprint. But then the sniper held up his forefinger. Looked through the cross-hairs of his rifle one last time. Wanted to see if he could recognise Schild among the few prisoners who were visible. Schild the traitor. Enemy of Israel.

Revenge thronging his veins, the man holding the deadly weapon concentrated on the cells he deemed possible. If the cells went up in twos and they were looking at the even-numbered side, that would mean B4-12 was six along from the left. And if the increments were in ones (again assuming they had got the correct side and there were twenty-one cells per level as the commander had said) - well, that would mean the cell furthest to the left. Or it could mean that B4-12 was furthest to the right - but on the other side of B Wing.

He concentrated on this side - no point thinking about a side he cannot see. The first cell, the one furthest to the left, had a towel in the way. And even infra-red sights cannot penetrate a prison-issue towel which, the way it was hung, covered most of the window area.

The second cell - six along - that was not much better. In it, he made out a prisoner in the lower bunk, head turned a hundred and twenty degrees from the window. Studied the back of the head. Saw how big it was, how narrow the neck. Realised, with a start, it was remarkably like the photos in the briefing. So looked again. And three times again. Became convinced he had found his quarry. Gently guided the laser onto the traitor's temple. Felt, through kid-leather gloves, the smooth curve of steel beneath his finger.

It was about a hundred metres, the distance. Ideal, in other words, for the SR-99's laser sight. It would be a clean shot. A lethal shot. But was it Schild? He carried on looking, the sniper, willing the prisoner to turn his scrawny head, allow a positive ID. Was still looking when, lightning quick, an arm reached out, yanked the tiny figure from the bottom bunk. And out of sight. That is when he knew. Knew it was his target. Knew it was Matthew Schild after all. And he learned something else, the sniper. Learned that someone was protecting him. Someone who understood that a little red dot can be a good reason to move.

"Ben zona!" he cursed under his breath. Gesturing to his colleague to be still, he carried on looking through his sights for a good five minutes. Then ten minutes more. But the chance had gone. Grudgingly, the man dissembled his weapon, packed it into his neat black rucksack. Motioned to the other man to begin climbing down. Less than a minute later, a small black moped puttered into life, made its way gently up a windswept Craven Road.

* * * * * * * * *

Can it really only be three months? Matthew Schild struggles with the concept. Really struggles. Because here he is, a heap on the lino floor after Djemil suddenly dragged him off the bed, barked at him to keep down. Managed to slam his head against the wall in the process. And yet it is not the pounding head that Schild notices. It is the searing perspective that, at this precise moment for some reason, wades into his conscious. Shows the Israeli how desperate his life has become.

And yet just three months ago ... It feels like another life. Standing there at the front of the conference room of Proactive Israeli Defence Services, on the edge of Lod Air Base, looking out towards the seven cynical faces of the Mossad top brass, ranged crescent-like in the front row. Three months since his boss nervously introduced him as Matthew Schild, PIDS's Head of Research and Development. Handed over the floor.

Even now, with all that has happened - even now Matthew Schild remembers how he felt as he got up from his seat, took the stage under the harsh halogen lights. Knew full well what the Mossad entourage were thinking. Were asking themselves how old this tiny upstart was. Wondering why the hell they had been dragged out to this crummy building by their boss. Why the General had commanded them to listen to the far-fetched claims being made by this defence company PIDS, a minnow within the industry. A minnow whose products were shunned by the home market. Were widely known to be flogged abroad to tin-pot dictatorships buzzing with stretched Mercedes and stretched truths.

But as he got to his feet, Schild also knew this was exactly how he wanted it. He wanted them to doubt him. Wanted his own boss to wilt under the searing stare of the Mossad head. Wanted it because this was his moment. The moment he, Matthew Schild, would reveal his genius to the world. Would obliterate everyone's doubts. Show them the madness of pouring billion after billion into fast noisy jets, drones, rockets, when the future of air power was clearly digital. The moment he would finally vindicate the PIDS strategy instigated by his far-sighted boss - the strategy of trawling Israel's top universities, finding bright young things who lived, breathed computer sciences. Software, not hardware.

But with opportunity, responsibility. Because up there, in front of the seven Mossad personnel, Schild also understood that he represented the new world order. Would have to guide the men raised on a diet of conventional weapons into a new military paradigm. So he started gently. Began by talking about the massive impact stealth technology had already had on military aircraft. Then, encouraged by slow nodding heads, moved onto the latest pilotless aircraft being developed around the world. Explained how some of the most advanced drones use bio-mimicry as their disguise. Look like pigeons with their flapping wings, pointy beak. Can stream live video and audio - even analyse chemical samples on the wing.

He illustrated his point. Brought up a video of a remarkably life-like bird flying over sand dunes, endless caramel hills.

"Yeah, but can it carry chemical weapons into downtown Tehran?" the Mossad head shot back, getting a giggle from his colleagues.

Schild reflected for a moment. Caught the watchful gaze of his boss sitting in the corner. Then somehow mastered his instincts. Replied courteously to the General that his R&D team at PIDS would treat the question as a gauntlet being thrown down. Used the moment to introduce minuscule drones called nano quadrotors - things the size of bumblebees that can fly into buildings, then photograph, even attack terrorists and insurgents.

Suddenly the director of the Mossad was gripped. All the more so when Schild plucked something off a white petri dish and chucked the thing into the air. Announced that this was PIDS's new drone butterfly. Weighed only 8 grams, could fly its diminutive camera over enemy forces, show Israeli soldiers exactly where the targets were. Invited the front row to watch as the tiny insect completed a figure of eight around the room, ended up hovering above the head of the most junior Mossad delegate. Displayed his bald patch on the projector screen. Then, with theatrical aplomb, flew directly into the butterfly net held out by a now-grinning Schild.

The antipathy evaporated.

"This is good!" the General shouted.

Schild merely nodded. In a more relaxed voice, went on to explain how insect-type drones could combine with iris-scanning technology. Then paused. Watched while the General worked out the implications.

"So we could drop a swarm of these things in a city, and tell them to seek out and eliminate a terrorist - by themselves!"

Kippen's appetite was whetted now. The time had come ...

"Matthew, do you not hear me? I'm asking you how you're doing."

Schild looks up, sees a being from another world. The earnest face of a young woman dressed all in black, an orange document in her hands, blond hair falling about her forehead. He rapidly recalibrates. With a struggle, remembers where he is. Tells Jenny Hughes he is fine, thank you. Sees, out of the corner of his eye, Djemil just staring at him from by the window. Flees the present by shutting his eyes again. Taking refuge back in the PIDS conference room.

Back to when he was educating the General about unmanned Combat Air Vehicles. Telling him about planes like the Grumman X-47 which has no pilot, but which the Americans have already been landing on their aircraft carriers. About the Chinese equivalent called the Sharp Sword which looks like a giant black bat, has its air intake where the cockpit used to be. How, very soon, these unmanned planes will be fighting each other in the sky. A computer game with global consequences.

Slowing his delivery, Schild added that PIDS had thought ahead. Already found another way. Seeing puzzlement in the General's fleshy face, realised he would have to spell it out. So told the Mossad entourage about the US drone, the state-of-art RQ-170 Sentinel, which the Iranians claimed to have hacked into, brought crashing down to earth on 4 December 2011. Impact with the ground: 140 miles inside Iran. Reassured them that Iran's claim was, of course, hokum, because GPS is not the primary navigation sensor for the Sentinel. The RQ-170 simply malfunctioned.

Then, without further ado, explained that aircraft like the RQ-170 are, in fact, vulnerable. That if the GPS component of the system is jammed, the drone can no longer check its longitude, its latitude, its elevation. Meaning that its autopilot, flight control systems can be reprogrammed to make the drone fly wherever hackers decree - fuel permitting.

"In fact, General," said Schild, taking a step back from his audience, "PIDS has not only dreamt up this technology. We have mastered it. Our new system will not only allow you to hack into drones like the Sentinel. It will also allow you to take control of manned aircraft. Any airborne plane in the world, in fact. That is why we have called it Lord of the Skies. Or LOTS for short."

Schild watched with delight as the General's brain soaked up the enormity of his announcement. Watched as, with painful slowness, the Mossad head understood that world air power as we know it had run its course. Patiently answered the ursine man's questions.

"So if we can bring down any drone fighter or bomber at the flick of a switch ... what are the implications?"

"It's no exaggeration to say that Israel will rule the skies around the world. As simple as that, General. We believe that LOTS represents the biggest advance in military technology since the nuclear bomb."

Silence filled the room after this pronouncement. Finally the General broke it.

"And this RQ-170 brought down inside Iran," he said, unleashing a coruscating stare. "Was it us, Mr Schild?"

The PIDS CEO, sitting quietly in the corner, leapt up to answer.

"I'm very glad you asked us that, General. The answer is a firm no. We would never do that."

The General nodded slowly.

"Well, I admit, your presentation is interesting. But I want to see this technology in action. I want all of us to watch you bring down the next drone that invades Israeli airspace from the Lebanon."

The top PIDS man thought about this for a moment.

"That should be possible, General," he said slowly. "If you can share with us intelligence about when Hezbollah are thinking of sending one in, we could muster at an outdoor location in the south Mount Hebron area. Then wait for the radar alarm to sound, watch the fireworks. Yes, that should work," he added, sounding more certain the moment Matthew Schild gave him a nod.

"One last question. Was this a team effort? Or was LOTS the brainchild of someone in particular?"

The PIDS CEO turned towards his protégé. Then back to the Mossad head.

"Lord of the Skies, General, is the exclusive creation of Matthew Schild who stands here before us. He is the creator."

Chapter 15

Shortage of staff the next day means bang-up all day long - news B Wing prisoners greet by pounding on their doors. Redefine deafening. The protest begins after lunch, carries on all afternoon. But Djemil escapes the din. Has a consultant's appointment down Healthcare at three. Follows the escorting officer off B Wing. Does not hear the clanging gates adding silently to the cacophony.

He barely nods at Liz Sherwyn before sitting down in Healthcare Suite 2, sullenness across his face.

"What's wrong?" she asks. "You said it was urgent."

"It is."

Djemil puts his face in his hands, then finally looks up.

"They tried to kill him last night. A sniper, outside. If I hadn't been awake, seen the laser ..."

"Bloody hell, Rash!"

"Yeah, bloody hell. And what it means is that the last text I sent, about him making up stories about the Mossad - that's all crap, right? It's them who are after him."

Liz Sherwyn fidgets with the file.

"OK, well at least tell me this. Is it true he can bring down any plane in the world?"

"What?" she says, surprise in her voice. But her eyes tell a different story. "Rash, come on! You know very well it's need-to-know, this stuff ..."

"And you need to understand - you, Anne, Sir Jack - you need to understand I can't do what you're asking me without knowing more. You've gone and put me in here, but at the same time you've tied my hands behind my back. So how you expect me to ..."

Sherwyn leans back.

"We think it is true," she says, the tone instantly more business-like. "Anne and I made a trip to British Aeronautics a couple of weeks ago, gave some of their software guys the gist of what we believe Schild might offer. They weren't able to comment on the feasibility of it. Weren't much use, to be honest. Just said it was "over the horizon" - I think that was their phrase. But they did give us a pretty good overview of air warfare today and in the future - drones controlled from bunkers in Nevada and - really soon, apparently - autonomous drones."

"How was that useful?

"It was useful ..." She has to think. "It was useful because of the common factor, which is the guidance systems they all use. British Aeronautics confirmed that being able to take control of the guidance systems of these drones, these planes, whatever, would mean you really do rule the skies."

"Which is why the Iranians kept banging on about the RQ-170 Sentinel when it came down? Because they knew it would be the west's worst nightmare."

She raises an eyebrow.

"You two obviously talk a lot."

"For fuck's sake, Liz, what the hell do you think we do all day? We share a room the size of your bathroom. Been hearing each other piss, shit, for the last three weeks."

He pauses, as if listening for an officer outside.

"I'm sorry. I shouldn't have gone off on one. But please, will you listen to what I'm saying? Schild and I talk for hours every day. And every day we get to a certain point, and then I run out of ..."

"But you say he's terrified. Surely the threat of the Mossad is enough."

"No, it's not. Which means there is something else at play here. Something stopping him from choosing the obvious solution. And that's my point. That's why I asked to see you. This whole mission is being jeopardised because I don't know what this other thing is. Which strikes me as incredibly stupid given that all of you obviously do ... I can tell."

Sherwyn runs her hands through her hair.

"OK," she says. "There is another element to all of this. One your cellmate has obviously been careful to leave out. And you're right: it might help you to persuade him. But you will have to find the way."

She leans forwards.

"Saying the Iranians are claiming they downed the RQ-170 is a simplification. The truth is quite a bit more complex. Or it is if you believe the information we've got from our Israeli source. Apparently when the RQ-170 came down, the Mossad didn't believe for one moment the Iranians could have hacked into it. The chances of that being true were infinitesimally small, they reckoned. Even so, they were terrified in case it was. So they did everything they could to check. Woke up two sleepers, one of them in IEI - stands for Iran Electronics Industries - which is the state-run bit responsible for developing Iran's cyberwarfare capability. Got them both to dig around, see if any of their colleagues could shed light.

"Soon they had a fast-flowing river of information about the country's cyberwarfare efforts. It turns out the hacking claims were made originally by the head of the Iranian air force, a guy called General Mehdi Majidi. When the RQ-17 came down, he told the president it was the work of IEI which he had set up personally. Even though the department hardly existed at the time."

"Why?"

"Because Majidi is a man under pressure. He's been under-performing for a long time. Was already scrabbling around trying to save his job when, suddenly, this high-tech bit of the US Air Force dropped into his back yard. Saw, there and then, the chance to save his career. Naturally what Majidi said was music to the president's ears. Which is why Iran went on a PR overdrive. It was a massive propaganda coup for them, a massive embarrassment for the US. But here's the really astonishing bit ..."

"Go on."

"The Iranian president and his aides never questioned Majidi's claim. Never asked whether his e-warfare department actually possessed the expertise. Even though ..." - she waggles her finger in excitement - "... even though the Stuxnet virus had, not too long before, been able to sweep through Iran's industrial control systems, create havoc in their nuclear facilities. It seems that in their enthusiasm to believe Majidi's claim about the drone, the presidential team were blinded, somehow. Lost sight of reason."

"People are quick to believe what they want to believe."

"Yeah ... Well anyway, to begin with, it looked like the gamble of this Majidi guy was paying off. He not only kept his job, he got more funding for his e-warfare department. But then came the order from the president for him and his newly expanded e-warfare team to reverse-engineer the drone. In other words, to get the downed RQ-170 back up in the air, and build many others just like it. A tall order even if they had hacked into its guidance system. But given that they hadn't, and have no real understanding of how the thing works ..."

"So Majidi is a man in a fix."

"Yes, but wait. It gets excruciating. As I said, there were two sleepers. The other one - i.e. the one not in IEI - it turns out he was a friend of Majidi's from their days together in the Imperial Iranian Air Force. Even better, was the navigator of the F4 Phantom Majidi used to pilot. And apparently, according to our source within the Mossad ... apparently Majidi has solemnly promised the president that Iran will be leading the world in drone technology by 2017. Or so he admitted to his friend. Why the hell Majidi made this promise, the friend has no idea. Can only guess he was enjoying the presidential praise too much. But the upshot is, his rash act has made a desperate man even more so. It's not just Majidi's reputation at stake now. It's his life. If his claims are exposed as lies, he could be convicted of treason and executed."

She sits back after her summary.

"So you see, there's quite a bit to this."

"So it would seem ..."

Djemil's voice trails off.

"But how does all this fit in with Matthew Schild?"

"I'm coming to that. Apparently Majidi's been drinking a lot recently. When he's really down or desperate, he's taken to turning up at the hotel his old navigator friend runs these days. The two of them get drunk together. And the last time Majidi was there, he let slip, late into the night, that in the entire world he knew of only one man who might save his skin."

There's a knock, and a nurse sticks her head around the door of the consulting room. Tells them there's a stand-fast roll check going on and the numbers don't add up. She needs to know how many prisoners are in the room.

"Just me, Miss," says Djemil, turning around with a smile. Liz Sherwyn confirms the prisoner's words with a nod.

The door takes for ever to close.

"So now I finally know all this ... how do you propose I persuade Schild?"

Liz Sherwyn breathes in hard.

"Rash, the only reason I told you ..." She struggles for the words. "I guess I told you because I think you deserve to know."

"OK. But as far as Schild's concerned, what does the Iranian thing mean?"

"To be honest, we don't know. We don't know whether the Iranians have made contact with Schild. Whether they have tried to recruit him. And we don't know, either, whether Schild has any sympathies for the Iranian cause."

Djemil looks thoughtful.

"So this visitor Matthew Schild had - what's her name? - Farideh. He said she was a girlfriend from London. And he has a letter from her in the cell offering to help in any way - to pass things on to the right people. Presumably you know who she is."

"Rash, you don't need to worry about that."

"Ah no, that's right, Liz. I don't need to worry about that. Just like I don't need to worry about those three guys who knocked at Schild's squat, because they were just common-garden criminals with balaclavas on. And as for Schild, he's just this normal Israeli I have to protect in case of a diplomatic incident. You feed me all this shit, then expect me to be your little foot soldier. Risk my neck, ask no questions."

"Rash ... "

"You're a bunch of fuckers, the lot of you. You know that? Treating me like ..."

A flush enters Sherwyn's cheeks.

"Well OK, then. You know why that is, don't you? Because after Yemen, Anne doesn't think she can trust you with that level of information any more. In fact, she's even not allowed, she told me, because you went and lost your clearance. Which is precisely why she had to put you on poor performance, take you off internationals. In fact, as far as I can make out, Rash, you're lucky you've even got this mission right now. I mean ..." She looks around the room. "Have you even got a clue why you're here? It's because I, like an idiot, stuck my neck out for you. Said you deserved another chance. Could be trusted as long as you were somewhere close, somewhere we could keep an eye on you ..."

"Well fuck you!"

Djemil bounds up, starts marching around the room. When he speaks - from below the lofted window - his voice trembles and his clenched fist is gently tapping the wall.

"You might want to know that what Anne is accusing me of is a hundred per cent wrong - her making out I leaked information. I had to because of her own fuck-up, creating that shambles in Yemen. Men died because of her, Liz. Everyone out there knows it. But obviously no-one in

Vauxhall Cross. We needed back-up, we told her we needed back up. And yet, sitting there in her fancy office with her river views, she chose to believe the Yanks instead. Refused all air cover."

He swallows hard.

"And so when I spent three months in a stinking pit thinking I was going to end my life as a little number on a Home Office memo - going through mock executions every other day, getting pissed on through the roof, having kids lob snakes, scorpions at me - one thing became incredibly clear to me. I knew I could never live with myself unless I exposed Anne's incompetence. Told the powers-that-be how massively out of her depth she is. That more men, more women will die unless she is stopped from having any operational duties."

His voice drops to a growl.

"And here's another thing you should know: I've personally put in a grievance against her accusing her of negligence. On behalf of my fallen comrades. So how fucking dare you accuse me of mishandling information when you don't know half the story."

He turns, still holding the bottom of the window ledge.

"Do you not see what she's done here? Put me in prison - literally - given me a high-profile task, one which, like you say, is in full view of the great and the good. And now she's trying to make me fail by not giving me the information I need. So that when I do fail, it will prove everything she's being saying about me." He runs a hand over his head. "The bitch is trying to ruin me."

Sherwyn stares straight at him.

"I don't believe you," she says. "No way would Anne be allowed to carry on managing you if you'd put in a grievance."

"Except that HR were sitting on it when I got sent in. Obviously couldn't be arsed to check who I report to. Too busy sacking soldiers."

"Then you should have flagged it up yourself, Rash. You knew about it so it was your responsibility. What I will say is, I don't believe for a minute Anne would try and set you up to fail. She's got far too much at stake here. She needs this operation to succeed as much as you do."

"The operation," says Djemil. "But not me, necessarily. She's going to try another way. Get me to fail, get the operation to succeed."

He comes to sit back down.

"Just so I am clear," he says, the voice quieter yet strangely more intense. "You're saying you won't take me out of here until I persuade

Schild to play ball? And you're also telling me that the plan from the outset was to - knowingly - put me in prison with Schild in the full expectation that the Mossad would come after him. The idea being that the whole thing will scare him enough to make him play with us Brits? The fact I might get killed ..."

Sherwyn fumbles with her bits of paper.

"This whole thing ... it's been bloody difficult for me, Rash. Every day I'm worried sick ..."

"What? That the Mossad have killed me?"

Djemil leans across the table.

"Let me tell you a secret, Liz. I'm a bit worried as well, as it goes. In fact you can tell Anne from me. If I ever make it out of this place, I will make her pay."

* * * * * * * * *

Standing by the same bus stop as before, Liz Sherwyn gets out her phone, dances her finger on the glass. Puts the thing to her ear. Scanning around her, she moves a few yards away from some mothers with their toddlers before giving a rundown of the meeting with Rashid Farouk. Her voice is haltering, shaky. Her brow, furrowed.

"But Schild has told him so much, Anne!" she stutters. "He's a got a pretty good idea of the risk now, but he's still going on about how he's got no bargaining power, that he doesn't know ... No, not about Iran ... I didn't breathe a word. Of course not. But I'm still concerned we're in danger of prolonging the process. Like I was I saying this morning before I went in, if Schild thinks he has more than one option, he's going to bide his time ..."

She runs an ink-stained hand through her hair. Takes a few steps north as a bus rolls up, opens wide its doors, lets rainwear-clad passengers come tumbling out.

"Yes, I did look," she continues, sounding glum now. "But I couldn't tell. The pupils looked a bit big, but it was gloomy in the room. It could have been the light. I mean ..." She takes a few steps. "Unkempt? A bit, I suppose ... But again, that might just be prison. Maybe that's how they all look after a while. I'm sorry, Anne, I really don't know. I couldn't tell. I will say one thing, though. He was a bit aggressive. No, angry's probably better. Like they get when they have PTSD. I'm not saying that's the reason. Just that ..."

Walking aimlessly in a mini-circle, she shakes her head.

"Yes, I suppose so. But equally, it could be his predicament that's doing that. I mean, if I was in his shoes ... No, OK. But he also told me how the stuff is getting in. Said hardly anyone knows - not even the prisoners on his wing. And I don't think he'd have done that, Anne, if he was also ..."

Liz Sherwyn carries on speaking. Walks north another ten paces, then about-turns. Walks south.

"What? Now? I'm in a public place, Anne. OK, hold on. Let me find somewhere quiet." She starts walking up a side street, then into the car park of a block of flats. Checks around her. "Ready," she says into the phone, before holding the screen in front of her face.

Some text appears. She pulls it closer. Reads:

INTERCEPT, SOURCE 42 - LONDON, 07.24HRS

"Update me, Commander. I'm hoping our snipers left no calling card?"

"None whatsoever, General."

"You're sure."

"Absolutely. No trace."

"And this ... this sniper. What went wrong? How could that not work? After your failure with the repairman ..."

"Sir ... it was a combination of unfortunate circumstances. The agent played safe, couldn't be confident ..."

"We've no time for playing safe!"

"I know, Sir. Our agents will be inside the prison very soon. They committed two separate crimes in the catchment area last night ... I briefed them just before, myself. They know what they must do, and preparations have been made. Unfortunately, due to time issues, General ... they are on

Israeli passports and will be using their own names. Of course there will be nothing to link them back to us."

"Just answer the questions, Commander. Who did you pick?"

"I mobilised Avraham and Mizrahi."

"Will they get help?"

"I think so, yes."

"You think so ... I thought you assured me London prisons are full of corrupt staff."

"That's still the case, General. But to find those staff, we had to go through some prisoners first. So we have established some links. Already used them for the light ..."

"So it's come to this. The Mossad depending on criminals! Well you just make sure they have no idea who we are."

"They have no idea, General. We are paying cash. Made it clear our offer is final, no questions asked."

"Glad to hear it, Commander. Let me know when it's done."

The message disappears. And when it does, Liz Sherwyn slams the phone back to her ear. Sounds frantic when she speaks.

"Anne, I'm still outside the prison. I can go back in, say it's urgent. Show him the message. Warn him." She starts shaking her head, disbelief across her face. "But that's just not fair. I'm sorry. He has to know." A pause. "Why not?" Another pause. "Fine, the other way's going to work. But there is still Rashid to think about. He still needs ..."

Liz Sherwyn starts shaking her head again. A few seconds later ends the call before putting the phone back in her jacket pocket. Cuts a lonely figure as she walks briskly up Craven Road.

Chapter 16

The heating must be on overdrive the next day in the prison chapel, because Tony McKenzie can't stop yawning. Immediately catches the gaffer looking at him. Worse, one of those earnest prisoner Equality / Listener reps. It is the final Equality, Diversity and Safer Custody meeting before the Equality audit and all twenty-five of the attendees - staff, prisoners, even a civilian advisor - all of them are seated chummily around four tables pushed together. Have been in the large church-like room off the central atrium for over an hour and a half now. Managed to make it seem cramped, sweaty - and there are still three agenda items to go.

He knew it would be like this, McKenzie, what with the audit looming and Simmering's three-line whip issued at the Morning Meeting yesterday: every Head of Department in the prison on Tuesday afternoon must attend, apologies not accepted. But somehow it is even more unpleasant than he expected. Trust Jenkins to rustle up an "unmissable" Headquarters meeting. Probably the only one he'll go to all year.

Still, at least he's got a bit of space either side of him - the prisoners giving the Security governor a wide berth, for some reason. McKenzie takes full advantage. Looking grave and concerned, and nodding unusually slowly as if soaking up the finer points of the discussion that is going on, he picks up a biro, continues a doodle of a shark on the Agenda sheet in front of him. He is half-way through making the big fish swim around item number five, has yet to put the gills on. There are about five of them, if he remembers rightly, and they need to be quite far forwards. Only question is, sloping up? Or down? He can't bloody remember.

Resolving to google "great white" the moment he gets back to his office, McKenzie sprinkles in a few smaller fish to emphasise the scale of the fearsome predator before tuning his brain back into the meeting. Charlotte is speaking and she is expounding the difficulties in getting her Equality Impact Assessments completed. Apparently the Equality and Diversity policy for the prison states that every process that does, or could, affect certain groups of people, however indirectly, has to be put through a giant procedural mangle called an Equality Impact Assessment. The idea, she explains, is that everyone's views, including prisoners' - in fact, especially prisoners' because they're the "service users" - that all these views get taken into account, used to modify prison policies if need be.

She completed the internal process for all the prison's key policies ages ago, she tells the room. What she hasn't done yet, though, despite her best efforts, is involve the outside community. That's despite her ringing up countless organisations - cultural centres, places of worship, that kind of thing - asking if they wouldn't mind having a quick read through some of the prison's more important policies, check they're not discriminatory in any way.

"And the amazing thing is", she says, the astonishment clear in her voice, "not one of the people I talked to said yes. Not a single one! Even though I told them Prison Service Headquarters said we have to do this. Told them how important it was for our more vulnerable prisoners - and that it's one of my performance objectives for the year. And now because of their refusal, I'm really worried the audit might suffer as a result. As we know, it's going to be on us in no time. But what else can I do?"

As Charlotte looks around the room, the fiery look in her eyes suggesting the question is probably rhetorical, Simmering, up at the head of the table, starts muttering things about ivory towers and only being able to do one's best - "as long as we keep a record of all the calls we've actually made." McKenzie joins in the support. Shaking his big head to also convey sympathy and disbelief (although actually thinking: "You'd have had more luck if you'd gone in person, you cute fox"), he gravely looks back down at the Agenda sheet and, once more picking up his biro, sets about adding in some fins.

By the time the big man resurfaces - for what must be the twentieth time that meeting - they are on Any Other Business and Brannigan is asking the top governor if it would be possible for him and the other Equality / Listener reps to move from wing to wing more easily. Without being escorted by staff, in other words. At the moment, the prisoner explains, the movement of the Equality reps is restricted and he is worried it is hampering their vital work. In fact, in his professional opinion, he has no doubt prisoners are suffering because of it. Maybe even self-harming.

Charlotte jumps in to back up Mr Brannigan's request. Normally she'd place security above equality. Way above, she says, shooting McKenzie a winsome smile. It's only ... well, with the audit coming up, there is just so much that needs doing. Getting the notice-boards in shape, ensuring a constant supply of Racist Incident Reporting Forms, making sure that filled-in ones get collected on time. So much!

But Simmering knocks back the pleas. Says he agrees about the importance of the work carried out by Mr Brannigan and his fellow reps. Ultimately, though, agrees even more with Charlotte's initial point that security has to come above everything else. Adds that this is what makes prisons so fascinating: trying to achieve great things within these kinds of constraints!

Looking around the room, as if to see whether the passion he feels is shared, Simmering moves to get up.

"There is one more thing, Governor ..."

It's Charlotte again. Simmering sits back down.

"I don't know if you know, but we had two new Israeli prisoners arrive in Reception last night. They're on Induction at the moment. I just want to make sure everyone here is aware as they seem quite vulnerable. I don't believe either of them live in the UK. So ... well, I just think they might need some support. Once Induction is over, could we think about locating them in the same cell, for example?"

"Yes, well ... Thank you for raising that, Charlotte," says Simmering. "It does sound like peer support could be a good idea, as long as there are no security concerns. Of course that is something we would need to explore thoroughly before any final decision."

He nods McKenzie's way as he says this. Moves a second time to get up.

But Charlotte is faster.

"And another thing, Governor! As well as these two new Israeli prisoners, we've got Mr Schild on B Wing. He's also Israeli. So that got me thinking. I suspect there could be quite a few more Jewish prisoners in Hatcham than we realise. As you know, I've only had Equality and Diversity for three months. And while the prison's made great strides in its care of Muslim prisoners, the Jewish population still has quite a low profile. It might be that Jewish prisoners feel reluctant to identify themselves ..."

She looks towards Simmering for a reaction, or a nod of support. But he blanks her. Seems to have no idea what to say.

"So I was thinking, maybe we should take a proactive approach and celebrate Jewish New Year which is coming up - Rosh Hashanah, it's called. On 17 September. I was talking with Rabbi Joseph about it. He was explaining it commemorates the creation of the world. It's also a judgement day, when God balances your good deeds against bad. A time to ask for forgiveness ..."

Now Simmering does spring into life. Makes McKenzie jump, go wrong with a giant five-tentacled squid which has begun attacking the shark.

"That sounds a great idea! Asking forgiveness for wrongdoings! I like that."

He laughs, a grandstanding, teacher-in-front-of-class type laugh.

"Well, it is about other things as well, Governor. But I'm glad you approve. Obviously it will need preparation. I've not asked the Israeli prisoners if they'll help yet. It's still a bit early. They need to settle in first. But I will. Afterwards, I'm hoping we can hold our own version of the special meal traditionally eaten at home. It includes things like apples dipped in honey, carrot stew served in bread ..."

"Yes, yes, fantastic. Do it. Great ..."

Dosing out encouragement like chaff, to ward off any more incoming Equality missiles, Simmering tries to stand up a third time and makes a bolt for the door. This time succeeds. But only because Brannigan is telling Charlotte all about the valuable work he has been carrying out on B Wing.

"Oh thank you, Miss! Thank you!"

* * * * * * * * *

Next morning, one of those blustery days that aeroplanes seem to whine about so much, Governors McKenzie and Jenkins are conducting a security check of the Reception yard. Planted in their customary spot, they eye each prisoner boarding a six-cell van, mistrust coursing through their veins. They do not speak to each other at first. Prefer, it seems, to wait until they create the right atmosphere. A big enough cloud of smoke. Finally, though, Jenkins opens proceedings.

"You need to reassure me, Tony."

A big head turns his way.

"The bug. Have you got it back? It's been days now."

The head shakes from side to side.

"Not yet."

"For fuck's sake, what are you doing! Trying to get us both put away?" Jenkins stamps a polished shoe on the drain cover. "In case you don't realise, Tony, our careers are hanging by a thread here. Until you get that thing ..."

"Chris, I'm well aware of that."

The smaller man raises his eyebrows.

"I just haven't found the right time yet. It's because we're being careful. We've got to be as discreet getting it out as putting it in."

"We?"

"Yeah. Me and Janet."

"Janet!" says Jenkins, looking at the heavens.

They fall silent after this. A cooling of the atmosphere, perhaps. Or maybe just their concentration on a twelve-manner that has just rolled up outside the Reception door, has its passenger door lying open until a prison officer walks out and, from the looks of it, asks for it be shut and locked. Whatever the cause, the two governors are halfway through a second cigarette before McKenzie breaks the spell.

"You missed more pearls of wisdom from the lovely Charlotte yesterday. Right at the end of that meeting you managed to bunk off, when it's clear the thing has finished and everyone is itching to get out, she starts banging on about these two new Israelis we've had in. How vulnerable they seem. Vulnerable my arse, Chris. I saw the two she was on about. Down Induction, when I was doing my rounds the same evening. Probably the least vulnerable prisoners I've ever set eyes on."

"Actually, it's funny you should say that."

"How do you mean?"

"Well, I was talking to the Reception SO in the Gate this morning, and the amazing thing is he picked up on them as well. Starts going on about these two scary Israelis he had in the other night. I remember it because he's not exactly the kind of bloke to get spooked."

"No, he's not." McKenzie looks thoughtful. "In fact, I hope they don't add to our theme, Chris."

"Theme? What are you talking about?"

"I'm talking about that other little Israeli we've got in who's already a problem child - you know, Schild. The one who had the hundred on his head. And now with these two new ones in as well. You never know, it might mean ..."

Jenkins turns to him.

"Oh bloody hell, Tony! I know exactly what you're thinking. I can see it in your face. You think these two new guys are from Mossad, don't you? Going back to your secret agent theory again."

"No, I'm not!"

"Yes you bloody are. I know you too well. So let me remind you: this, here ..." The Head of Residential waves his arm at A Wing, at Reception, at the mighty grey wall behind them. "All this is Hatcham, Tony. Hatch. Am. Exciting stuff like that doesn't happen here. So when our SO friend down Reception said they seemed scary, these two Israelis, he meant scary for Hatcham. Like they might become a pain in the arse, throw their weight around. Be another Lopez. Nothing more than that. So you need to get it into your head: our job is boring, Tony. It's about KPTs, it's about audits, it's about your bog-standard London criminals who rob your granny for a fix. Not bloody ..." - another arm wave - "... not bloody secret agents and assassins."

"I suppose you're right. It's a bit of a shame, though."

The two men fall quiet, look straight ahead, the gusts of wind standing no chance against their close-cropped hair.

"Oh well," says McKenzie, flicking away his butt, somehow making it boomerang, almost fly into Jenkins's trousers. "At least we've got this Jewish festival to look forward to. Carrot stew, apples in honey ... Tell you what, though. We've got to get her revved up for Chinese New Year. I love all that shit - Peking Duck, plum sauce, spring onions. Ooh yeah! Give it to me baby!"

He starts gyrating and rubbing his belly. But only two gyrations in, Jenkins spoils the fun.

"Simmering!" he hisses.

At which point HMP Hatcham's Head of Security curses mightily, cups a big hand under his chin. Feigns deep thoughts about penal reform.

Chapter 17

So chronic are the time-out-of-cell figures for the week thus far that Simmering gives Duty Governors carte blanche to authorise staff overtime for its remainder. A concession Tony McKenzie, duty dog this evening, grabs with both hands. Persuades enough B Wing staff to extend after their Main shift, allow prisoners to have a shower, make some phone calls.

"It will make tomorrow easier for you, I promise," he tells the staff.

Even so, the prisoners on B4 landing only get forty-five minutes out of their cell. A period that expires at seven forty-five.

"OK, lads! Let's have you away," shouts Officer Damian Siddle, walking up the narrow gangway. "Bang up!"

Following the general shout with a more targeted approach, the earnest young man stands by the doors of certain cells, calls out the inhabitants by name. Even then, only 50 per cent of prisoners comply. But half of forty-two becomes twenty-one. Half again, ten. Within a couple of minutes only three or four stragglers are left on the landing. Same again in the showers.

Djemil, Schild are on the landing. With no phone calls to make, and showers spurned in favour of a strip wash ("better not risk it, Matthew"), they have spent the time out of cell just hanging over the bars. Watching. Pretend not to notice as Siddle makes his way up the landing again, says to them: "Bang up, lads." Carries on without a second glance.

But the occupants of B4-12 do not bang up. Instead Schild jabs Djemil in the ribs. Looks towards the gated area between B and F Wings.

"There," says the tiny man. "That guy. Second door on the left."

Realising Schild means F Wing itself, Djemil looks to the place indicated. Can see only the back of a prisoner's head at first - a prisoner who is busy talking to another. But then the conversation appears to finish and the first prisoner turns around. Shows his face side-on.

"Him? You think he's one, Matthew?"

Schild does not reply but he looks petrified. Starts walking back into the cell. Reveals, as he does so, a dark patch around his groin. A pithy answer to a simple question.

Looking up, Djemil sees Officer Siddle heading back towards him. Starts ambling in the other direction, towards F Wing. Reaches the end of the landing. Is now just ten yards from the man Schild picked out, only the sterile area between them now. That and two sets of bars.

There is nothing remarkable about the prisoner on F Wing physically: five foot tennish, thickish build, Mediterranean looks. Yet there is something. Standing in the recess of a doorway so Siddle can't see him, Djemil tries to work it out. Watches as the guy asks an officer to let him back into his cell - the kind of new-boy compliance that would normally shout victim, get Birdman and his merry band of taxers slavering. Yet here the polite behaviour is not weakness. Allied to confident body language, controlled movements, it says something quite different. It smacks of the military - the way the guy seems so sure of himself, but is still inclined to obey orders. Djemil knows a mirror when he looks in one.

The F Wing officer opens the cell door. As he does, the prisoner happens to look left. Catches Djemil's eye before the Londoner can look away. And in that split second of recognition - for that's what it is, a kind of recognition - in that split second, a message is sent. I am like you, it says. We do the same job, but we have different employers. And I am here to kill the man you are protecting. If you are collateral damage - well, too bad. It's nothing personal.

What's funny is that, standing there in the doorway on B4, Djemil understands this. It will be nothing personal. Just two missions that happen to be on a collision course. His, theirs. A second later, Siddle appears. Tells Djemil, in a flash of frustration, to bang up straight away or get a written warning.

Without a word, prisoner Djemil HA2684 makes his way back to B4-12. Says to himself: any time now.

* * * * * * * * *

Standing by the sink and washing out his boxers, tracksuit bottoms using the last of the soap, Matthew Schild refuses to answer any of Djemil's questions. Instead scrubs away as if he cannot hear. Acknowledges his cellmate only after he has meticulously draped the pieces of clothing on the heating pipe that runs along the exterior wall - drainpipe-thick, clenched by sturdy brackets six inches off the ground.

"Of course I hear you," he says eventually, returning to his bunk.

"So what do you say?"

"I say I agree. We've run out of time. It was them."

Djemil knits his brow.

"Well don't you think now would be a good time to agree to work with us? You do know that the offer still stands, Matthew? All you have to do is say yes, and ... look ..." He pulls the mobile phone out from his pocket, waves it in Schild's direction. "You just say yes, and I will call the powers-that-be tonight. Can call in the next five minutes if you want. Put the wheels in motion. Get us both out of here by lunchtime tomorrow. Just think, tomorrow night you could be having dinner in a safe house, guards out the front, out the back ... I've said this many times, Matthew, but I'll say it again. Work with us and you will be safe. You'll have a new life, will be able to carry on your work. But if you don't ..."

"You're sounding frantic, Mr Djemil," says Schild, a faint smile appearing on his face. "Like you're afraid. I thought you said the Mossad were a bunch of pussies. Aren't those the words you used?"

Djemil stands up, then rests his head between the window bars, as far as it will go. Mists the glass as he speaks.

"You know what? I am afraid now, Matthew. I don't mind admitting it. That's why I wish you'd just agree to work with the UK. Because then we could both get on with our lives. Instead of fearing for them." He looks round. "But you won't agree. I can see that already. And I think I know why."

Schild does not say anything.

"You're waiting for a better offer, aren't you?" Still no answer. So Djemil sits down, tries again. "Mate, it's obvious. Your life is under threat, and you were so scared when you saw that guy, you pissed yourself. So the fact you won't agree has to mean one of two things. Either you've gone mad and have found a way of deluding yourself. Or you've got another option. Or think you do."

He looks over for an answer, but the eyes of the diminutive Israeli run for cover.

"I'm right, Matthew. Aren't I?"

Now Schild looks up.

"Yes, Mr DjemiI, you are right. I have another option. But not the one you think. My other option is about peace. It's about not giving LOTS to anyone."

"LOTS?"

"Lord of the Skies - my aircraft-hacking system. You're saying the only way I will survive is if I work with the UK, give LOTS to them. Let them rule the skies. But doing that will only add to the war machine. It will only make the world an even more dangerous place. OK, so it might mean I survive - at least until the Mossad finally track me down. But it would make me a prisoner of the British. At their bidding for the rest of my life."

"Better than dying."

"I'm not sure. And I'll tell you why. It's because I have changed. I want to make amends, be a force for good. For peace. I told you I ran from Israel when I realised the Mossad knew about the RQ-170? How I brought it down on my own?"

A nod from Djemil.

"What I didn't tell you is how disgusted I had become with my work. Spending day after day developing drones that will use chemical weapons, track down targets on their own, exterminate human beings like pests. Or hacking into UAVs, missiles, turning them against their controllers. It's disgusting, all of it. And I can't be part of it any more. I doubt you've read much Rabelais, Mr Djemil. You don't strike me as that sort ..." He smirks. "But Rabelais said science without conscience is the soul's perdition. And ... well, I see now that he was right. So yes, OK, I might lose my life. But what I really don't want is to lose my soul."

As Schild stops speaking, Djemil takes a rollie, unlit, from his lips. Puts it down on the window sill.

"I don't believe you," he says, spinning around. "I don't believe you've suddenly become a pacifist. Not after working for years in defence. People don't just change like that."

"You don't believe a lot of what I say, Mr Djemil. And to be honest, I expected you to react like that. Because to believe I am a pacifist, you'd have to admit something else. You would have to admit that you've been stitched up. Given an impossible task. Sent in here to persuade me to work for the UK war machine when your masters knew very well I was living in a squat of peace activists in London. That I used to go on anti-war marches with my girlfriend, that I employed my hacking skills to help bring down banks. All part of the same system, Mr Djemil - the convenient cycle of war. They didn't tell you any of that. Did they?"

The question festers in the cell.

"I have to say, I'm surprised how badly they're treating you, Mr Djemil. Shocked, actually. Sending you in here like that. Letting you risk your life in the process, treating you like an expendable commodity. In fact, if I was you, I'd be angry. Really fucking angry."

* * * * * * * * *

Early afternoon, and Djemil HA2684 is watching the pink giraffe take off in a hot air balloon, wave goodbye to the sad green donkey. He has been following the animals' adventures for over an hour now, choosing the children's TV programme over the view of the bleak exercise yard outside. At one point, even leans forwards, as if to see how the donkey reacts. Then leans back. Lights up a cigarette.

The two cellmates have not spoken to each other since yesterday. Literally not exchanged a word. Instead, Djemil has been menacingly quiet. Staring down the Israeli if he ever dared look his way, unleashing salvos of abuse at no one in particular, for no apparent reason. One time, even pounded the window bars over and over again, until the dull thuds hugged each other, formed the same thunderous backdrop. Schild took the hint. Curled himself up on his lower bunk, tried to make himself not there.

Djemil did speak to someone, though. He spoke to Brannigan. At about nine - not long after the night shift came on duty - he got off his bunk, hit the cell bell. Told the night officer he felt depressed. Couldn't see a way forward. Needed a Listener. It took a while but Brannigan eventually came. Looked serious as staff gave him a rub-down search, let him into cell B4-12. Took Schild off somewhere else.

Half an hour later, Brannigan's understanding, his grasp of Djemil's problems, had obviously done the trick. Because as the tall Listener was unlocked from cell B4-12, searched a second time, prisoner Djemil seemed a different person. Told the staff he hadn't felt this calm in ages. Could see, now, what had been worrying him. Had it all in perspective.

The night Supervising Officer ignored him. Instead, looking like a man who had lost a bet, he put Schild back in the cell, slammed shut the heavy door. Took Brannigan away. As Djemil clambered back up to the top bunk, missing a rung or two before launching himself onto the thin mattress, the Israeli skulked back into the bottom berth. Pulled up the duvet.

Now, though, it is early afternoon the next day and darkness has most definitely reclaimed Djemil's mood. As the pink giraffe floats back down to earth, and the green donkey skips around joyously - "Ee Aw! Ee Aw!" - the Londoner just looks vacantly at the screen. Carries on looking as the credits roll lazily upwards to a bass tuba ditty, the kiddy colours trampled flat by the gloom, the closeness of the cell. As if the whole world is on standby.

Then, a clunk. The sound of the observation flap being lifted, then shut. The door opens and there, on the landing, stands Officer Jenny Hughes. She has a no-nonsense face on. Informs Djemil, Schild they are having a cell spin. Must put on their shoes, make sure they've got nothing in their pockets, and follow her to the "sterile room." Slowly the two men react. Wiggle feet into trainers. Tie long laces.

Schild is ready first. Shuffles through the doorway, his T-shirt hanging limply off his scrawny body. Djemil joins him a few seconds later. Squints when Jenny Hughes nods down the deserted landing towards the Association Room, indicating she will follow.

"OK, gents, in here," she says, opening the door when they get there. "We'll do the cell, then have you searched. Won't take long."

Djemil, Schild enter the Association Room and the door slams shut, the stackable plastic chairs, expensive-looking table tennis table around the perimeter doing nothing to soak up the noise. But leaving an empty space, boxing-ring size, in the room's middle.

Heading towards the chairs by the near wall, Djemil lifts two off the pile, sits down on one. But Schild does not follow. Prefers to stay by the door. Looks around nervously.

"You think it's OK?"

No answer. Just a grunt from Djemil as he puts his elbows on his knees, his head between his hands.

"Don't you think there was something a bit ..."

But Schild does not finish the question. He is pointing manically towards the table tennis table. Starts hyper-ventilating. Tugs desperately at the door handle.

Zombie-like, Djemil follows the jabbing finger. Rotates his head. Is looking at four plimsolled feet peeping out from underneath. For a second, he does absolutely nothing. Nothing except blink. But then he leaps up. Charges towards the table like some demented beast: "Arrrgh!"

It is too late. With depressing ease, the flat surface pushes back powerfully, the pairs of shoes divide - one left, one right - and two figures in prisoner garb appear. They ignore Schild, now cowering in the corner. Come straight for Djemil.

The Londoner lurches back to evade flying fists. Bobs and weaves like a boxer. Trades blows, thumps, thwacks. But then a glint, a flashing, as a silver sliver slices at his face. Yanking back his head, Djemil gets pummelled in the stomach. Manages to twist around. Times the twist perfectly to receive a disgustingly well placed kick to the groin. Crumbles, gasping, onto the ground. Scrabbles mindlessly at the floor.

As one of the attackers gets him in a headlock, Djemil rams a knuckle into an eye socket. Somehow getting to his feet, manages to kick the second man. But then, another glint as the knife comes again - slish, slash - the sharpness this time finding Djemil's forehead. At the same time, a crunching kick to his knees. Again the Londoner falls. Blood streaming from his forehead, he throws a punch on the way down. Misses his man. Is suddenly on the floor with two Mossad agents pinning him down. One about to plunge an ISAK knife into his unshaven throat.

* * * * * * * * *

Moods don't get much fouler than the one McKenzie is in now. He has had a lot of shit days recently, but this one takes the shit biscuit. It started with a prang to his car - some fucker on the Archway Road pulling out without looking, telling McKenzie, once they'd pulled over, he was being aggressive, people like him ought to be locked up. Then, when the tall angry man got to work, there were the latest MDT results waiting for him on his desk.

"Not brilliant news," said Janet before scuttling off to safety.

McKenzie slung his green sports bag into the corner of the room, took off his parka jacket unusually slowly (those last precious seconds not knowing!), finally picked up the sheet of paper. A second later, unleashed the loudest "Fuck!" Janet had ever heard.

The day went downhill from there. With suspicious timing, Simmering chose that very Morning Meeting to ask McKenzie, in front of the usual crowd of senior managers, if he had any news on the MDT rate. As if he knew. Two dozen pairs of eyes swivelled towards the beleaguered man.

McKenzie met the question with silence at first - in truth, because of deliberation about what to say. Should he play it straight, admit what a travesty his stint as Security governor had become? Or deny any update? Give himself time to improve the figures à la Jenkins? Save his skin. Risky given Simmering's timing (if he did know ...).

The hesitation only aroused suspicion. Nudged Simmering into saying, in that lethal jaunty voice of his: "Not so bad you can't even tell us, I hope, Tony!" Put McKenzie even more on the spot. Meant he couldn't think. Could only listen as his mouth, dry as the Sahara, uttered the words: "We've hit twenty-five per cent, Governor."

There were gasps on all sides. Loudest of all from Charlotte Rosesmith who shook her head in disbelief, laid a pale hand on her forehead and exclaimed: "Governor, this is terrible!" To which Simmering, from operational solidarity if nothing else, said sharply: "Thank you, Charlotte, I think we're all aware of that." Followed it with an equally sharp: "Tony, a chat afterwards, please."

They did chat afterwards. A bit of a one-way chat, as it goes. Back in his office, Simmering told McKenzie that the game was up. He could not support him any longer. Or rather, could not be seen to support him. Told McKenzie he was going to find another Head of Security. Not quite yet. Not until the Equality and Diversity audit was out of the way: "Even keel and all that, Tony!" The gaffer couldn't have made his succession plan any clearer if he'd gone himself, screwed Charlotte's nameplate onto McKenzie's office door.

Fuming, but also, it must be said, experiencing a strange kind of relief - the kind a beaten cage fighter might feel as he is being stretchered out of the ring - McKenzie stalked back to his office. Shut himself away the whole morning. Just him, his demons, a mountain of paperwork. Declining Jenkins's invitation for a Security check ("Go on, mate, tell me ..."), he also snapped at Janet the one time she dared to open the door, replenish the mountain. Even forewent the gym. Could not face the thought of Jenkins with his happy-chappy face, his smart-arse comments. No, he needed to be alone. Let his conscious absorb the calamity of his career at its own pace.

Coming up to two o'clock, the Security governor's mood has become a huge black hole, sucking in even the slightest speck of optimism before obliterating it utterly. He has been here before, McKenzie. Knows he has to break glass. Something. Opts to take the black dog for a walk. So shuffling together bits of paper - replies to prisoner complaints, allegations, concerns from prison visitors and the like - he orders them into what will make the most efficient route around the prison. Sets off on his travels.

He starts with the Visits department. There, tells a member of staff they are needed for an investigation. Arranges an interview time, gets them to sign a bit of paper. On his way out of the Visits Hall, has to sidestep a small boy who keeps pointing up at his face, won't stop shouting: "A monster, mummy! A monster!" Next stop, the gym. Same drill: informing a member of staff they will be interviewed for an investigation, then getting the signature.

Returning onto D Wing, McKenzie zig-zags his way up to the fours, walks to the end of the landing. Lets himself onto the steel balcony that borders the central atrium. Looking down, he notices Simmering and a Custodial Manager three floors below. They are talking to each other and the CM is nodding dutifully. Brown-nosing, McKenzie supposes. That's fine by him. Just as long as they don't look up, either of them.

Creeping past lest they raise their sights, McKenzie lets himself onto B Wing. Caresses shut the gate like a thief in the night. A Hammer Smith howl greets him the moment he withdraws the key. Makes him shiver for some reason. Not like me, he says to himself as he sets off down the empty landing and glances at the paperwork in his hands. He has gone only a few steps when a noise stops him - a clunk from the Association Room on his left. Instinctively feeling for his radio, he realises he has none. Peers through the glass slit just to check. Sees a man about to die.

* * * * * * * * *

Trainee prison officers always ask the question, if there is a fight between prisoners and you're outnumbered, do you rush in and help? Jeopardise your safety to rescue others? And McKenzie's answer was always that, technically, you should not. You should summon aid, wait till there are three of you per prisoner (or three of you in riot gear if there might be sharp things around), and then intervene. That way you're safe, can apply Control and Restraint properly and, barring those cases where only immediate intervention will be any use, should prove more help overall.

Whenever McKenzie said this, he always wondered how he'd really react. Would he go in? Risk his own neck for the sake of others? He doubted it. He prided himself on his perspective too much. Thought he respected the "system".

How wrong he was. A scalded cat in his reactions, he double-takes for a split second - fuck me, that's a knife! - manages to hit the green alarm button on the wall outside the room and, after fumbling for the right key upon realising the door is locked, charges in, a wild rampaging animal. The last thing on McKenzie's mind is his safety. He is not sure how many prisoners are in the room, has no idea what the fight's about, or who is against who. Just runs, tries to keep up with his clenched fists which cleave the air. His one aim: get that fearsome-looking thing away from that guy's throat.

It turns out to be a fairly stratospheric ambition. The prisoner at knifepoint has his hands over the knifeman's hands, which in turn are on the knife's handle. Already too many hands, not enough handles. So instead, McKenzie tries to put the prisoner holding the knife into a headlock. Realises, around about then, there is another prisoner on the knifeman's side. Unwittingly incurs his full attention. Gets kicked in the face. Feels hands tighten unfeasibly hard around his throat. Is suddenly on his back, struggling to breathe. The Association Room swims, swirls, sways.

If McKenzie had time to think, he would realise he was about to expire. Fortunately he does not. Instead, unthinking rage kicks in. Pure unadulterated rage. All those months being under the cosh, trying to stem the tide of drugs coming into the prison, seeing the MDT rate climb, climb, climb, and being humiliated in morning meetings in front of people far less experienced, less knowledgeable. All those years working his arse off, only to see fresh-faced fast-trackers like Charlotte sail past him up the ranks, talking to him like he is a piece of dirt on her shoe. And then that smart-arse Jenkins with his crafty short cuts - not only getting away with them, but often landing strivers like him, McKenzie, in hot water in the process. And now this fucker, whoever he is, trying to squeeze the life out of him.

Fuck it makes him angry.

As McKenzie's breathing labours, and he stares into the slate eyes of the man trying to stop it for good, the rage, distilled over weeks, months, years - now beautiful and wondrous in its purity - it surges around his body, this rage. Finds, at this precise moment, the very outlet it needs for expression. With the strength and viciousness of a madman, McKenzie places his own hands around the aggressor's neck, applies inhuman pressure. Manages to use his greater weight, his dorsal strength (those competitions with Jenkins!) to manoeuvre himself on top of the other man. Nudge his head nicely into position. Punch his lights out.

More hands land on McKenzie back. As they do, the crazed man leaps up, eyes blazing, jaw clenched. Is about to swing. Then, through the fog of rage, makes out the CM, startled but with half a dozen staff behind her. Other things, too, are happening. Cries of "Lock on!", "Take the legs!", "Alarm bell, B4 Association Room!" As the commands ring out, bring order to the chaos, McKenzie understands. His role is done. Shoulders slumping, he sits down, coughs violently holding his throat. Barely hears the commotion around him. Could not care. It's so wonderful being alive.

Gradually his breathing steadies. And as it does, his friend Adrenalin draws back the curtain. Shows him the mess. The knife-wielder under restraint - still struggling but oddly silent. The prisoner who was fending off the knife who McKenzie recognises as Djemil. Djemil! Another prisoner - Schild, by the looks of his scrawny frame, his oversized head - on his knees over in the corner, shock shining from his face. Finally

McKenzie's own aggressor, his prone body showing just how well the man from Security hit the most important key performance target of his life.

A nurse pulls back the man's eyelids. Tells the CM she's worried.

The CM pulls out her radio, calls for an ambulance. Her voice shakes.

Chapter 18

The Morning Meeting after the "Association Room fight", as it becomes known, is almost as painful as Tony McKenzie's injuries. First Simmering's breezy greeting: "Heard you've been in the wars, Tony!" Then the po-faced account by Charlotte Rosesmith who, McKenzie learns for the first time, was actually Duty Governor for the day. She relates the alarm bell in the Association Room as if it was just another incident.

"Then at fourteen twelve hours, alarm bell B4 landing. Fight involving Mr Djemil HA2684 and Mr Schild GR5899 versus Mr Avraham GR2434 and Mr Mizrahi GR2435. Intervention by Governor McKenzie, prisoners Mr Avraham and Mr Mizrahi currently out at hospital."

Simmering, to his credit, has no truck with downplaying the whole thing. Says it was clearly attempted murder, that he got it referred to the police the moment he heard about it. Believes it raises some extremely grave concerns. How, for example, the prisoners accessed the Association Room in the first place. The implications of that are impossible to overstate. Adds that the knife represents another massive security breach. Points to pre-meditation. A carefully planned execution. One that must have involved a member of staff.

What he doesn't understand, Simmering continues, is why. Why is everyone out to get this small harmless-sounding Israeli Matthew Schild? He asks McKenzie if he has any ideas. The large head shakes left to right, winces as it goes. Jenkins, opposite, raises his eyebrows, as if to say: "Go on, tell your Mossad theory, Tony, I dare you."

Then Simmering asks McKenzie how he's doing. Says he's impressed he's come in to work today: "An example to us all!" Jenkins kicks McKenzie under the table: "Not to me, you're not." McKenzie kicks him back: "Wanker."

Charlotte finishes her account of the incident. Provides more detail, more colour now, as if to satisfy the top governor's desire for drama. Assures Simmering that all the right paperwork for the incident was carried out before updating the room on the prisoners' injuries. Mr Avraham, the Israeli prisoner without the knife - "the one unfortunate enough to mess with Tony!" - he regained consciousness after a couple of minutes, got sent out to hospital. Had a brain scan. The brain was OK, but he suffered a fractured cheekbone, two broken ribs, severe bruising to his throat.

Two of the other prisoners also sustained injuries, she continues. Mr Mizrahi went out to hospital too, received treatment for a broken finger, a dislocated jaw. As for Mr Djemil, he suffered severe bruising around his groin area and face, a stab wound to his arm and lacerations to his forehead.

"Went out as well?"

Charlotte looks awkward.

"Actually no, he didn't, Governor. He was due to be taken out but he refused to go. Said he'd kick off if we tried to take him."

The doctor was uneasy, she admits. Therefore so was she. But she thought it through. Decided they couldn't very well do tests on Mr Djemil in hospital if he was not going to comply. So persuaded the doctor the only option, unless it was life-threatening, was to keep Mr Djemil in Hatcham, treat him as best they could. He is currently down the CSU.

"That's a bit odd," says Simmering.

Lastly Charlotte updates the room on Mr Schild. Says the tiny Israeli did not have a scratch on him. Adds that he had injuries of a different sort: emotional ones. As Jenkins raises his eyes to heaven, the Head of Equality, Diversity and Safer Custody describes how she went to talk to the vulnerable Israeli herself, assess his mental wellbeing.

"Given that Mr Djemil didn't go out to hospital and is still here in the prison, Governor," she says, with a little cough, "I was going to recommend that he and Mr Schild both return to their previous cell, B4-12. For Mr Schild's sake. Obviously there's no danger from Mr Avraham or Mr Mizrahi now. And I'm assuming when they get back from hospital, we'll locate them both down the CSU."

"Till we get them a transfer," says Simmering darkly. "I don't know who they are, these two new ones. But assaulting a member of my senior staff like that - Belmarsh strikes me as the place for them. While they are on remand for attempted murder, that is. Will you get onto that please, Tony?"

The tall man nods.

"As for the others - Mr Djemil and Mr Schild - that's fine for now, Charlotte. But we have to get to the bottom of this Mr Schild issue. I appreciate he's not the instigator of these incidents. But he keeps getting targeted. I want to know why."

He nods at Tony. Seems to remember something. Nods at Charlotte too.

* * * * * * * * *

No post-Morning Meeting security check today. McKenzie needs to ring the hospitals first, determine the ETAs of the Israelis, then get on the blower to Belmarsh. What about a good long check after that, he suggests to Jenkins. Ten do?

The way McKenzie walks stiffly into his office, stands for a minute just contemplating things - the paper-strewn desk, the soothing sombreness of the light - it's like he is savouring life anew. Or feeling pre-emptive nostalgia, perhaps, before he gets booted out of Security altogether. Gingerly he flicks on the lights, waits while they splutter into life before sitting down at his desk, picking up the phone. Soon lost in the maze that is Belmarsh's switchboard, he shouts next door. Persuades Janet to make him a cuppa: "Go on! For an injured old hero!"

By the time she pads back in, sets a very full mug down on the desk, McKenzie is on his final call. Motioning her to stay, he finally puts down the handset. Manages to spill, then sip his tea.

"Right Janet," he says, turning towards her. "To business."

"Aye. I'm waiting, governor."

"That thing ... did you get it?"

"Did you ask me to get it?"

"Yes I did, Janet."

"Well then."

Sucking in her cheeks, she reaches inside her bra, pulls out the grey rectangular object before placing it into his hand. It is still warm. McKenzie shivers as he takes it.

"Well done. Really well done ..." His voice trails off. "So ... go on then. How did you get it? Without anyone seeing you?"

"That's for me to know and you to wonder, Mr McKenzie."

"Come on, Janet. Don't be a pain."

Her small face crumples.

"I'm sorry ... sorry!"

"It's OK, Tony. I know you're having a difficult time." She reaches out a hand, withdraws it awkwardly. "I promise you, no-one saw me. None of the prisoners, none of the staff. No-one."

"And you promise you haven't said a word to anyone? Even at home?"

Janet sighs, frustrated now.

"You know very well I live on my tod. But no, I've not said a word. To anyone. Brownies' honour."

"OK. Sorry for asking. I just needed to check. Maybe I'm becoming a bit paranoid. But promise me one thing. If you ever get the slightest whisper you've been seen, come and tell me."

"What would you do then?"

An almighty guffaw.

"Janet, I have no idea! Prepare myself for the guillotine, I suppose."

"You don't have to worry," she says. "There's no evidence. Even the CCTV's not working. I've checked. You can forget ..."

"How do you mean?"

"The CCTV. On B Wing. I didn't know it wasn't working till I checked this morning ... you know ... for this. Seems like the picture was on pause or something. So you had the image of the wing, alright, but not in real time. It's OK, I've rebooted it ..."

Her voice trails off as if smothered by the consternation in McKenzie's face. Head pointed at the ceiling, he blindly grabs his pack of cigarettes, pulls one out. Lays it on the desk.

"This fight in the Association Room ... Think it might be connected with the CCTV going down?"

Her head cocks sideways.

"Are you asking me?"

"I'm asking you. It seems a big coincidence, no?"

"It seems a massive coincidence, Mr McKenzie. And I'll tell you another thing. When I was in the loo this morning, I got talking to the CM who was on the Centre yesterday afternoon. And she said she saw an officer come out the end of B4 - you know, the fours landing - then go onto the Centre and onto A4. Literally a few seconds before you passed by. She didn't do or say anything, the CM. Couldn't. She was with Governor

Simmering at the time. But she did wonder what the officer was doing up there, she said. Why they weren't in staff training. Made a mental note to challenge her later on."

"Her?"

"Yes, her."

"Well who was it? Did she see?"

McKenzie sounds impatient.

"Jenny Hughes?"

"What? Definitely? Probably?"

"You're probably best talking to the CM."

"Right, I will."

McKenzie stares into space, deep in thought. Finally asks Janet to submit an SIR.

"Not about you-know-what, obviously. In fact ..." - he opens his jacket pocket, inserts the little bug inside a near-empty packet of Marlboros - "... let us never talk about that again. No, I want you to do an SIR about the CCTV being off. When you discovered it, the fact you've just told me. All of that."

She nods, gets up purposefully. Is already pulling a biro from her shirt pocket as she walks towards the door.

"Oh, and Janet," he calls out. "Brace yourself for death by investigation."

* * * * * * * * *

"I thought we said ten? Or can heroes arrive any time they like?"

Jenkins makes a big point of looking at his watch, then at McKenzie who is limping from the door of Reception over to their drain cover. But the Security governor ignores him. Reaching his usual place on the left, he stops, lights up, before letting his arm perform its well practised arc, cigarette flaring with each inhale.

"So come on, then, how are you doing?" asks Jenkins, his voice more conciliatory now. "Or do you hurt so much you can't speak?"

"Let's just say I feel like I've gone twelve rounds with both the Klitschkos - with one hand tied behind my back. I can hardly walk, find it difficult to brush my teeth, everything hurts. Apart from that, yeah, brilliant thanks."

Passing the cigarette to his left hand, he opens, then shuts his right.

"Not surprised it hurts," says Jenkins, noticing. "Not every day you punch someone unconscious. Have to admit, even I was impressed when I heard, Tony. Didn't think you were capable. A shame Charlotte wasn't there to witness your derring-do."

"I'm sure she had a very important meeting."

"Of course she did. Making the world fairer for us all," says Jenkins, somehow making his breathing out sound sarcastic. "Besides your hand, no other injuries?"

"Only emotional ones."

"Yeah, I can imagine. Gentle flower like you." He spits something out of his mouth. "So go on, then. Why so late, Tony?"

McKenzie tells him. Gives Jenkins the bones of the conversation he had with Janet up in Security, then of a chat he had literally ten, fifteen minutes ago, with yesterday's CM. Caught her - the CM, that is - going into one of Charlotte's ACCT reviews. Managed to prise her away, ask her what she'd seen from the Centre just before the Association Room fight.

The CM looked a bit sheepish, continues McKenzie. Told him that, just before the fight - "my fight", as he puts it now - told him she was ninety-nine per cent certain she saw Officer Jenny Hughes coming off B wing on the fours, then cross the Centre, go onto A Wing. Admitted that, a minute before, she'd also heard a cell door being opened, then shut. Did nothing about it, even though the prison was meant to be in patrol state. Told herself it must be drug workers, maybe a nurse dishing out meds.

"So she bloody leaves it!" says McKenzie, incredulous. "And so does Simmering! Neither of them does a fucking thing!"

Jenkins joins in the disbelief with a shake of the head, a couple of tut tuts. Throws the butt of his cigarette like it's a dart before swivelling it dead with the sole of his shoe. Lights another.

"So what do you reckon?" McKenzie asks.

"How do you mean?"

"About the CCTV. It was turned off on B Wing yesterday. Think there's a connection with the fight? I mean, common sense says there must be."

Jenkins kicks imaginary stones.

"Not just common sense, Tony. I know there is. From what you've told me, Jenny Hughes is guilty on both counts: meddling with the CCTV, organising the fight."

"Whoa! Hold on! You don't know that. I mean, for one, the CCTV could have been turned off hours, even days before the fight. And two, I was talking to one of the camera operators this morning. He reckoned it would be possible to have the cameras on pause and not notice. Don't forget the whole nick was on lockdown, there was nothing much happening."

"He's talking crap, Tony. For a start, that's his job ... to bloody well check."

"Yeah, OK. Maybe. But you get my point? There's still no proper proof the events are connected. I mean, if you wanted to pause the cameras - and someone obviously did, because when we unpaused them this morning, they started working straight away - if you wanted to do that but keep the clock running, you'd need to know how to operate the system. And the chances of that being the same person as the one who organised the fight are not exactly going to be big, are they?"

"You're hardly Bill Gates, Tony. But no, I agree with you. Which proves my point."

"And what's that?"

"Before she moved to B Wing, Jenny Hughes worked in Security with me. She was my number one camera operator. She knows that system inside out."

* * * * * * * * *

Conversation was curiously scarce in cell B4-12 the morning after the Association Room fight. Little of the concern one might expect from Schild towards Djemil. Just a mumbled comment or two about how Djemil's employers were the ones really responsible, he ought to sue. Apart from that, the slight Israeli lay as usual on his bottom bunk, eyes shut, while the Londoner sat in his customary chair, watched easy TV. Both men skipped their evening meal. Djemil, presumably, because he'd have found hobbling down three flights of stairs tricky at best, Schild because he dared not go alone.

He suffered a long painful night without sleep, Djemil. At one point even asked the night nurse for painkillers, got two Paracetamol for his pains. In the morning, when the nurse's replacement comes to check on him, she decides his symptoms worry her. Orders him down to Healthcare. Reluctantly the Londoner consents. Commands Schild to stay in the cell. Says he'll be back by lunchtime.

But Schild does not stay cooped up. Wanders instead onto the landing come Association, leans over the bars. Is there for some minutes before he nods at Shorty who is passing on the threes below, head almost brushing the walkway above. The giant man pretends not to notice, ambles on past. But within a spookily short time, is on the fours sidling up to Schild.

"What's up?"

In a low voice - so low, the six foot eight figure has to almost get down on his knees to hear the tiny man - Schild tells him what he wants. Causes Shorty to suck through his teeth, go for another amble. But he returns a minute later, the giant. Nods silently before walking off again - this time, Schild in tow.

They have gone only a few yards when Shorty stops abruptly, makes a hand signal in the direction of the threes. Seconds later, a heated argument erupts - Jarvis having a set-to with someone down by the phones. As Officer Siddle strides along to intervene, calm both prisoners down, Shorty and Schild walk down the stairs at the other end of the landing. Enter a cell.

In it is Birdman, impassive on a chair by the window. Hunched over, he sits reading a book, his posture emphasising his distinctly unbird-like heft, the ill-defined neck which bunches up, fold by fleshy fold, above his maroon sweatshirt.

"Jarvis doing his stuff," says Shorty.

"I hear him," says Birdman, ponderously looking up. "Getting mouthier each time, and they still don't twig. Not the brightest, are they?" He chuckles, wheezing slightly. Turns his eyes to the skinny man behind. A hardness invades his voice. "You want to see me?"

Schild nods.

"Sit down." He points to the school-type chair. "I heard you had a bit of beef yesterday. You lucky you got your friend with you, Mr Djemil."

Birdman lifts his eyebrows. But Schild stays schtum.

"So tell me why you're here then. Why you want to see me."

"I want to ... I want to book a flight."

The sides of Birdman's mouth curl up.

"You want to book a flight. And you think I can help?"

"Uh-huh. I've heard ... you can deliver things."

"OK ..." Looking thoughtful for a moment, Birdman nods over at Shorty who immediately exits the cell. Space and daylight double. "Why don't you tell me what it is you want delivered? Then I'll see if I can help."

"I want to send something out. A message."

"A message ..."

"Yes."

From his sock, Schild pulls out a carefully folded bit of paper. Is about to pass it over when Birdman snatches it. Unfolds it. Knits his brow as he looks at the series of curves and dashes on the page.

"What the fuck is this, man?"

"It's just ... it's something I need to tell someone. It's Arabic."

"Why can't you use a phone like everyone else? Hey, listen. If you want to borrow ours, I can do it for ..."

But Schild shakes his head.

"The person I'm calling is tapped. And if they get a new phone, a new number, I can't trust that either. Plus, they don't do prison visits, this person. Not now. But they could pick up a message from someone on the out. If you just tell them where to ..." He pauses. "Take it from me, I need a flight."

"You're into heavy shit, man," says Birdman, sucking through his teeth. "I don't need heavy shit. I've got a business to run. I mean, fuck, why am I talking to a man who had a hundred large on his head, had these other two fuck with him ..." The voice trails off. "OK. This information ... what's it going to do to me if it goes AWOL?" Birdman directs a chubby finger

Schild's way. "In fact maybe you should tell me what this shit's about. Then I'll consider doing a flight for you."

"I promise you, it's not a risk. But I can't tell you what it is."

Birdman sucks through his teeth again. Acts uninterested - "Huh." Fails utterly to hide his curiosity. Seems enthralled, almost. Like he reckons Schild might be part of the big time. As in BIG.

"OK, man, here's what we're going to do. The way I see it, you bring a risk to my operation. I don't care what you say. So I'm going to charge you ten times the regular price. You take it or you ..."

He points to the door. But Schild nods. He will take it. So they talk numbers, logistics, bank accounts, and finally the two of them touch fists. Taking one last look at the message, Birdman folds it in two before placing it, carefully now, towards the back of the book he was reading. Then, with obvious effort, he stands up, leans heavily against the window bars.

The cell door miraculously swings open.

"Jarvis just got himself banged up on 53/4," laughs Shorty, navigating his huge frame under the doorway.

"Yeah, he's over-doing it, man. I told him. Can't gauge it, can he? Got to do just enough, not be a fucking drama queen." A pause. Then a flick of fat fingers towards Schild. "This one, we're done. And be careful. With Jarvis banged up ..."

"Nah, it's alright. He's still a draw."

On the way back up, Schild passes the wing SO remonstrating with Jarvis at his cell door, Siddle standing uncertainly at his manager's side. Jarvis is refusing to let the SO shut it - his foot is in the way. Five minutes later, he is walked down to the CSU.

Chapter 19

Jenny Hughes lics on the stained mattress, stares up at the mildewed ceiling of her bedroom. Seems oblivious to what surrounds her: the clothes strewn across the balding carpet - crumpled black trousers, white shirt, dirty underwear - the detritus from food take-aways, a key chain. Over the window, on which condensation has, here and there, massed into giant drips, plunged downwards, orange curtains hang limp, pathetic in their thinness against the sharp eastern light.

She has nothing to do now, Jenny, but wait. Wait for the early morning knock. The one that will lead to her arrest, her trial, eventual imprisonment. There is no rush. She knows too well these are her last moments of freedom for a long time. Ironically cannot stop thinking about her colleagues beginning their working day at the prison: the B Wing SO standing there in the crappy staffroom, geeing up the troops in his customary careworn fashion; the tuts, rolling eyes, of officers as he tells them one of their number has phoned in sick. How she wishes she was one of them! Almost chokes with sadness remembering she can't be. Not now.

Disbelief engulfs her as, for the millionth time, she relives the moment. The sickening feeling as she escorted the two Israelis from F Wing down to the B Wing Association Room - a feeling that only grew stronger when, minutes later, she opened up Djemil's cell, led him and Schild along the landing as well, thinking with every leaden step, "Fuck, am I really going to do this?" Then doing it. Opening the door of the Association Room. Ushering them both in - one, the same man who, only weeks before, had crashed his fist into Lopez's solar plexus, made the vile monster bend over double, sink wondrously to the floor. Who made her believe, for a few days at least, that the past might be escaped after all.

The front door slams, makes Jenny Hughes grip the side of the mattress. So this is it. They have come. But then she hears the clack clack clack of her neighbour's high heels down the garden path. Almost laughs at the anti-climax. Gets quickly sucked back into reflection. Asks herself: did she really have no way out? And what about now? Is it definitely too late? Even if she came clean, told them everything? Would they still not believe her?

No, that's a silly idea, she decides. For a start, her credibility is shot. Or certainly will be once they do their digging, find out about her and Lopez. And secondly, if she did tell them, she would probably end up retracting it. Knows how dangerous Samuels has become. Remembers (how could she forget!) that quiet Saturday afternoon a few months back when she slipped into Security on her own, had a shifty at his file. Read there in black and white how the chubby kid she and Lopez used to mock, taunt on their Waltham Forest estate - how, these days, he is suspected of two shootings, a kidnapping, the masterminding of a murder ... But so far the CPS has failed to land a punch. Witnesses keep bailing out.

She flinches - literally - contemplating the awfulness of her predicament. A second later, becomes vaguely aware of something positive floating around in her brain. So chases it. Grasps the moment she heard about Governor McKenzie's heroics, just minutes after locking the four prisoners in the Association Room. Heard the sickening thumps, the cracks from inside before fleeing, panicked, to join in with staff training during a tea break. By the urns, overheard excited chatter about the Head of Security saving a prisoner's life.

"Which one?" she asked someone weakly.

"Jameel?", shrugged an officer, stuffing a Custard Cream into his mouth.

She could have kissed him. Sashayed, lunatic-like, into the classroom. He was safe!

The doorbell rings. Another wave of sweat. Followed, this time, by a lop-sided smile. Then a second ring. Slowly, like some arthritic old dear, Jenny Hughes crawls to her feet, trips on her key chain walking out of the bedroom. And carries on down the stairs.

* * * * * * * * *

Especially important, this security check, because it is getting dark - about seven o'clock or so - and you never know what you might see in prison grounds in the dark. Blankets tied together, hung out of a window ready to be climbed down; a man shimmying down a drainpipe, wire-cutters in mouth; a tall ladder resting gently against the perimeter wall, each rung a precious step to freedom. Just as well there are two highly alert men in suits standing in the Reception yard, keeping everything safe and secure.

As you might hope, no escape attempt is apparent. And yet the two men are definitely exercised about something. McKenzie, in particular, seems in a lather. Keeps jabbing his cigarette. Contorting his long face.

"And if I ever see that Jenny Hughes again, I'll tear the cow to shreds, I swear to God."

"Sounds like you won't have to, Tony. Not unless you take a trip over to HMP Holloway. It won't be a bundle of laughs there, I promise you. I used to work there."

The two men take a drag of their cigarettes, blow out clouds which have scarcely begun their mushrooming when Jenkins asks: "Go on, then. How did it happen?"

"What? Oh, that! Well now ..." McKenzie pulls his lapels together as if about to give a recital. "Straight after our chat the other day, when you went on about Jenny Hughes knowing about the cameras and everything, I go to the gaffer, tell him what I know. Or what we thought we knew ..." He points to himself and Jenkins. "And straight away Simmering says refer it to the police. So with a little help from our oversized Police Liaison Officer, who did some work for once instead of frightening normal-sized folk down the gym, our Jenny gets the knock first thing yesterday.

"So anyway, they take her down the station, do the full interview. And straight away she coughs. Couldn't wait, according to the PLO. Even declined a solicitor. Just wanted to get it over with, get charged, know where she stood. And get this: even tried to fess up in the car on the way to the cop shop, apparently."

"Yeah, but to what?"

McKenzie turns to Jenkins.

"That, me old mucker, is a good question. Because the answer to that leads to something bigger altogether."

"Go on."

"Well, she admitted disabling the cameras, making it look like they were still running."

"Like we thought."

"And she admitted unlocking the four prisoners in patrol state - our two new Israeli friends, plus Djemil and Schild - then chucking the lot of them in the Association Room. But apparently ..." - McKenzie stabs the air again - "... apparently she denies knowing what the repercussions would be. Kept on telling the coppers she had no idea they were going to beat the crap out of each other."

"Yeah, right."

"Obviously it makes Jenny Hughes an accomplice to attempted murder, the whole thing. What she hasn't done yet, according to the PLO, is say why she did it. Apart from some cock and bull about following orders. Or being told to - some bollocks like that."

"Well of course she was acting for someone."

"I agree with you. But it's meaningless unless she hands over names."

McKenzie's big face lights up.

"That's what's so amazing about this whole thing, Chris, don't you think? There's obviously so much going on. You know, big stuff. Yet no-one's breathing a word. Jenny Hughes is taking take the rap instead of pointing the finger. And so are Djemil and Schild. Yeah, I didn't tell you about that. I had a long talk with both of them. Separately, of course, so they couldn't compare notes. And ... well, you know what I'm going to say, don't you? I got bloody nowhere. Djemil did his smooth surfaces thing: 'Just trying to keep my head down Guv.'"

McKenzie mimics the Londoner's accent.

"And Schild ... well, he looked like he always does. A frightened little mouse. I'm not sure the guy's all there, to be honest. He strikes me as a bit - how would Charlotte put it? - intellectually challenged. Anyway, I didn't get a squeak out of him either. He just looked at me with his big eyes, kept his trap firmly shut. As for the other two ..."

"Who?"

"The other two fighters ... er, Avraham and Miz ... whatever his name is. The PLO said they might as well be mute. Three times his cop-mates pulled them out the CSU, gave them the third degree. And three times they learnt fuck all. Both prisoners just kept staring at the wall, by all accounts. Kept on saying 'no comment.'"

"Must get boring."

The two men light up another, the glow showing night is really kicking in now. Chances are, they're the only two senior managers left in the nick. The gaff is theirs.

They talk easily, McKenzie, Jenkins. Let the conversation slide around like a fat-tyred car on ice. No prescribed route, no barriers. It skids, inevitably, onto colleagues, onto pay, finally onto other staff who, over the years, have also turned out to be rotten apples. The patronising solicitor who was bringing in drugs; the prim fast-tracker caught shagging the bad-boy gangster in his cell; the officer caring for his dying wife who smuggled in phones so he could pay for her palliative care. Rotten apples, the lot of them. Even the last poor sod.

None, though, quite as rotten as Jenny Hughes, they decide.

"Rotten to her filthy disgusting core," says McKenzie, opening, closing his fist.

As the daylight dwindles, the two governors carry on reminiscing about all the corrupt staff they have encountered over the years - the temptations they succumbed to, the silly situations they put themselves in. Finally turn to go in. And as they do, feel remarkably good about themselves.

* * * * * * * * *

Turns out McKenzie, Jenkins are not the only two senior managers in the prison. Because at the end of an unlit Admin corridor, in John Simmering's office where the blinds are drawn and the illuminated desk lamp spreads a warm and gentle glow, the top governor is having a quiet chat with Charlotte Rosesmith. They sit opposite each other, either side of his impressive desk, and both of them wear earnest expressions. There, however, the similarities end. Because whereas Simmering's straight-backed, shoulders-down posture is one of the upstanding public servant, Charlotte looks filled with trepidation with her arched back, her tightly crossed legs and delicate clasped hands.

"In a way, it's good this is happening now," says Simmering, leaning across the desk.

"How come?"

"I'm afraid it comes with the grade, Charlotte. Things of this nature - accusations, falsehoods - they're part and parcel of our role. A senior role, I should say. How else are the guilty going to defend themselves? When a fox gets caught in a trap, it lashes out, tries to bite anything within reach."

The crumpled body opposite does not respond.

"Listen," he continues gently. "I know it's difficult to imagine but, in time, this will stand you in good stead. In fact I hope that, one day fairly soon, you will look back and see this difficult period as formative. I think highly of you, Charlotte, as you know. Very highly indeed. And I think you will go far. In fact, if you asked me right now, I'd go as far as to say Area Manager could be within your reach one day." He puts a hand up to ward off disagreement. "No, I mean it. But to get up to that level, Charlotte, you are going to have to learn to take unpleasant episodes like this in your stride. Not let them get to you."

She manages a faint smile.

"John, I'm so grateful for all your support. Not just now, but ... Without you ..." Her eyes fill with tears. "What hurts ... What hurts is who it is. The fact it's Jenny Hughes. I didn't tell you, but after the Lopez incident, we had a long chat together about working in a prison, how hard it can be to be a woman in a place like Hatcham. And I became her unofficial mentor, in a way. Thought she appreciated it. She certainly seemed grateful at the time. Wouldn't stop thanking me. Kept coming to my office, saying I was the only reason she was still in the job. So for this to happen ... I just can't believe the way ..."

She tries to blink away the tears.

"Come on," says Simmering. "You can't take it personally. The way Jenny Hughes is behaving now, it's because she is terrified. She will do anything to try and save herself. Absolutely anything. But you ..." He puts down the pen, leans back majestically. "From what you've told me, you have nothing to fear, Charlotte. Nothing at all. Just think - tomorrow evening, it will all be over. By the time you have your tea, the police will know Officer Jenny Hughes was the only one responsible. Her and no-one else."

Chapter 20

Not many things surprise Tony McKenzie. Far from it. This, after all, is a man who graduated from juvenile miscreant creating havoc on the outskirts of London to upstanding foot soldier serving in the Gulf (two tours) through to - well, via a few tortured and, it must be said, rather boozy years adjusting to civvy street - through to the Prison Service, whose operational ranks he climbed in pedestrian but dogged fashion to reach the heady heights of today, the noble office of governor grade in one of the capital city's prisons. A proper prison. Where stuff happens.

Commensurate with his varied, oft hard-won experience has been the growth of confidence within Tony McKenzie. Not for him the short-cut approach of Charlotte (to airily pick someone at random!) who wanders from fee-paying school into university, wanders out again with a fancy qualification or two, thence onto a fast-track scheme and, from there, straight into a governor-grade job. Wafting in like some expensive perfume. No, every inch of progress McKenzie has earned. Fought for. Tooth and nail.

In fact when he thinks of his career, McKenzie, he sometimes sees an image of Roman soldiers in formation holding shields over their heads to form a human tortoise, then inching forwards, slow but sure. He is that tortoise. Has got up at 05.45 hours every day, give or take, for the last twenty years, hoisted increasing loads onto his wide bony shoulders, sometimes jeopardising his marriage in the process - and very likely his long-term health, what with the security checks out on the Reception yard with Jenkins the whole time.

So was it worth it? The jury is still out, in McKenzie's head at least. But there is no denying that the kids enjoy their odd family holiday to Florida. And, as he has heard many a time, his wife wonders how they ever did without their new conservatory (which the tortoise bought after much persuasion and attempts to hide inside his shell!). What is not up for debate is that McKenzie's sure-footed advance means that, these days, he can take the job in his stride. He has seen it all. Heard it all. Done it all. Nothing that happens in Hatcham prison can faze him.

But then the phone rings. And within a few seconds of him answering, McKenzie's composure gets blasted to bits. Doing the blasting at the other end of the line is a well-spoken woman. She begins innocuously enough. Asks if he, Governor McKenzie, would like some help getting down the MDT rate. When he admits (rather rashly, in retrospect) that yes, he could do with all the help he can get, she tells him about a pigeon that is regularly bringing drugs into the prison. Explains, rather rapidly, that that is why the MDT rate is so high. Goes on to identify the bit of the prison the bird routinely lands in: "Does B3 mean anything to you?" Adds that such things have been known to happen in Mexico, according to her "extremely brief research on the web."

McKenzie's brain has not even begun to process the information when the woman launches her second devastating (again, politely delivered) strike. She tells him about the bug. The bug that McKenzie ensured was placed in the utmost secrecy in cell B4-12, yet which somehow this posh-sounding woman knows all about. The bug that will end his career, even put him in jail, if she ever chooses to tell the authorities. The bug that ... Permutations of his demise run riot in McKenzie's head. He braces himself for the blackmail demand that will surely follow.

But out of the darkness, light. Instead of threats, the woman offers hope.

"I wouldn't recommend putting any more bugs in prisoners' cells," she says. "I'm not sure you're allowed to do that, Governor McKenzie. And we don't want you to get in any trouble."

Then there is a click. She is gone.

For a full five minutes, all McKenzie can do is stare at the yellow wall behind his desk as shock, awe magimix his brain. Stop him from thinking straight, make his whole body quiver uselessly. When, slowly, some reasoning ability does return, the big man's first instinct is to scour his conscious. Try to work out who the hell could have tipped this woman off. Barely has he begun a virtual interrogation of every possible candidate before Janet's little face looms large. Is followed close behind by the ratty features of Jenkins. Their appearance stands to reason. She and Jenkins are the only people who know about the bug. Or at least, the only people he has talked to about it.

But then McKenzie remembers the bird. If the pigeon does exist, like this mysterious woman says, Janet and Jenkins could not possibly know about that as well. Not unless ... He comes up with a variety of scenarios to somehow include the bird as well, but they are just too far fetched. Too silly. He scotches Janet from his list of suspects. Minutes later, scotches Jenkins too. Experiences relief both times.

Eyes resting on the phone - so far the only confirmed culprit - McKenzie hears the woman's voice again. There was a brisk matter-of-factness to it. At the same time, it was also gently patronising. Or maybe that is a whiff of conspiratorial empathy he can detect: "We don't want you to get in any trouble." Either way, she definitely sounded posh. Could be Charlotte's mum, the way she signed off in that plummy voice.

The silly idea enters McKenzie's head as a joke to self. Rapidly mutates into a hypothesis. Gives him a spasm of terror as he thinks it over. Could Charlotte have found out about the bug from Djemil or Schild - maybe during one of her ACCT reviews - then got, if not her mum, then one of her posh friends to play a practical joke on him? He mulls the idea. Seriously mulls it. Eventually decides it does not stack up either. Charlotte, with her sensible shoes and so much to lose, is hardly going to mix it with the criminal fraternity. She is just not the sort. Besides, what about the pigeon? How would that fit in?

Charlotte gets scotched.

Calling out to his staff and getting no answer, McKenzie lights up a cigarette. Finds comfort in the smoke. Starts blowing out circles, watches how they belly-dance, contract uncomfortably between the thick bars over his desk, then linger as if stuck to the glass somehow. It is only as he is watching this aerial display that McKenzie stops looking back. Looks forwards. Sees the hope the call offers. Maybe even the chance to save his job.

No, OK, so he does not know who the caller is. But she was right about the bug, the woman, and he cannot see any harm in taking her at her word about the bird. After all, the MDT rate is up there in the ether and he is a man without a plan. So what on earth has he got to lose? Besides, come to think of it, giving it a whirl will be easy. Jenkins has often gone on about a mate of his who runs a pest control business. Keeps on about how the guy got "proper rich" by hitting rats on the head, wrestling with cockroaches. Also, if McKenzie remembers rightly, by flying a bird around hospitals, schools, that kind of thing. To frighten off the pigeons.

Clouds clear from the rectangles of sky between the bars, unshroud a shy sun. Let it cast rare rays into McKenzie's office, blinding him in the eyes. Squinting as he picks up the phone, he dials the extension for the Head of Residential. Conveys his sophisticated plan.

"Jenkins, mate ... you would not fucking believe it ... wish I was ... but help me ... your millionaire friend with the eagle ... all right, hawk ... got his number handy? ... I need it ... pronto ..."

* * * * * * * * *

The shock of the phone call obviously numbed a few brain cells because it is only in the afternoon that McKenzie registers the blindingly obvious. He has a little pile of SIRs, near a dozen in all, diligently indexed under the title "Birdman." In his metal filing cabinet, top drawer. There waiting to be whipped out the moment the Birdman word meant something. The moment which now has surely come.

Frustratingly, Duty Governor shenanigans mean McKenzie cannot go through the SIRs until about six. By which time the wine-like air of a late summer evening is wafting over Hatcham's glowering grey walls, and a blackbird, dainty on the Dannert wire, is singing out its heart, chirpy yet melancholic. It's all so sad and beautiful, McKenzie actually slows as he leaves the Admin corridor, steps outside into the inner perimeter of the prison, so he can consciously drink in life's riches. Then, with a mighty sigh, he opens the door into the Gate Lodge, starts climbing the stairs back up to his office.

It takes a second to dig out the Birdman SIRs. Only a few more to flick through them, remind himself what is what. He reads one from Damian Siddle dated 16 August. It is about Samuels, Longman and Jarvis being in a cell together, how they were talking warily about Djemil, deciding whether to react to his felling of Lopez. One phrase jumps out at him: "Mr Samuels I have heard referred to as Birdman." Good, well at least that corroborates the identity of Birdman, thinks McKenzie as he shuts the thing before slapping it down on the desk.

He shuffles through the other SIRs. Grows curious as to when the Birdman connection was made first. Is soon pulling out one from Charlotte Rosesmith noticing that it pre-dates all the others. Thinks: unbelievable, she has to be first at everything! Then, opening it and scenting a lovely perfume smell, finds himself lifting the form to his nose. Immediately feels very silly. Lays the form back on the desk. Reads:

Sir, at approximately 10.40 hours on 22 May, I was walking down the threes landing of B Wing on my way to an important meeting with some Listener reps when I heard one prisoner say to another: "Birdman? That's Samuels, everyone knows that." Later, at the end of the Safer Custody strategy meeting, I asked one of my most trusted Listener reps - Mr Brannigan HA2022 - if he had any idea who this Birdman character was. Mr Brannigan did not hesitate. He said it was common knowledge that Birdman was indeed Mr Samuels HA2214. I do not know if this is of significance, but I am forwarding this information to Security in case it forms part of a bigger picture.

Toying with his biro, McKenzie rereads the SIR. Wonders why it actually makes him feel a bit angry. Decides it is because Charlotte does not mention who the first lot of prisoners doing the talking were. A bit sloppy on her part - any officer recruit knows that supporting information like that can be useful. Then he spots something else: the way Charlotte calls Mr Brannigan one of her most trusted Listener reps. As if she has any idea who is trustworthy! It is not that McKenzie has anything much on Brannigan. No intel off the top of his head, at least. But that is not the point. It is the naivety of the young fast-tracker that irks him. The idea that a governor, or any member of staff for that matter, can trust anyone. No they can't, Charlotte!

Shutting the SIR with its two small sins, he nudges it back into line with the others, then puts the lot of them back in the top drawer. Good. That's his plan of attack for tomorrow sorted.

There is no doubt about it. Progress is in the air.

* * * * * * * * *

From the way Samuels HA2214 reacts when the Dedicated Search Team open up B3-17 first thing next morning, tell him he's going to have a cell spin, it's as if he is expecting it. Because the chubby man accepts the news without resistance. Merely nods to the shaven-headed trio who inform of the fact, makes some quip about how tough they think they look with their short haircuts, their fancy trousers with pockets all over. Then starts bumbling around his cell, muttering something about trying to find his burn.

He shows only a whiff of anger, Samuels, when he is told to forget his burn, take nothing with him. But it is only a whiff. Nothing more than a sucking through the teeth, a slight slowing down as he exits the cell, tries to stare down the lead man.

The strip search passes quickly. Samuels is surly, taciturn throughout. Nevertheless complies. Shows he has nothing on him. The search of the cell by the active drug dog - a springer spaniel with long floppy ears called Annie - that is also soon finished. To the team's amazement, not the slightest sniff of drugs anywhere.

The search of the cell by humans takes longer. Not so much because of the number of objects in it - although the amount of stuff in Samuels's cell does move one of the DST team to comment that B Wing staff wouldn't know volumetric control if it fucked them up the arse. No, it's more because of the thoroughness with which they carry out the process.

The three officers run their surgical gloves through, in and around everything. All the cereal boxes, fruit juice cartons, packets of soup; the page of every single book, magazine, notepad piled high on the single bedside cabinet; the formidable number of toiletries - shampoos, shaving creams, skin balms; the duvet cover, duvet itself, pillow, mattress - with particular focus on the seams; the stereo, the stereo's battery compartment, its plug, the inside of the plug; the window ledge, behind the mirror, all of the walls. They even tip up the bed, the three of them, see if anything tumbles out of its hollow legs. Shine a torch up.

But nothing. Nor do they find anything of interest elsewhere. When, half-way through the process, Governor McKenzie turns up, asks how it is going, jokes that he cannot trust them to do a proper job on their own, they tell him nothing has been found. Set storm clouds rolling across his face.

And yet there is nothing they can do. The cell of Mr Samuels is as clean as a whistle. No drugs, no mobile phones and, above all, no pigeon. McKenzie even goes into the cell himself. Opens a narrow slit of window as wide as it will go, starts feeling for pigeon shit that "should be bloody caked here outside." Swears fulsomely when he finds none. Says he cannot understand it. The DST team raise eyebrows at each other. Whisper about a knock to the head during the Association Room fight.

Letting loose one last salvo of expletives, McKenzie looks at his watch, then at the staff.

"Right. Better crack on with the next one," he commands. "Mr Longman and Mr Jarvis. And do me a favour, will you? Check like I did - feel along the outside of the window for pigeon shit. Don't smirk, guys. This is important. Make sure you do that, please. And one of you, report to me once you've finished. I'll be in my office."

But McKenzie does not move. He stays standing there on the threes while the staff escort Samuels HA2214 back to cell B3-17. Watches as the prisoner, with a smug smile, thanks staff for their efforts, tells them better luck next time. But the smile evaporates the moment Samuels turns to walk back into his cell. Sees the mess staff have left behind.

"They've fucking turned it over, guv!"

"Give you something to do, Mr Samuels," says one of the DST officers, slamming shut the door.

As fruity phrases pierce the steel barrier, McKenzie puts a hand on the young officer's shoulder.

"We do not wind them up, OK? That is not in your job description."

The tall governor gets a reluctant nod, a few mumbled words of apology. Then, as he is walking away, a call from the same officer to come back.

"What is it?"

"This, Governor," says the officer, taking something out of his thigh pocket. "No idea what it is, or if it's important. But we found it in one of Mr Samuels's books. All weird scribbles and wiggles. Some kind of code, we reckon. The only thing I can make out is the word Matthew at the end. Do you want to have a look, or shall I bin it?"

McKenzie takes it. Has a cursory read.

"I haven't got a clue either," he says, stuffing it into the inside pocket of his suit jacket. "But let me hang onto it. Oh, and thanks for your efforts, guys." He glances towards Longman and Jarvis's cell. "Go get 'em."

* * * * * * * * *

Gym time. Or rather, that nasty period just after when prolonged exertion followed by hot shower, rushed change saturates shirt cotton with sweat, makes it stick to your back like a second transparent skin. Thus afflicted are Governors McKenzie, Jenkins. Standing in the CSU exercise yard - handy cooldown area - they puff away, wait for the wind to work its wonders.

It was particularly strenuous, today's workout. The reason? No contraband was found in the cells occupied by Jarvis and Longman either, despite the best efforts of the DST team. This caused utter disbelief in McKenzie - and profound frustration. Led to furious grappling with heavy dumb-bells come lunchtime - a zeal returned with interest by the ever-competitive Chris Jenkins. Guttural grunts, shouts of "Come on!", scary thuds as thick metal discs came crashing down onto ribbed rubber mats after reps of six, or were precariously replaced onto bar holders by shaking arms - the caveman antics soon created an exclusion zone around the two governors. Intensified their own private arms race.

Now, though, that race is won (who by, neither man will say!) and frustration has given way to physical exhaustion. What the exertion has not done, however, is quell McKenzie's bewilderment about the cell search fiasco.

"I still can't believe it," he says, not for the first time. "I mean, how the fuck could we not find anything? The drugs are coming in by pigeon, and Samuels is called Birdman. Plus he and his sidekicks are obviously running the whole of B Wing. So how could we not ..."

"Must of got a tip-off."

"But no-one knew about the search till this morning, Chris. They can't have - I didn't tell anyone. Even the DST guys - I only briefed them when they got in at seven."

For a good ten seconds, the middle distance claims their attention. And then Jenkins, out of the blue: "It's faulty intel, Tony. Got to be. I mean, this pigeon thing you're so damn sure about all of a sudden. What makes you so sure? What I'm saying is, I don't get why you suddenly asked me for the number of my pest controller mate. What was it? An SIR? A cosy little chat with a prisoner? Or did you just wander out for a smoke, find a bird stuffed with drugs on the exercise yard?"

McKenzie studies his shoes, says "Uh-uh" to each suggestion. Finally stops the guessing game.

"That's the amazing thing, Chris. I got this phone call ..."

Five minutes later, the Head of Residential still cannot get over it. Having passed through the predictable phase of disbelief, plying McKenzie with question after question, he has, with each answer, chiselled away at his own incredulity. Now inhabits that childish realm of unadulterated astonishment. A realm McKenzie is starting to find boring.

"So you've really no idea who she is?"

"You've asked me that."

"Yeah, but ... you must have some idea. Some tiny little thought that's crossed your mind."

"I've told you! I thought about Janet, thought about you, even thought about Charlotte."

"We all do that ..."

"Crossed you all off my list."

"And you didn't recognise her voice? Nothing that ..."

"Chris!"

"Yeah, sorry." Jenkins puffs thoughtfully. "So she told you about the pigeon, this woman. How did you get from there to finding out who controlled the bloody thing? OK, so you reckon Samuels is Birdman. But there's hundreds of prisoners, hundreds of pigeons."

"Actually, that was the easy bit," says McKenzie, going on to to tell Jenkins about the Birdman SIRs he has been collecting over the last few months, how he only recognised their significance yesterday. Not straight away, he admits. A few hours after.

Jenkins pulls at his shirt, tries to make it billow.

"Well, the fact you've got a few of them - SIRs, I mean - it does sound like the Samuels-being-Birdman thing is pretty reliable. Especially if one was from the lovely Charlotte. So it must of been the tip-off about the pigeon that was wrong, Tony. I mean, it's not as if you know who the hell this woman was. She could have been anyone."

McKenzie is shaking his head before Jenkins even finishes.

"I disagree, Chris. I reckon the intelligence is probably spot on, and Samuels and his gang are just wily fuckers. Bullying the other prisoners to keep their gear - you know, like they were doing with Schild a while back. Besides, last night, I had a useful chat with one of the Listeners when everyone was locked up."

"Let me guess: Brannigan."

Jenkins almost spits out the name.

"Yeah, OK, I know what you're thinking. But believe you me, it was worth it. For a start he corroborated the Birdman SIR thing as well. Said it was Samuels all the way. Not just the fact he is Birdman but also that he's running the drugs supply. Basically running the whole of B Wing."

"And let me guess. Brannigan wanted a kickback ..."

"Well ..." McKenzie looks uneasy. "Of course everything's a trade-off. You taught me that, Chris. And so, yeah, I had to overlook a couple of things we found in his cell. But the net benefit to the prison ..."

A couple of slow nods from Jenkins.

"Yeah, I suppose if I was in your shoes ... Besides, the fact that what he told you backs up the SIRs and the phone call ... But you still need proper hard evidence, Tony. You know, a drugs find."

"Chris! Why do you think I'm so pissed off?"

Jenkins chuckles.

"Well, at least we got a good weights session out of it. We were knocking out our PBs in there today. Haven't done that for a while. You should get pissed off more often."

"Yeah, and now I'm bloody freezing," says McKenzie, putting on his jacket. "Listen, I'd better get on. See what other wild goose chases I can find."

"I think you mean pigeon chases, mate."

Chapter 21

The injuries incurred by prisoner Djemil HA2684 were obviously more acute than he was letting on because when his presence in Healthcare is demanded a second time, one day later, the Londoner accepts without hesitating. Tells the officer he'll join him on the ones as soon as he's put his trainers on. Once again sternly instructs Matthew Schild to stay in the cell.

When Djemil does return, not long after eleven, the skinny Israeli is standing by the window, tapping his teeth with his fingers. He turns the moment Djemil enters the cell. Quickly cedes the window spot. Stays on his feet.

"We need to talk," he says.

The Londoner raises an eyebrow. Starts rolling himself a cigarette.

"This offer ..."

"Which one, Matthew?"

"Come on, Mr Djemil. Are you going to make this difficult for me?" Schild sits down on the bunk. Waits for Djemil to finish making his rollie, light the thing up. "What guarantee do I have?"

"About the offer? Nothing. Nothing apart from my word. Nothing I can show you ..." Djemil has a drag. "But you could talk to my boss, discuss it with her. Here, I've got a phone ..."

"And what would that prove? She could be anyone."

Another drag.

"We've thought of that. To a point. We can't give you proper proof straight away. Not till we get you out of this place. But my boss will be able to tell you things about your life in Tel Aviv - things that a regular scammer could not know. Not unless they've been spying on you for years. Or bought the info from the Mossad - which I think you'll agree, Matthew, is not very likely."

Schild leans forwards, elbows on his knees.

"You know a lot will depend on what your boss says."

"So you're not interested, then? Fine."

"No, no ... I am."

"Good," says Djemil. "Well, it took us a while but we got there in the end. What my boss says, by the way - that's beyond my control. But I tell you what, I hope to God she does say the right thing because I really want to get out of this shithole. It's doing my head in." He looks at his watch. "OK. It'll be lunchtime soon. So I suggest we do the call this afternoon - when everyone's banged up. Let me text her."

* * * * * * * * *

Schild falls asleep after lunch. As if his decision has brought him calmness, somehow. Restored control. By the time he comes to, Djemil is sitting on the chair next to him, mobile phone in hand.

"When you're ready," he says. "She's expecting us."

Not replying, the Israeli hauls himself off the bunk, goes for a piss. Once the toilet starts quietening down, gives Djemil a nod.

Turning on the TV, the Londoner twiddles the volume. Dials a number.

"Anne? Yeah, he's right here. No, I didn't ... and, if you don't mind, I suggest now is not the time for that. Here, I'll pass you over."

Scowling, Djemil hands the phone to Schild. The tiny Israeli looks at the device stupidly, as if it might give him an electric shock. Then puts it to his ear.

"Hello?"

"Hello Matthew," the voice says. "My name is Anne Forbes-Pelham. I understand there is a possibility we may soon be colleagues."

There is a pause.

"It's a possibility. But it depends on you winning my trust. By proving to me who you work for. For all I know ..."

A shuffling of papers down the line.

"Matthew, I quite understand. In your position I would feel exactly the same. But before we go into that, please allow me to make two things clear."

"What is it?"

"The first is that even after we meet - and I hope we can very soon - we won't be able to force you to cooperate. You can still refuse to work with us. You'll be able to take your chances back in prison any time you want. It's very important you understand that."

Schild starts the teeth tapping again.

"And the second?"

"The second ... well, as I believe Mr Djemil has already explained, ultimate proof about who I represent will have to wait until you are released. Only at that point will you know for sure who we are. There is no way around that, I'm afraid. However once you come to our premises to talk terms with us, there will be no ambiguity whatsoever. That, I can promise you. Until that happens, all I can do is provide you with information over the phone, and from that information, it will be for you to judge the kind of organisation I work for."

"Right, I get it. But I still have no idea about you, Mrs Forbes ..."

"Anne Forbes-Pelham. And no, you don't. But may I suggest we begin with establishing who I work for first? If you have any more questions after that ..."

"Go on, then. I'm waiting."

More shuffling.

"Good. Let me start, then, by saying we know you were living in a squat in Alwyne Place, Islington from the end of June to the first week of August. That you told the people who were living there that you were a hacker who operated under the name Permy8. You joined the squat just days after you met a young woman called Farideh at a music festival in East London. You smoked a joint with her there, shared some sort of drink made from crushed ice. But you did not kiss until you were kettled together a few days later during an anti-capitalist demo outside ..."

"That ... all this shows you were following me," says Schild. "It says absolutely nothing about who you are."

"I don't disagree, Matthew. So now, let me move onto Tel Aviv. Specifically onto your early days at Proactive Israeli Defence Solutions where you were recruited personally by its CEO Ishmael Lotz. PIDS was in deep trouble when he took over and Mr Lotz's strategy was to massively increase the focus on Research and Development, and to harvest talent from Israel's top universities - computer science faculties in particular. You were only twenty-three when he gave you a golden handshake, persuaded you to abandon your doctorate. But you won his confidence extremely quickly. Within three years you had been made head of R&D for the entire organisation. There you ..."

"And all this you could find on the internet. Even by looking at my LinkedIn profile. This is zero proof!"

"Matthew, please bear with me. Despite your position at PIDS, we also happen to know you were a regular visitor to the Hezbollah-affiliated web site Al-Manar."

A slight pause.

"And you could find that out with a bit of hacking, a bit of code-breaking..."

"Yes, but hold on. What hacking could not tell us is that you discussed Hezbollah's strategy with a man with links to the Iranian regime in the middle of a sports field in Kfar Chabad on 24 April at 06.23 hours. Which - correct me if I'm wrong, Matthew - we could only know by eavesdropping on you using a highly sophisticated drone, or by obtaining the information from an organisation that operates a similar piece of hi-tech. Wouldn't you agree?"

No reaction from Schild.

"We understand a key focus of your work when you joined PIDS was bio-mimicry. In particular, building on the work of the University of Pennsylvania, whose GRASP Lab created a swarm of 20 miniscule drones - nano quadrotors, I believe you call them - that could fly in formation, even avoid each other. You took this a step further. With your team, you developed bee drones that could be dropped into a town or city and were programmed to kill or incapacitate any target whose iris pattern matches one identified on the user's database. I should say, this line of work is of particular interest to us," she adds casually.

"What else? Ah yes! You also created a drone butterfly which weighs only 8 grams but provides a ciphered video link. It can enter buildings undetected, this butterfly, and provide special forces with a layout of the interior before they go in. You demonstrated this micro-drone to seven senior members of the Mossad at PIDS HQ back in May. Despite initial scepticism, it appears you won them over, Matthew. Convincingly, by all accounts."

Schild looks at Djemil in astonishment.

"How did you ... That means that ..." Standing up, he walks to the door, the phone still to his ear. "OK. Enough! I believe you. At least for now. But I still need to know the terms you are offering. Mr Djemil here ..." - another glance at his cellmate - "... he says I can be protected. That I will be able to live safely, have a good life. A well resourced team to continue my work."

"We can promise you all that, Matthew."

"On top of that, I want a salary of one million pounds a year - plus options."

A few muffled words at the other end.

"That shouldn't be a sticking point either, Matthew. Although it will depend on you agreeing to work with a major defence contractor we have in mind, one we believe will be ideally suited to your line of work. We hope to schedule a meeting with them within the next few days."

"Well tell them I want to be able to pick my team. Do things my way," snaps Schild. "And anyway, before that, I need to see an email from you confirming the terms we've just discussed. Sent to my personal email which you will have, no doubt. Only then will I ..."

"Matthew, that won't be a problem. I will get the Ts and Cs sent from the Attorney General's office within the hour. They will confirm salary, accommodation, your new identity and, of course, the expectations in full from our side."

"Good. I will expect it. Then, assuming I'm happy ... what then?"

"You need to explicitly agree to the terms and conditions we are offering, Matthew. My email will make clear how to do this. Once you do, we will get you out of there. By tomorrow morning, probably. In the meantime kindly hand the phone back to Mr Djemil. He and I will take it from here."

* * * * * * * * *

What should be a moment of triumph and eager anticipation - successful completion of the mission, imminent release from HMP Hatcham - these positives have precisely the opposite the effect for Djemil. Plunge him into a dark and brooding mood. A mood that only darkens once the email to Matthew Schild pings through on the phone. Contains in its body text enough noughts to elicit an ecstatic punch of the air by the Israeli. Even a brag about the lifestyle he is about to enjoy: "Better than you could ever imagine, Mr Djemil."

Both men decline exercise in the afternoon. Spend the rest of their last day together reading, watching TV or, in Djemil's case, simply standing by the window, every so often smoking, but always with eyes pinned on the empty yard outside. Pinned, you would guess, on the disc of grass in the yard's centre which, today, is pockmarked by white objects - paper from the looks of it, the way they flutter, tumble in the wind.

At one point, when they finish their tea and stack the light-blue plastic plates, bowls by the door - "Our last supper, Matthew" - once they have done that, Djemil asks Schild about the phone call. Wonders, he says, what Anne Forbes-Pelham actually said to convince the Israeli. What evidence did she give him? But Schild is evasive. Prefers not to talk about it. Mumbles something about his career, his time in London - "that kind of thing." Djemil looks thoughtful when he hears this. Lights up another.

Hours later, when Matthew Schild has his eyes closed on the lower bunk, appears soundly asleep, Djemil studies the curious life-form he has been sharing a cell with: the weedy arms lying by his side, the neck so thin a guillotine would not blink. And, for some reason, he imagines strangling that slender neck. At first recoils at the idea. Feels genuine shock he should think such a thing. But then starts to rationalise it. Thinks, no wonder he wants to lash out after what Schild has put him through. Especially the way he was gloating earlier - on top of stirring things up about Anne.

Through the window bars, Djemil watches an officer walking around the tall metal fence that encircles the exercise yard, then veering off, letting himself onto E Wing with one fluid key action. And as he looks, Schild's words the other day toll like heavy bells in his head: "treated you as an expendable commodity ... I'd be angry, Mr Djemil. Really fucking angry." He tries not to listen. Really tries. Does everything he can to focus on life after jail: the hot debrief he will endure tomorrow on the seventh floor; the question of whether Anne will remain his manager, dig out another dead-end assignment for him; or whether HR will get there first, put him on gardening leave while they fudge the outcome of his grievance. But through these thoughts, over and over, the clang of Schild's words: "I'd be angry, Mr Djemil. Really fucking angry."

Grimacing, he squeezes shut his eyes. Makes himself remember his good intentions only five weeks ago when Anne summoned him for the initial briefing. How he tried so hard then to be positive! Kept repeating to himself as he walked down the corridor to her office, don't let her beat you, Rash. Just keep your head down, do what she wants so you can escape the shroud she has thrown over you, get yourself back onto Sir Jack's radar. Remind him you are the same man who spent nine months infiltrating Al-Qaeda in Sana'a. That you only agreed to work for Anne in the first place because of his charm offensive. His pleas.

"It's OK, Rash. You're going to be OK," he whispers.

Moving his head in a circle, he tries to relax his shoulders. Tells himself he does not want to be angry. Wants nothing more than to get on with his life, be treated fairly. And yet the anger - he can feel it eating him up, turning him into his own worst enemy. In this oven of a cell, there is no escape.

* * * * * * * * *

The observation flap was only open for a couple of seconds. But it was obviously long enough for the fours officer to spot that prisoner Djemil HA2684 was distressed, because he went immediately to discuss the issue with the Wing SO. Returned to cell B4-12 a couple of minutes later. Discreetly, sensitively asked Djemil if there was anything he could do to help. A phone call with the blessing of the SO, for example. A chat with the priest.

Djemil was non-communicative at first. Looked angry, even, when the officer asked him to walk down the landing to the gated area where they could have a chat "away from eyes and ears." However the officer persisted. Kept saying how he did not want to be a nuisance, but that he had to check Mr Djemil was alright - especially as he has now been put on an ACCT. Even offered to make the desperate-looking prisoner a cup of tea.

The tea, Djemil declined. The free phone call too. Only when the officer began insisting there must be something he could do for him - only then did Djemil cave in. Reluctantly accept there might be one way of lifting his spirits. A visit from a Listener, perhaps.

* * * * * * * * *

Seems Brannigan's visit did the trick. Because although it is dark in cell B4-12, and Hammer Smith's howls mix with the scores of B Wing TVs, stereos, form a boggy soundscape into which prisoners' shouts splatter, rapidly sink, Djemil, on his top bunk for once, feels incredibly calm. Elated, even.

The anger has not gone. Fuck, no! What has, though, is any confusion about the course of action he will take. How he will deal with his resentment about the charmed, affluent life that Matthew Schild is poised to walk into. And more importantly - much more importantly - how he will channel the rage he feels against Anne. The rage which started when her strategy first came into focus - putting him in prison, discrediting him before the grievance procedure could even kick in. Has now become a churning torrent.

And now - here, this evening - the solution. A solution so eloquent, so simple that Djemil cannot believe it did not cross his addled mind before. It is beautiful, the way it will kill two birds with one stone. As he lies on the top bunk - his body three foot below the ceiling, three foot above Schild's - as he lies there, he cannot stop marvelling at the simplicity of it all. Savours the ephemeral power that, right now, is his. Will remain his only until the cell door opens and the two of them are led down to Reception where they will be discharged, collected by armed escort before being driven swiftly along the river, along to where Schild will inherit his new life. And Anne Forbes-Pelham will bask in the glory of Yusuf Djemil's making.

Chapter 22

It is Damian Siddle's first ever night shift and, true to form, the conscientious young officer does all he can to prepare for it properly. Arrives twenty minutes early, collects his fish knife to cut down any swingers, installs himself on the tatty sofa in the B Wing staff room. There, has a read-through of the staff handover book. The entries in it this evening are pretty run-of-the-mill: arguments between prisoners, threats to do themselves in, one bereavement - life, condensed. Nevertheless Siddle reads every word of every entry from the last few days. Even makes one or two notes in a jotter.

Finally shutting the book and putting it back on the table, he looks up as if he has remembered something. Starts unzipping his rucksack. Takes out two boxes of Tupperware: dissected fruit in one, pasta-based mush in the other. Is trying to find space in the staff fridge when the B Wing SO pops his head round the door.

"Here nice and early, Damian. It's your first set of nights, isn't it? Prepare yourself for mayhem with your body clock. There's a reason they give you a week off after."

Siddle smiles at his manager - a whiff of humouring to it, maybe - but says nothing. Shuts the fridge.

"Not too bad a day today," the SO continues breezily. "Only one alarm bell, association on every landing, only one new ACCT. Good start to your week, I'd say."

Siddle smiles that smile again.

"Yes," he says. "Hopefully I'll have a quiet night."

"Not now you've used the Q word, you won't! But nah, you'll be all right. Got the usual Officer Support Grade coming in. Good as gold, she is. Mind you, just as well, because we've still got seven ACCTs open, two of them on the fours. Sorry about that. We meant to do some cell moves today, make it easier for you night owls to do your ACCT checks, but we ran out of time, I'm afraid. So you'll have a lot of climbing to do, the two of you. Keep you fit!"

As he is speaking, the SO puts on a red ski jacket, plonks the seven documents down in front of Siddle. Then, touching a non-existent cap, bids goodnight "to one and all." Disappears. Returns a second later.

"Forgot to mention: we took the Kavanaghs' stereo out of their cell today. Kept refusing to turn it down, so in we went. Any more of that, we'll split them up. I'm telling you this just in case they bend your ear, tell you porkies. Toodle-loo!"

The OSG, when she turns up, does indeed turn out to be as good as gold. Comes armed with a family-sized box of croissants, oodles of maternal warmth and, after making a coffee for them both, insists on patrolling B Wing for the busiest two hours of the shift: nine to eleven o'clock.

"I know the boys," she says proudly. "I'll settle them down."

Siddle does not argue. Agrees to begin the night patrolling F Wing with its (by and large) more settled, less demanding prisoners. Past eleven, once the prison quietens down, just one of them will cover the whole of B and F Wings. They will take turns. Two hours on, two hours off.

Siddle flies solo first. Encounters no serious problems during his stint from eleven to one. Handing over to the OSG, he tells her he will be on the Centre if she needs him. Then, somewhat tentatively, walks off B Wing to join four other officers and the Night SO clustered around a counter laden with important-looking documents, a prehistoric-looking phone. Soon looks enthralled as he listens to the officers' tall tales, competitive in their gore: the hard nut on D Wing who became a gibbering wreck after he saw a ghost in his cell; the funny smell in the governor's office on A Wing, not ten yards away, where they carried out hangings into the second half of last century; the prisoner discovered dead in his cell whose stone-cold body staff warmed up on the hotplate to make it look like he'd just died, hide their negligence. Every tale, according to its narrator, "a hundred per cent true".

The atmosphere of Hatcham at night, with its four huge accommodation spurs, its thousand-plus souls locked up, its long turbulent history swirling around, filling the massive volume of the central atrium - in this atmosphere, the stories seem plausible somehow. Likely, even. The lone pigeon flying up and down B Wing only adds to the fantasy. So, in a weird way, does the control panel on the Centre for the alarm system which, every six seconds or so, bleeps softly with metronomic knowingness. A heartbeat.

Eventually the Night SO looks at his watch. Says with a raised eyebrow: "Mr Siddle, time to give your OSG a break, I believe."

It is past three by the time the new officer recruit returns to the B Wing office, apologising profusely. The OSG tells him to stop fussing. Says there are still some croissants left. That she's had no problems either. Turning round from the kettle she is about to pour, she points to the piece of paper with a list of the ACCT prisoners, their locations.

"Easier than carrying the documents around," she tells him a second time. "And don't forget to take your shoes off before you go on your travels. Don't want to wake them."

Siddle pads in stocking feet up to the fours. Will start at the top, work down - another tip from the old hand. Opening the hatch of the first prisoner on his list, he switches on the inspection light then, a few squints later, is scrawling a tick next to a name on the bit of paper. Moves onto the second ACCT prisoner. Reaching the cell, he again peers through the Observation window, again turns on the light. Thirty seconds later, is still there, hands cupped around his eyes now.

Suddenly Siddle jumps back from the door. Looks down the wing, blinking stupidly, then back at the door. He pulls out his radio. Sounds frantic as he says: "G4DP, Code Red, cell Bravo 4-12! I say again, Code Red, cell Bravo 4-12!"

* * * * * * * * *

Duty Governor Tony McKenzie gets the phone call that a prisoner has been found dead at 03.34 hours. The voice at the other end of the line is shrill. Conveys the seriousness of the situation with staccato syllables, sharp gasps. Looks like he did it when his cellmate was asleep, the voice says. Yes, Mr Djemil's down the CSU. Been full searched.

McKenzie reacts fast. Obligatory phone call to Simmering out of the way, he speeds down the motorway, arrives at Hatcham in record time. Is talking to the night staff on duty before quarter to five.

Officer Damian Siddle is a mess. McKenzie finds him sitting with the Night SO, head in his hands, right leg jigging up and down like a flesh-and-bone pneumatic drill. When McKenzie asks him if he is alright, the young man looks up but does not even manage a nod. The Night SO answers instead. Tells the Security governor that Damian is still in shock. It's his first.

Asking one of the night staff to make them a cup of tea, McKenzie sits down with Siddle, asks him to relate exactly what happened. Writes down every word the young man says. Has him repeat bits.

"So you say he was just standing there, holding up Schild's body?"

"Like I said ..." Siddle pauses, as if every word is an effort. "Like I said, I couldn't see at first. It was quite dark in there, and I think Djemil and, er ... the body were actually blocking out the inspection light. But then my eyes adjusted. And I realised that what I thought was the gloom was actually them."

McKenzie writes this down.

"So you radioed for help? Then waited outside the cell for it to come?"

A nod.

"And Schild? Did you look back into the cell? Try and see how he was? If there was any chance ..."

"Yeah, of course. But I already knew he was dead. Could tell from the way his body was hanging - like it had rigor mortis. Which I suppose must mean he died before Mr Djemil woke up ..." He shakes his head. "I spoke to Mr Djemil. Told him help was on its way and I ... I asked him if he was OK. While he was holding up the body. I feel so stupid ..."

"And what did he say, Mr Djemil?"

Siddle bows his head, runs his hands through his hair.

"What did he say?"

"It was a bit weird, actually," says Siddle, looking back up. "But I suppose he must have been in shock too. He just looked at me. Said in this calm voice: 'I just lost it, guv.'"

"I just lost it, guv," repeats McKenzie as he writes it down. "Anything else?"

Siddle shakes his head.

"Did you ask him what he meant?"

"Not then, I didn't. But I did a few minutes later, when we were down the CSU. Mr Djemil said he was talking about Matthew Schild. About his life. As in, he'd just lost Schild's life for him. Funny way to put it, though."

"And he was calm at this point, Mr Djemil?"

"Calmest in the prison, I'd say. The Night SO said it was weird, how calm he was."

Siddle hunches forwards, looks like he might be sick. And as he does, McKenzie slurps his tea. Draws a giant question mark on his bit of paper. Writes right in the middle: WHY SO CALM?

* * * * * * * * *

Matthew Schild's death affects the whole prison. Descends like a thick fog along all four residential spurs, dampening moods, muting conversations. Not just the wing staff, who speak to each with less performance than normal, seem to tone down the acting. Also players like Birdman, Jarvis, Longman - even they seem to walk with a bit less swagger, exchange high fives with a touch less slap.

Nowhere, though, are the signs of despondency greater than in the Morning Meeting. The twenty or so staff in the Boardroom have had less than an hour to absorb the news. Fail utterly to disguise their consternation. Questions crawl like maggots over a corpse: "Who was Matthew Schild?"; "Was he on an ACCT ?"; "Was there a cock-up?"; "Who was he sharing with?" Quickly mutate into death knells: "This might be what breaks the camel's back ..."; "I wouldn't like to be in Simmering's shoes ..."; "Well I wouldn't like to be in Charlotte's!"

It is almost ten past eight by the time Simmering, Tony McKenzie enter the room, a glum expression across each man's face. The gaffer wastes no time getting started. Asks McKenzie to give a run-down of the day's events, beginning with the death of Mr Schild. McKenzie does. Says the cause of Mr Schild's death was hanging, and it looks to have been a suicide. Confirms, nevertheless, that Mr Djemil HA2684 is down the CSU. Also that cell B4-12 has been sealed. The Scenes of Crime Officers should be in by half nine, McKenzie adds - just in case the death was not a suicide. He will oversee proceedings personally. Will meet the SOCOs at the Gate.

Nodding, Simmering turns to Charlotte Rosesmith. Asks her for the response plan to the death in her role as Head of Safer Custody. Seems satisfied when she describes the prisoner and staff notices she has already distributed, the wing visits the chaplaincy will be making, her intent to have all ACCT documents reviewed by the end of the day. Not forgetting the visit she made to the CSU first thing to check that Mr Djemil is OK.

"Talking of which, what about Mr Djemil?" Simmering asks. "As I understand it, it wasn't Mr Schild on an ACCT, it was Mr Djemil. And he is now down the CSU ..."

"I was extremely concerned about that as well, Governor," says Charlotte, sounding like she is pouncing on some prey. "We should avoid locating any prisoner on an ACCT down the CSU, whatever the circumstances. Especially someone as distressed as Mr Djemil. He's actually been using the Listeners quite a bit recently, Governor, and it's why one of the B Wing officers saw fit to put him on an ACCT in the first place. So given the fact he has just been through this highly traumatic event and now finds himself down the CSU as well ..."

McKenzie's face has turned red. But as the Security governor opens his mouth to say something, he gets stopped by a kick under the table, a little shake of the head from Jenkins.

Instead it is Charlotte who carries on.

"I intend to have a discussion with Tony about Mr Djemil after this meeting, Governor. Clearly Mr Schild's death is a terrible blow for the prison. But it is vital that all of us learn lessons from this tragedy - no matter how experienced we may be."

"That's fine, Charlotte," says Simmering with a little glance at McKenzie. "But obviously ... well, we all appreciate coping with a tragedy in the middle of night state ... it's a difficult situation. But by all means, decide with Tony where Mr Djemil should be located now. You should probably be part of that discussion as well, Chris. And one of you let me know your decision, please."

* * * * * * * * *

The sun streaming through the window of cell B3-17 lands on the most expensive smile in East London, makes Birdman's gold tooth glint brilliantly. Because what started as a sombre, curiously respectful chat with Jarvis and Shorty about the deceased quickly became an hilarious, gently mocking anecdote about one of the tiny Israeli's final acts.

Jarvis slaps his tree-trunk thigh, says he wishes he could have been there instead of having to play the decoy. Asks Birdman if he will tell the story again.

The chubby man nods: delighted to, he says. But hold on, give him a sec. Let him get on top of his smile first.

A hand signals he is ready.

"So he comes in, all serious. Won't look at me, is shaking like a fucker. Like I'm going to kill him or something. Can hardly speak. Finally gets out that he wants to book a flight!"

Jarvis bursts out laughing, slaps his leg again.

"So I'm thinking, you what? He must mean a fight. I dunno, some MMA-type shit maybe. He was such a weird little guy, could be anything. Anyway, so I look at Shorty by the door - I mean, he's the one who brought him - give him, you know, that look, like what the fuck's he on, man? And he ..." - Birdman points the giant's way - "... he just does this."

Birdman shrugs, holds out his two palms.

"So I look back, and the shrimp carries on. Says to me again, he wants to book a flight. And I'm thinking, OK then, let's run with this. See where it goes. So I nod, all serious now. Ask him where to? And he shows me this letter. In code, it was, the whole thing. Looks at me like, you know, I'm going to fly it there through the window on my magic carpet or something. And I'm still thinking: fuck, what are you taking? Don't say it, though. Still being all serious - no, no, professional, that's it - I negotiate a price. Tell him it will cost him two large ones. And the guy doesn't fucking blink! Just nods like, yeah, whatever. And you know what? Someone pays it into our account the same day."

They laugh again, the three of them.

"Him sending a message out like that ... it's like he knew he was going to die," says Birdman, bringing down the mood.

"Wouldn't surprise me," says Shorty. "Not with Djemil as his cellmate. Told you that guy was a psycho."

"Well, he's left us alone, so we were right to leave him alone."

Shorty grunts.

"But Schild," continues Jarvis. "He might have been a fruit loop, but obviously he came here, asked you to fly something out ..." - he looks over at the chubby man - "... because of your nickname. What I don't get, though, is how he was expecting you to do it."

Birdman lights up a rollie.

"No idea," he says after a drag. "Maybe a drone or a pigeon - that's all I can think of. And I agree with you. It must have been the name that made him think that."

"How did you get that name, anyway? It's not like you've got a fucking pigeon. Or is there something you need to tell us?"

They laugh, the three of them.

"Cheeky fuckers. No, I'll tell you how I got it. I got it the last time I came back into this place. It was that woman governor who gave it me. The fit one. What's her name ..."

"Rosesmith?"

"Yeah, yeah, yeah. That's the one. She's down Reception the day I come off the van, doing her checks or whatever it is those top governors get paid for. And so there I am at the desk, checking in, like, and out of nowhere she goes to me: 'I can't believe you're back here again, Mr Samuels! Know what I'm going to call you from now on? Birdman, that's what. Because you keep coming back, doing more bird.'" He shrugs. "And since then, it's bloody stuck. Everyone uses it - even you guys."

He looks sternly at Jarvis, Shorty. Bursts out laughing when both of them look down bashfully. Then starts tapping the side of the chair. Speaks the moment they look back up - the laugh gone, his eyes ablaze.

"Gentlemen, I've got an idea. An addition to our service offering..."

Chapter 23

It's a world full of surprises, Hatcham. Take today, for example. Two days after Schild's death, Governor Tony McKenzie is squinting at Chris Jenkins from his big office chair, genuinely struggling to understand what the hell the guy is on about.

"Come again, Chris."

"I kid you not, Tony. Just talked to him now. Says he wants both of us to go because it's important we're seen there. Not normal procedure. He said as much himself. Well, what he actually said was the prison has a right to have a representative there, but that this right is not normally taken up. If you get my drift. But this one is out of the ordinary, he says. So he wants ..."

"And you're sure he means both of us? I mean he was your prisoner ..."

"Both of us, Tony. He was emphatic: Security, Residential. He kept on saying it."

McKenzie wrinkles up his nose.

"What about Charlotte? Surely it's more her thing. I mean - Jesus! - how much more Safer Custody can you get?"

"Tony, don't go there. She was with Simmering when I was talking to him. Kept complaining about how her figures were fucked. Bad for the audit, she kept saying. Didn't seem to give a toss about poor old Schild. And the amazing thing is, Simmering was just sitting there, taking it. Kept on nodding at her. Started going on about the broader picture, the cumulative effect. How it won't count against her ..."

Jenkins leaves McKenzie's office within minutes of delivering the bad news. Two hours later is waiting for him in the car park as arranged. Climbs into the Insignia's passenger seat.

"Missing my netball fix," he says.

"Perv," says McKenzie, firing up the car.

They are at the local hospital within minutes. Spend longer trying to find a place to park, then the autopsy department located in the bowels of the hospital, than they do on the journey itself. Finally settled in the cramped observation room, they start chatting with come coppers also present, wait for the body to be wheeled in. Fall silent when it is.

Schild looks tiny on the industrial-looking metal trolley. Tiny, but also scarily similar to a living being. As if he, too, can hear the autopsy team talking about their weekend. About the leaving party it sounds like they all went to. The torrid journey home one of them had.

The body is lifted easily onto the dissecting table, and the moment it is, the room falls quiet. The team, the observers outside - everyone watches as the pathologist hunches over, starts examining the rings around the dead man's slender neck. Closer and closer he peers before gently touching the reddish brown marks with blue latexed fingers. Finally he begins dictating notes. Sprinkles his measured rhetoric with anatomical terms, abbreviations, the odd figure.

He stands up, the pathologist. With zero ceremony, makes a deep incision along the corpse's forehead with a scalpel. Tucks in fingers as if into an orange, gives a visible tug before peeling back the skin and, with it, Matthew Schild's long brown hair. Keeps on going until he can drape the hirsute material along the hard surface behind. Puddles it like posh curtains. From another technician, takes a small circular saw. Makes the thing whizz round. Wastes no time in cutting a neat hole in the top of the Israeli's skull before carefully extracting the brain and plonking it onto a cool metal tray.

The organ glistens under the lights.

"That's a big'un," says the pathologist, now starting to slice the thing as if it was pastrami.

The whole autopsy procedure lasts about two hours. Quick going, a nurse will say to McKenzie afterwards.

"We don't call him Rapid Robin for nothing."

Jenkins talks for most of this time. Shares silly jokes with the coppers, joins in the banter as they talk about other autopsies they've been to, go to town describing the most gruesome road accidents they've ever seen.

But McKenzie does not join in. Instead the tall man stands slightly apart, his solemn face taking in every small part of the process, occasionally changing position to get a better view. Even when the pathologist plunges his hands into Schild's stomach area, pulls out yards, yards of intestines which he then places onto the plinth where they spread gradually outwards like strands of spaghetti finding the limits of a pasta bowl - even then McKenzie does not shift his gaze. Carries on staring through the glass, as if mesmerised.

Only once, in fact, does the big man's focus waver, make him place a large hand over his mouth, then a hand in his pocket. It is during the scrutiny of the scrotum when the pathologist matter-of-factly carves the thing open, lets the balls come tumbling out. Like a warped version of the national lottery - but, this time, with no winner.

* * * * * * * * *

Dropping Jenkins off at a tube station on the way back, McKenzie shares a parting joke about chicken dumplings before pulling out into the traffic, crawling south. By the time he makes it back to the nick, the tall man, it's gone half five and staff are clogging up the main Gate. Prolong the time it takes for McKenzie to actually get in.

Janet McKechnie is one of those staff. Looking slightly sheepish, even though it is the end of her shift, she tells McKenzie she's left the translation on his desk. Getting a blank look back, reminds her boss that he asked her to translate the letter they found in Mr Samuels's cell. It was in Arabic or something, so cost a bit more than normal. She got it done into English, she adds helpfully.

Climbing back up to his tower, McKenzie catches himself vowing the letter will make sense to him. Must do. He laughs at his determination. Wonders where on earth it comes from. Straightforward curiosity - hallmark of a good Security governor? Or is it because he has a hunch the letter may finally give him an insight into the curious Mr Schild and - who knows - maybe even Mr Djemil? Either way, he decides, now reaching the top step and wondering if he should cut down on the fags - either way, the idea of the letter has put a spring in his step. Fostered some indistinct hope.

It takes him a while to find the thing - partly because it turns out to be a slip of paper rather than a letter. Also because the translation - on company-headed notepaper, he sees - is hiding the original Arabic version which has been paper-clipped behind. But once he does locate it, McKenzie, he sees immediately that his expectations are going to be exceeded. Because the note signed by "Matthew" is not just cryptic. It pours flammable fuel onto his smouldering conspiracy theory.

He reads it. Then reads it again. Cannot stop his hands from shaking as he goes into the kitchenette to make a mug of tea. Returns - almost runs - back to the desk, where he reads it for a third time. Does the hand-cupping around his chin thing. Keeps on shaking his head.

Farideh,

I am not entirely confident this letter will reach you. I have sent it using the pigeon which brings in all the drugs to the prison and I suspect the bird has never carried a letter before. What's more, the crook who runs the poor creature does not exactly inspire confidence! Still, I needed to be sure my message to you could not be intercepted. It is too important.

Another element of uncertainty is you, angel. In your letter you talked about your father's friends and I am reasonably confident I know who they are. However I have no proof. Not as much as I'd like.

But time has run out. I have to act. You know I came to prison because there are people after me and soon they will have their revenge. So I have nothing to lose. I am giving you the information they seek. If you are who I think you are, you will know what to do with it. If not ... well, as I said, I have nothing to lose.

Please understand, the pigeon that brings you this message must be a dove for peace. Technologically your country is far behind and it is vulnerable. But if you access the information on the server (Address overleaf, Password: columba) and deliver LOTS into the right hands, you will make your country safer. Maybe even the entire world.

This is too painful, Farideh, so I will not dwell. But before I go, let me say that I know you were sent to find me. To seduce me. No doubt you believed in what you were doing. But I hope you felt it became more than that. I certainly did. Which is why, in my last moments, I will be thinking of you.

Matthew

By the time McKenzie checks that Schild did have a visitor called Farideh, his brain has moved onto other things. Specifically, what the hell LOTS is and whether he can access it himself. Phoning his wife to tell her he'll be back late from work, something's cropped up, he walks to the bookshelf in Janet's office. Gets down the book he mocked her so mercilessly about buying: The Internet for Dummies. He must remember to put it back.

Returning to his desk, McKenzie pulls the translation close to. Laboriously types in the lengthy web address spelt out in the note. It is not like the addresses he is used to. Has lots of funny dashes, squiggles, dots. A complete pain to type in, in other words. He gets there on the third attempt. Knows this when a request for a password suddenly flashes up.

Strengthening his resolve with a sip of tea, he excitedly types in "Columba." Soon realises his mistake. Types in "columba." And then "COLUMBA." Then, out of desperation, "cOLUMBA." Tries every permutation he can think of. No joy.

The frustration that he won't find out what LOTS actually is - not tonight, at least - is enormous. Nevertheless, there is nothing he can do. So with a final "Fuck it!", McKenzie shuts down his desktop PC. Cannot believe the machine chooses this very moment to update its software.

With the thing grinding away, he looks around for something to do. Knows, from experience, he has a few minutes to fill. Starts flicking through the mail on his desk. Grows curious about a sober-looking letter originally addressed to Simmering but on which the gaffer has written: "Forward > Tony McKenzie." Opening the envelope, he sees it is from the Israeli embassy. They have heard about the tragic death of Matthew Schild, the letter says. Urgently seek the young man's property on behalf of his bereaved family.

Cursing, and wondering why on earth the letter has come to him and not Jenkins, McKenzie soon concedes that he probably is the correct recipient. The police's Scene of Crime Officers conducted a forensic search of Schild's cell after the death, and then handed all his property over to the prison. Handed it, if McKenzie remembers rightly, to one Janet McKechnie.

Hauling himself out of his chair, he opens the door of Janet's office once again, sees a large transparent bag in the corner. On it, a clearly labelled tag: "Schild HA2313: Property." Inside, the usual fare: a tatty book, some clothes, a cheap digital watch.

Deciding to add in the note that was found in Birdman's cell - might as well keep everything in one place - McKenzie starts looking for a pair of scissors to cut open the bag's nylon cable tie. Starts scanning the surface of Janet's desk, then rummaging through the three drawers that drop down to the floor. But the woman is too neat for her own good. Scissors are nowhere. Cursing some more, he walks back to his own office. Fails once more to find anything to cut with.

The one upside of his unsuccessful search is that the software update is now complete. Shutting down his computer with a "Die, you bastard!", McKenzie folds Schild's note in two - the translation, the original still paper-clipped together - ends up stuffing both of them into his inside suit pocket. Then, with a last look round, he switches off the lights.

Only when he is five miles up the motorway does Governor Tony McKenzie remember he forgot to put Janet's book back. What a dummy!

Chapter 24

They may have been charged with attempted murder and be deemed extremely high risk by Simmering, but prisoners Avraham GR2434 and Mizrahi GR2435 languish in Hatcham's CSU. The reason? Beds in the high-security prison HMP Belmarsh have become particularly scarce over the last few weeks after the Home Secretary rounded up teachers in London with supposed Islamist sympathies, filled the place up.

However, what would normally be an irksome bottleneck for Hatcham's top governor is, right now, manna from heaven. Because the two Israeli prisoners might just help the prison squeak though its Equality and Diversity audit. Especially as, by some miracle, the first day of the audit happens to coincide with the first day of Rosh Hashanah - the Jewish New Year which Charlotte Rosesmith pledged to celebrate in her most recent Equality, Diversity and Safer Custody meeting.

The celebration is modest, she warns the auditor as they stroll down to the CSU together. However it is significant. It will be the first time in its 170-year history that Hatcham recognises the festival. The auditor nods approvingly. Mumbles something about oak trees and seeds.

When they get to the CSU, the two of them, it becomes clear the young governor was not lying about the modesty of the occasion. Only seven people are present: the two Israeli prisoners, the rabbi, Charlotte Rosesmith, Simmering, Chris Jenkins (there to show "Residential solidarity") and Brannigan HA2022 who - if you believe what the lanky Listener tells the auditor - has been helping Charlotte organise it all. Governor Tony McKenzie is not there. Simmering decided the presence of a man who, not long ago, punched one of the celebrants in the face might not be conducive to a good audit score.

For security reasons, things are taking place in the adjudication room. With the queen looking down sternly from her lopsided photograph on the wall, and after a few prayers for the deceased Matthew Schild from the prison rabbi, two kitchen staff proudly bring in traditional Jewish dishes prepared specially for the day: chicken soup, honey-sweetened carrots, and lettuce salad with grapefruit and almonds. Brannigan distributes paper plates, plastic cutlery all round and, as he does, Charlotte talks through each dish. Cannot stress enough how lucky Hatcham is to have Mr Avraham and Mr Mizrahi with them.

"A tremendous chance for us to learn!" she beams.

Brannigan cannot agree more.

"Oh yes, Miss! Such a steep curve!"

The prisoners at the centre of it all look rather less impressed. Avraham gets engaged in conversation by Simmering, asked if he has ever been to Jerusalem. Hears about the top governor's "absolutely fascinating" trip to Bethlehem where he got baptised a second time. Mizrahi fares even worse. Finds himself cornered by the auditor, has to field endless questions about his experience of the prison, everything from the standard of kosher food to the lack of Hebrew translations in Induction. Exasperated, finally, by the length, the earnestness of the interrogation, the prisoner tells the auditor his only real gripe is the prison's lack of provision for Krav Maga. Avraham overhears. Bursts out laughing. The auditor is not sure he gets the joke. Notes down "Better Krav Maga facilities" just in case.

* * * * * * * * *

Riven by key performance targets, po-faced inspections and exacting audits the Prison Service may be, but there is still a place for a wee nod and a wink if you know the right people. Fortunately John Simmering does. Turns out he joined the Prison Service fast-track in the same year as the man now leading Hatcham's Equality and Diversity audit. But while Simmering stayed on the steep winding road to governorship, as keen fast-trackers are meant to, the other chap performed a hand-brake turn. Opted for a Headquarters job instead. Less stress, an easier commute.

Now, as the two of them sit in Simmering's office, reminisce fondly about various acts of debauchery and the plastic bed sheets at Training College, it soon becomes apparent that the nod and the wink are positive. In fact, better than that. Hatcham has sailed through its Equality audit. A truly remarkable improvement given the travesty of the last one, he adds, before looking at his watch, muttering something about the traffic.

Two hours later, Governing Governor John Simmering still struggles to hide his delight. Betrays his mood by making tea personally for Charlotte Rosesmith who sits cross-legged on the other side of his desk. He keeps squeezing the tea bag against the side of the cup with his spoon, then turning round, showing Charlotte the results.

"Strong enough?" he asks for the second time.

With a demure smile, the young woman takes the proffered cup, lifts it to her mouth, then tilts it so the warm fluid trickles gently between her lips.

"I can't tell you how glad I am," she says, gently repositioning the vessel on a coaster. "I mean, I was pretty confident after all the work we've put in. Especially with your unstinting support, John. But until it's in the bag ..."

"Absolutely right, Charlotte. There's never any guarantee until it happens. Before that, everything else is just groundwork. You do everything you can, you lay the foundation, you hope. But until you get that seal of approval ..." As his voice fades away, Simmering lifts his own cup. Looks a bit flushed as he, too, takes a sip, finds a coaster. "On a personal note, Charlotte ..."

His rather dainty hand pulls at his lower lip.

"On a personal note, I'm just glad your work has received some proper recognition finally. You've been through such a difficult time of it recently, what with those spiteful accusations from Jenny Hughes ..." - he spits out the spiteful - "... and, now, the death of Matthew Schild - a death which, like I said at the time, occurred despite the remarkable way you've been transforming Safer Custody. It was really unfair. So you were due some luck, and I'm glad it has finally come your way. Which reminds me: you never told me how the police interview went."

Charlotte looks up, surprise on her face.

"About the allegations from Jenny Hughes?"

"Yes. I'm sorry, I meant to catch up, ask you about it before ... I know they didn't take things any further. And of course I never expected them to. But were they tough on you? Did you have to try hard to convince them?"

Now, a wide smile across the pretty face.

"No, it was fine, John. The moment I went in, I could tell they were just going through the motions. Doing it because they had to, not because they believed any of the rubbish she was coming out with. They were thorough, though, I'll give them that. And so they should be with such a serious allegation. But I always felt we were on the same side, somehow. That they knew the real story."

"I'm pleased," says Simmering, sitting back and resting his elbows on the arms of the chair. "So that's two things to celebrate then - your police interview and the Equality audit." His hand moves back to his lip, then back down onto the armrest. "I was going to say ... how about we go for dinner tonight? Celebrate the victory of the innocent!"

"Don't you mean the innocent and the diligent, John!"

* * * * * * * * *

Under an hour later and, as the pigeon flies, not more than fifty metres removed from the top governor's office, prisoner Brannigan HA2022 takes his penis out of Governor Charlotte Rosesmith's vagina, wipes its still-swollen head on the inside of his grey T-shirt, then hurriedly pulls up his striped boxers, dirty-pink tracksuit bottoms. At the same time, the Head of Equality, Diversity and Safer Custody gives a prim little cough, wipes herself with a hankie then bends down, pulls up white knickers followed by the dark blue trousers of her work suit. Key chain jangling, she fastens her belt, moves the key pouch back to its full frontal position.

Appearances restored, the two lovers each take a seat in the corner of the B Wing Association Room. Sit there out of sight from the lit slit of window that runs up the door. Are quiet for a few minutes. Quiet just being. At one point, Charlotte reaches across, starts stroking the hand of Brannigan. He does not respond.

It is peaceful in the large room. Just the the occasional clunk of a closing door and, if ears are not mistaken, the dubstep favoured by the Kavanagh brothers who must have been given their stereo back. Through the two large barred windows, day is giving way to night and the spotlights around the exercise yard have resumed their brutal reign. Light up the lovers' faces in the dusky room.

"Well, you can't ask more of a Listener," says Charlotte, giving his hand one last stroke before placing it gently on his lap. "You leave this client much happier."

"You know me, Governor Rosesmith. Always trying to spread a bit of happiness."

He turns to her. Demands a kiss.

"Listen," she says, giving him a quick peck before gently pushing him away. "I've been thinking. Our little operation. I told you about the hawk?"

"Yeah, you did. How the fuck did he find out? Especially after all them meetings, when you kept giving him the third degree, showing him up in front of his boss. Fuck that was funny! He didn't have a clue, did he? But we'll get another one, Lottie. Even two, maybe ..." Edging his chair away, he looks over at the young woman who is now vigorously shaking her head. "What's wrong?"

"We can't, Ray. Not now."

"What do you mean we can't?" he asks, an edge entering his voice. "Why not? It was working, there was no risk to it. You were the one who kept saying the screws don't have a clue. Even that thick-as-shit Security chief."

He laughs thinly.

"You say there's no risk, but there bloody is, Ray."

"At the start, maybe."

"Yeah, but it's massive. Have you got any idea what would happen if someone like McKenzie stopped me, found a bloody bird in my bag? I wouldn't just get sacked. I'd get arrested, made an example of. Maximum sentence, newspaper headlines, all that crap. And don't forget what I had to go through to get us the bloody thing," she adds with a shudder. "Coming in night after night, doing all those pretend spot checks on the ACCT system, checking up on my merry band of Listeners, all that bollocks. I still can't believe they bought it."

"Too busy looking at your tits."

"Plus all that business with the seeds - trying to get that horrible bloody bird to trust me, then it going on dirty protest when I'm on the way over to your dodgy mate's place, all over my gym kit. Besides, what about those times I've had to stick my neck out for you? Over-ruling the SO, stopping you getting a cell move, getting moved off the wing. And ... And!" she crescendos to stop him speaking. "Remember, way back, me trying to pin it on Samuels. Really bloody obvious - first SIR I'd ever done."

She looks meaningfully at him.

"What I'm saying is, you've got to trust me on this. It worked, our little operation. It worked because I judged things right, pushed people's buttons. And I'm really glad it did. My debt's paid off and, like I told you, I'll be getting a mortgage for a little flat soon. I might even ask you round to come and play, when you get out. But everything else, it's just too risky right now. I mean, we're lucky as it is and I don't just mean the bird."

"So what do you mean?"

He sounds sullen.

"Come on, you know exactly what I mean! That favour you asked me to do. That one-off." She makes sarcastic quote marks with her fingers. "You promised me the four of them were just going to meet, do some sort of deal. So I do what you asked because I trusted you. And then they bloody try and kill each other!"

"For fuck's sake, Lottie, we've been through this. I didn't know! I swear on my mother's life. There's no way I'd have done it if I knew. They asked me, those two new geezers, if I could make this meeting happen. Offered me shitloads but didn't tell me what it was about. And OK, so I didn't ask. But of course I'm going to say yes, with that amount of money. And don't forget we went fifty fifty, you and me. Straight away, you went and said, 'No problem'. Went on about how you had that Hughes screw eating out of your hand. Would be easy money."

"And Ray, that's my point. It was too easy. You never told me how much they were paying till after. An insane amount! If you'd told me, I'd have said no way." She pauses. "It's like that bounty you were trying to persuade me to go for. I could tell immediately it was too hot. If I hadn't told you to put it Samuels's way ... "

"Yeah, yeah, yeah. You can judge it, I can't. But you still got Jenny Hughes to help make it happen."

"Because you said you owed him one. I was trying to keep you safe, Ray. Safe from the big boys."

She sniggers. But Brannigan does not get the joke.

"And anyway, it's not like you can always judge it," he says.

"How do you mean?"

"I mean like when you got Jenny Hughes to do the light in their cell. You did all the groundwork, and then fucked it up by ordering the whole world to your stupid Equality and Diversity meeting. Including the Works geezer who Samuels ... "

"Yeah, but only because Simmering bloody showed up in my office. Was right by me when McKenzie rang, asked if ... Oh, for fuck's sake, forget it! I've told you all this as well. I don't even know why you're still going on about it."

Brannigan turns away from her. Blows out his cheeks. After a few seconds, turns back.

"Listen, yeah. Maybe when things cool down a bit, we can have a think about another bird."

"Ray, I've said. No way. Not ever again. And we couldn't even if we wanted to. That hawk McKenzie's been flying around. He's just going to do that any time the drugs in this place go up. Scare the pigeons." She rubs his arm. "Don't be like that, you sexy criminal. It's been exciting and we didn't get caught. But now we have to stop. Doesn't mean we can't carry on having fun."

She kisses his cheek. Squeezes his groin. Then, looking at her watch, mutters something about going out this evening, needing to get ready. She gets to her feet. Pulls hefty keys out of her pouch.

"Come on," she says. "I'd better take you back. Lock you up."

* * * * * * * * *

For Jenny Hughes HM4434, the over-riding feeling when she arrives at HMP Holloway the next morning is not fear and foreboding, but relief. The women's prison represents a haven of safety, somehow. An end to the stress of subterfuge, of powerlessness. Maybe that is why, when the cell door is held open for her in the CSU, she does not shrink back in terror. Instead walks into the small gloomy room calmly. Appreciatively, almost.

The dimensions of the cell differ slightly from the ones she has searched hundreds, thousands of times in Hatcham. Holloway was built in the 1970s, Hatcham over a century before that. But the feeling of confinement presents no surprises. Comforts her, even. So, in a weird way, does the cleaning product that has been used, obviously with great abandon, to prepare the room. Its scent she knows so well. It reminds her of work - of better times. Same goes for the room's thick metal door, its impenetrable walls, the over-sized window bars.

Her CV will not endear her to her fellow inmates, so she undergoes induction down the CSU. Annoys the officer by pointing out things she has missed. Afterwards, receives a visit to her cell from the prison's top governor, a striking-looking woman with a loud voice, even louder dress sense. The governor tells Jenny she can start her adult life again. Must not give up hope. Obviously got herself in a fix, made the wrong choices. But can now wipe the slate clean. There is still time.

She nods, Jenny Hughes. Says she likes the idea. Then tells the tall woman it is difficult to start again - even think of it - when the sense of injustice is gnawing away at you. Fills you with a kind of rage.

"How do you mean?" asks the governor sharply.

The ex-prison officer looks at the ground.

"Because no-one believes me," she mumbles. "Just like I thought. I told the police everything that happened. Told them I was only following orders. That I had to do what she asked because she knew all about me and this prisoner, me bringing in mobile phones and stuff."

"Had to do what who asked?"

Jenny looks at Holloway's top governor, as if amazed she does not know.

"A governor at Hatcham. You know ... Charlotte Rosesmith. She told me she'd get me sacked if I didn't do some stuff for her, like letting these prisoners into a room during patrol state. It was because of her I did that. But I could see when I told the police ... I knew immediately it was a waste of time. Could tell from how they were talking to me. Plus, they asked me straight after why I'd not told the prison about Lopez ..."

"Lopez?"

"This prisoner I knew from the out."

"Ah, OK. So they asked you why you'd not informed them?"

"Yeah, about knowing him from old. And about him forcing me to do stuff, threatening me. But even when I answered all their questions, they just looked at me like everything that comes out my mouth is complete crap. Seems like I just can't win."

As the prisoner's face crumples, and her chin falls onto her chest, bobs up and down as she cries, the tall governor clears her throat.

"What you told the police ... did you see them write it down?"

"No," says Jenny Hughes, shaking her head. "I didn't see. Just felt they were taking the piss, laughing at me. I don't know if they wrote it down."

Five minutes later, the top governor returns to the cell. Hands Jenny Hughes a notepad. Sternly instructs her to write down her version of events. Every tiny thing she can remember. To sign and date every page. Then to give it back to the Duty Governor when he visits her later on that afternoon.

"He'll be expecting it. And so will I," she says before turning heel in bright pink shoes.

Jenny watches the tall figure shut the door, then sits quietly on the bed for a few minutes, biting away at her fingernails. A minute or so later, she gets up and walks over to the window. Stares out at the gaudy flowerbeds that lie in the prison's central courtyard. Remains motionless for some minutes before turning around decisively. Sitting back down. And picking up the pen.

Chapter 25

The modern age's enrapture with all manner of anaesthetics, from social media and shopping to the endless pounding of treadmills in airtight cathedrals of fluorescence, might persuade newcomers to our civilisation that the dullness these pastimes help create is healthy. But no. Dullness is a scourge. In fact, with every day edging us towards our end, our senses fade slightly - our ability to see, to hear, smell, taste and feel. And they carry on fading, these facilities of ours to take biopsies of life, examine our own unique visions, sounds, aromas, flavours and textures, until we experience loss of sensation altogether. We die, in other words.

This rather grandiose intro explains why, although Tony McKenzie was only ten when he received his year's Project Prize at Vernon Terrace Primary School, the fact the memory keeps cropping up even now, thirty-six years on and, contrary to logic, gets more vivid with every repeat showing on the screen in his head - somehow this has a rejuvenating effect on the tall man. Why the memory remains so bright, so pungent, he cannot say. But for some reason, that third-person image of his ten-year-old self getting up, walking to the front of the whole school while the other children clap and his friends (Jenkins's predecessors) shout out 'Swot!' and much ruder things to try make him laugh - for some reason, that image refuses to stop following him around.

He has asked himself why this is. Has wondered, for example, whether it is just him delving into the lighter, brighter moments of his past for succour during those private battles with despondency which he has sworn to his wife, time and again, he never has. But it can't be. Because here is the memory again. And this time, he is definitely not despondent. In fact he cannot stop smiling. Three and a half decades ago, it was Salty, his old headmaster, doing the intro, uttering the plaudits, coaxing the small boy onto the stage. Today it is Simmering, the gaffer. Sure, the circumstances are different this time and McKenzie himself has changed - fuck, he should know, he had to buy new trousers at the weekend. But the feeling is identical. Governor McKenzie, Head of Security at HMP Hatcham, is once again aged ten.

"So, Tony, I gather you have some good news for us today?"

Simmering's stage manner risks spoiling the moment. But as everyone turns their eyes McKenzie's way, the tall man realises this is not about delivering information. It is about reporting a battle won. About staff reassurance. Giving the troops a little morale boost in what is probably going to be his last meeting as Head of Security. Poor bastards need it, he thinks, getting to his feet and pressing Return on a whirring laptop.

The projection on the wall changes from a page called Main Players to one headed MDT Rate. Below the title, there is a graph, cartoon-like in its simplicity. And on it, a thick red line which hovers way above the x-horizon before plunging dramatically downwards to a height only a quarter as high. The axes are labelled, so the graph demands little explanation. But McKenzie knows he has to say something. Wonders where to put his hands as he launches in.

"Right, well ... as the Governor says, some good news this month. We all know the prison has had a high - no, unacceptably high MDT rate for many months," he says, wallowing in mea culpa now the pressure is off. "This was obviously extremely concerning because it was leading to increased rates of violence and self-harm. In fact, it was harming the performance of the establishment as a whole."

Simmering opens his mouth as if he is about to say something, causing McKenzie to pause, raise his eyebrows. But the gaffer thinks better of it. Mumbles something about nothing. Waves on his man.

"So it was vital we get the rate down. I think we were all feeling the pressure to do that." He coughs. "And I'm glad to say, things do finally seem be improving. Whereas we were averaging about twenty per cent for coming up to six months - and let's remember, that means one in five of prisoners tested were proving positive for drugs of some sort - we're now down to four point nine per cent. A heck of an improvement."

"How do we know that we won't be back to the same disastrous rates next month?" asks Simmering, the d-word tripping off his tongue with remarkable ease. "That this is not just a welcome blip?"

"I don't think it will be, Governor. We're three weeks into the next month already, and the figures are looking just as good. Slightly better, in fact."

"Well that is good ... But what I want to know is, have you found out the reason for the massive drop? Unless we know what led to the rocketing in the first place, we can't be confident we can stop it happening again, can we?"

McKenzie studies the ground while he decides how to answer the question. Knows it is not straightforward. Because if there is one thing that he has resolved not to say a word about, it is the pigeon. The spiralling MDT rate, the awful violence, the chronic self-harm - the fact that all of it came down to a bird, and a really boring grey one at that - well, there's just something about it that makes him feel silly. Like he should have known.

He looks across the room. Sees Charlotte giving him that gorgeous haughty look of hers. Then catches sight of Jenkins, sitting behind everyone nearest the window, creased up and making a flapping motion with his hands. Obviously finding McKenzie's predicament hilarious: "Go on, Tony! Explain the massive drop without talking about the bird!"

McKenzie grimaces. Gives it a go.

"Well, Governor," he says, putting on a stately voice. "We've been focusing on disrupting the activities of a number of key players on Security's radar, people like Mr Samuels, Mr Longman, Mr Jarvis. As part of this focus we conducted a thorough search of their cells. And although we failed to find any contraband, we've tightened up on our lock-down searching of residential areas more generally and, importantly, have been reacting more quickly to any new intelligence. For example, we had five arrests last month of visitors bringing in drugs and I predict more. I've also made sure someone's staffing the CCTV cameras in Visits every day without fail - including weekends."

Looking out again, McKenzie sees Jenkins is now bent over double with the giggles. Immediately senses danger. Knows he must do everything he can to keep a straight face himself. So he looks away from Jenkins, immediately starts biting his lip, tries hard - incredibly hard - to think terrible despicable thoughts: starving orphans, the Eastern Front, Rwanda. Even the autopsy. But it is no use. The lips of Governor Tony McKenzie begin to twitch. A few seconds on, so do his cheeks, and then his eyes. Finally the whole big face crumples, helpless with laughter. The Head of Security in his own monthly meeting! He really, genuinely wants to kill Jenkins this time. Jesus, the guy's a cock.

"Well, I'm glad you seem so pleased by the improvement," says Simmering, sounding fantastically unamused. "And thank you to everyone here who has contributed to the dramatic fall. Well done. Keep it up."

The rest of the meeting is uneventful. Follows the usual agenda, identifies the usual culprits, discusses the usual issues. When, at the end, the AOB bit gets no takers, Simmering slams shuts his leather-bound folder, and everyone gets up, prepares to troop out of the stuffy room. McKenzie does too. Turning off the projector, he shuffles together his papers, is just about to swear under his breath at Jenkins who is walking past making cooing noises when Simmering calls out in that teacherish tone of his: "Tony, can I have a word?"

Nodding warily, the Head of Security goes to shut the door. Then turns back round to face the gaffer. Is suddenly, again, ten years old.

* * * * * * * * *

Worth a go, McKenzie tells himself for the umpteenth time as, the next morning, he guides the snout of his Vauxhall around the HMP Belmarsh car park, finds - to his surprise - a space hiding craftily in the corner. Minutes later is undergoing Belmarsh's security checks. Experiences, God knows why, a whiff of imposter syndrome. Is nevertheless soon talking shop with his Security counterpart who comes down to greet him. Asks the guy how Mr Djemil has been getting on. Whether rats have been smelt.

The Belmarsh Security governor - a jovial sort with ruddy cheeks, retro handlebar moustache - mournfully shakes his head. No rats, he says. But he does know who the guy is. Got the report from McKenzie, written the day after Schild's death. Very helpful it was too. Kept an ear out for snippets, of course. Anything that might give the game away. But since Mr Djemil came through the doors, not a sausage. Not that he expected anything, to be honest. Not with Djemil on detox. Too busy clucking.

"Just like all the others we get from you," he says with a grin.

McKenzie meets Djemil HA2684 in the Legal Visits area. They sit opposite each other in a small meeting room, its confines, nasty lights, forcing a thorough epidermal inspection of the other. In front of McKenzie, a mug of tea from which curls of steam rise up, stretch out lazily like arms post-slumber.

"How are you getting on?" he asks, the voice flat.

"Better than where I was," comes the reply.

Letting out a grunt, McKenzie looks awkward as he reaches for his tea. He slurps it noisily. Puts the mug down.

"Mr Djemil, you know there is an investigation into the death of your cellmate Matthew Schild."

The faintest of nods.

"Just to make things clear, that is being conducted by the police. Then, depending on the findings, the Prisons and Probation Ombudsman will also hold an investigation."

"As long as the police conclude it was a suicide?"

"That is correct. And the reason I'm mentioning this is because it means I'm not able to discuss anything related to Mr Schild today. Although I will add that the pathologist's report was inconclusive ..."

"How do you mean?"

"The findings of the report said that strangulation could not be ruled out. That the marks around Mr Schild's neck ..."

Djemil shrugs.

"Well, if you can't talk about it, guv, why are you here?"

"It's the drugs. Now ..." McKenzie gives a little cough. "I know you've been on detox since you came into this place because you tested positive on Reception. Even though, I note, you tested negative during an MDT at Hatcham."

"Must of been lucky with the timing, Guv."

"Yeah, I thought as much. And obviously you were getting your gear when you were on B Wing. So ..." Another cough. "What I want to know is, would you like to tell me where were you getting it from?"

Djemil widens his mouth into a semi-smile. Visibly relaxes as he puts his hands behind his head, tilts back the chair.

"It was Brannigan, guv. You know ... the Listener."

"Brannigan? You sure you don't mean ..."

"I'm sure. I mean Brannigan. That's why the whole prison keeps asking for a Listener every other minute. Because you get more than a cosy little chat."

McKenzie sighs and sits bolt upright, as if to maximise surface area, help his body absorb the information.

"And do you know how the drugs were getting in?"

"A pigeon, from what I heard. Brannigan - maybe others - they trained it to fetch the gear from somewhere, bring it in. That's why they never got found out, I suppose."

"So ..." McKenzie rubs his chin. "So Samuels wasn't mixed up in this?"

"You mean Birdman? No, not as far I know. He runs a taxing and mobile phone business, by all accounts. Does the odd bit of enforcement on the side. Hires out muscle, all of that business. But drugs ... they're not his thing. At least not inside."

"So how come he's called Birdman?"

"I don't think it's got anything to do with the pigeon, if that's what you're thinking. In fact I know it doesn't."

For twenty minutes, Djemil tells McKenzie the ins and outs of life on B Wing. The prisoners who run things, the ones who enforce things, the staff who bring in stuff, turn a blind eye, take back-handers. Every detail, a gem of intelligence for the Security governor. By the time Djemil stops speaking, McKenzie has filled out four sides of A4 with his scruffy illegible handwriting.

Only then, once he stops scribbling away and finally looks up - only then does McKenzie realise how helpful Djemil has been. How they have been talking like colleagues, almost, not prisoner to governor. In fact, now that he starts thinking about it, he probably feels more comfortable talking to Djemil than he ever does talking to Jenkins. The idea alarms McKenzie. At the same time, excites him.

Makes him ask rash questions.

"So tell me, Mr Djemil. What were you really doing in Hatcham?"

Djemil looks up in surprise.

"Well ... you don't strike me as your normal kind of con. I mean ... weren't you in for something minor?"

"Drunk driving."

"Yes, that's it. And yet the other prisoners were all afraid of you. Plus you duffed up the mighty Mr Lopez, did a pretty good job protecting Mr Schild ..."

"Just because I drink and drive, it doesn't mean I can't handle myself, guv."

"No, fair enough," says McKenzie. "But the way you ... You seemed to get to the top of the tree very quickly, somehow. That's not normal for someone's first time inside. So you get my point? Why I'm curious?"

Djemil folds his arms.

"I promise you, I'm just one more prisoner, Mr McKenzie. A bit handy in a fight, that's all. Tricky childhood."

As he swallows the last of his tea, McKenzie knows he has already asked too much. And yet, already, there is another question on the tip of his tongue. One about the conversation he heard via the bug. The conversation where Djemil promised Schild a safe house, twenty-four hour protection, a good job. But how to play it? He can't very well admit to eavesdropping in the cell ...

"But you were protecting Mr Schild, I think?" he begins cautiously. "Looking out for him. Almost as if you were keeping him safe for somebody. Providing - how shall I put it? - providing close protection."

"Must be my time in the forces," says Djemil with another shrug. "You know how it is. You get used to watching out for people. Gets drilled into you."

The two men look at each other as he says this. And as they do, McKenzie once again cannot help thinking they are kindred spirits, somehow. Wonders whether it is just that ex-forces thing - they share the same values, have simply fallen down on different sides of the fence. Or whether it runs deeper than that. A commonality so strong, it knocks down cell doors, transcends prison walls, leaves the whole system in the dust. Definitely something, though.

Suddenly Djemil stands up, announces that he would like to return to the wing. He has a headache. Hopes the governor does not mind.

As the door opens and an escorting officer gives Djemil a rub-down search, the prisoner turns and looks back into the room.

"Thanks, by the way," he says to McKenzie. "Coming in like that, saving my arse. Couldn't have it done better myself."

The Security governor nods back gravely. Does not say a thing. But behind the po-faced demeanour and firmly clenched jaw, a young boy is running around, whooping and punching the air - feeling like this is the proudest moment of his life.

Chapter 26

Two plumes of clean white smoke joust and jostle against pure-blue sky. Yes, those two linchpins of repentance and rehabilitation are at it again, conducting yet another security check of what must be the safest Reception yard in the land. We who know them well will note the unusually smart appearance of Governor Tony McKenzie this crisp October morning. In particular the snazzy-looking herring-bone coat he wears over his suit. Looks like it is made of wool, boasts an oddly fussy buckle arrangement at the front.

"Nice coat, Tony," says Jenkins.

McKenzie does not answer. Instead, blowing out smoke ring after smoke ring, he appears fascinated by the way they lose their form the more they expand.

Finally, though, he does turn Jenkins's way.

"If you must know, it was an anniversary present from my wife."

"And you're daring to wear it here, in full view of the world, as a sign of your love. Very touching."

Another smoke ring.

"Are you going to be an arse all morning, Chris?"

"Sorry, mate. Only lightening things up. This weather ... makes me feel kind of chirpy."

"Well go and be chirpy round someone else next time."

"You can talk. You've not wiped the smile off your face since your cosy little chat with the gaffer. What did he say to you, anyway?"

McKenzie does smile now. A real letting-go of a smile.

"Oh, nothing, really. We just talked man to man. You know ..." He takes a drag. "Actually, come to think of it, John did mention something. Said basically to forget what he'd said about Security. Taking it away from me and all that. Reckoned I was doing a fantastic job. And, er ... I shouldn't really be telling you this bit, Chris, but since it's you ... said that in his eyes I was the second most important person in the prison. A kind of deputy was how he put it."

"I'm pleased for you, Tony. Really pleased. Compare that to two weeks ago. You were getting so much stick, I was genuinely worried for your career. I mean, an MDT of twenty-five per cent! You were becoming a living legend - and that's just among the prisoners."

"Nice of you to say so, Chris. Well hopefully that's all in the past now. I didn't say so in the meeting but we're actually on course for four point three this month."

"And that's why you're profiting from it, me old mucker. Just promise me one thing. When you're finally in the gaffer's comfy seat in two years' time, make sure you give me a nice easy post, will you? Let me ease gracefully into retirement. Head of Security will do."

The quip gets no response.

"Tony, what's wrong?"

"I feel like I don't deserve it."

"Don't deserve it? Fucking hell, Tony, you really are mad, aren't you! You've worked your arse off for months trying to get the MDT down. Tried every trick in the book, broke practically every rule. And now, finally, when you get a pat on the back for it, you react like ..." Jenkins is at a loss for words. "Don't you see, Tony? You won. You bloody won!"

But McKenzie is shaking his large head.

"That's just it, Chris. I'm not sure I have. I told you I went to see Djemil?"

"In Belmarsh?" Jenkins looks incredulous. "You went to see him in Belmarsh? You are bloody joking me. You and your Djemil obsession!"

"I knew you'd react like that. But why don't you listen to what I'm going to say? I asked Djemil about the drugs. That's basically why I went. And you know what he told me? He told me it wasn't Samuels behind the pigeon idea. It was Brannigan!"

Jenkins shrugs.

"Brannigan, Samuels - it doesn't matter, Tony. Because there ain't no pigeon no more. It's gone. Flown away, out of your life. And anyway, don't forget that, before this, it was Brannigan making out it was Samuels. And now it's Djemil trying to pin it on Brannigan. So they're all trying to pin the blame on each other - the whole lot of them. Which means it could be anyone. I have to say, though, if I had to take my pick, I'd still choose Djemil as the culprit. In fact that's probably why he's trying to put it on Brannigan now. So he can start the same thing over in Belmarsh - pulling all the strings, looking whiter than white."

McKenzie starts shaking his head again.

"What's wrong now?"

"Not wrong, exactly. But I just disagree with you about Djemil. It's funny, when I was talking to him, it was like we were on a level, somehow. Like he wanted to help me out. Saw me as a kind of colleague."

"Oh, here we go. Let me guess what you're going to say next. You're going to roll out your spy story again. Go on about Djemil being SAS, Schild being Mossad ..."

"Not Mossad. He was their target."

"Yeah, right."

"Chris, I know my theory sounded mad when I came up with it. But that's only because we didn't have the evidence then. All we had was the recording from the bug in the cell ..."

"Which we decided was a wind-up, Tony. That's what made you panic, get it back."

"Fine. But don't you get what I'm saying? When we talked about the conversation, we decided either Djemil or Schild - or both of them - we decided they must know about the bug."

A slow nod from Jenkins.

"And from my conversation yesterday with Djemil, it's clear he also knew about the pigeon."

Another nod, even slower this time.

"If you say so, Tony."

"Which means that Djemil - or maybe Djemil and Schild - they both knew about the pigeon as well as the bug!"

He says this with great excitement, McKenzie. Does the cigarette-stabbing thing. But the ratty face looks back at him nonplussed. Makes the tall man blow out his cheeks in frustration.

"Chris, it's significant because ..." He takes a slow thoughtful puff. "It is significant because the only other person who also knew about the bug and the pigeon was ... the woman on the phone!"

McKenzie heaves a sigh of relief as he finally gets there.

"So what you're saying, basically, is that the woman on the phone is a contact of Djemil's."

"Exactly! And then we had the Association Room fight, don't forget - two Israelis trying to kill a third one, and by that I mean Matthew Schild. Well, what if ... No, come on, at least hear me out. What if Djemil was from MI6, and those two Israelis were from Mossad? I mean, throw in the posh woman as well ... You've got to admit, it all adds up."

"Course it does, Tony. In fact we've got a lot of Krav Maga on the wings right now. The doctor's giving out cream ..."

"So you think I'm talking bollocks?"

Jenkins snorts out smoke like a dragon.

"Tony, listen mate. Your argument stacks up. On paper. But yeah, I think you're talking bollocks. The pigeon thing, I'll believe. Prisoners are clever like that. Always trying to find new ways to rule the roost. But not your MI6 theory as well. That's just too much. The way I see it, Djemil or Schild found out about the bug, probably because Janet put it somewhere bleeding obvious. Then they found out about the pigeon, most likely because Djemil was in with Birdman and his cronies. Or in with Brannigan. One of the two. And then one of them has gone, told their posh friend on the out about both these things. Simple. As."

Jenkins kicks at a pigeon in front of them. Watches as the urban angel flies up to a window ledge on the Admin block, starts strutting its stuff like it is on the stage. The bird dances left, it dances right, the thick metal bars a backdrop to the performance. And now, suddenly, behind the bars, entering stage left, the shadowy shape of a man's torso.

"Oh fuck! That's Simmering."

And with that, the two governors flick away their fags, march briskly back into that breeding ground of so many tall tales, Hatcham prison.

* * * * * * * * *

Unbelievable! For once in his life Governor Tony McKenzie is about to get a flyer, sneak home and - who knows? - maybe show his wife some love.

Then his radio blares into life.

"G4DP to Victor One, over."

Wearily, he takes the thing out of its holster.

"Go ahead."

"Victor One, can you call figures 2113, G4DP over."

"That's received, Victor One out."

Grumbling, McKenzie sticks the radio back onto his belt, dives into the nearest wing office to find a phone. Calls the number. Knows very well who it is. Wonders what chestnut Charlotte has for him this time.

When he gets through, Governor Rosesmith thanks him for calling. Says in her prim voice that she is Duty Governor today, has a planned intervention going on. Really needs to be there - "to support the staff, Tony." Problem is, a representative from the Israeli embassy has also just turned up. Out of the blue, apparently. Is waiting down the Gate right now. Insists she made an arrangement by phone that she'd be coming in to pick up Matthew Schild's property - and no, the woman can't remember who she spoke to. But she has all the ID, the paperwork, is ready to go. All the Gate staff need is for a governor grade to go down, get her signature on various forms, hand over Schild's prop ..."

Glad that such a ball-ache might at least be vaguely interesting, McKenzie toddles off down the Gate. Freezes en route as he realises he cannot remember where Schild's property has got to. Thaws when he remembers Janet saying something about Legal Visits - "stop it cluttering up your office, Mr McKenzie."

When he gets to the Gate, McKenzie sees the embassy woman through the sliding glass doors. She is smartly if soberly dressed, with shoulder-length hair, a green skirt and jacket, and a brown attache case. Charlotte in twenty-five years' time, he decides, motioning to the staff to let the woman through.

"Anne Stekel," she says, holding out a hand as she walks towards him.

"Tony McKenzie. I believe you've had to wait a while. I'm sorry about that. It's not the most attractive waiting area."

"No need to apologise. It was absolutely fine. I'm just relieved my visit was not wasted."

"Well, I certainly hope not," says McKenzie, now letting her through the door of the Gate Lodge and shutting it behind them. "But actually, just to make sure, do you mind if I check your ID before we go any further? I know the Gate staff will have already. But obviously handing over someone's belongings ..."

"No, no, I quite understand," says the woman, before rooting around in her bag and handing over a dark blue passport and an identity card from the Israeli embassy.

Studying them and failing to find fault, McKenzie hands them back. Suggests they walk over to Legal Visits where they can do the necessary paperwork, collect the property.

"You have an English accent," he remarks, guiding her along the perimeter wall.

"Everyone says that! Yes, I spent most of my teenage years in London. Just down the road, in fact, near the common. So I have to say, it's very strange being here," she adds with a glance at the mighty slabs of grey concrete to her right. "To think, just a mile away - but a different world! I had no idea."

"No. Not many people do."

When they get to Legal Visits, McKenzie locates Schild's property without any problem and, lying on top of the bin liner-sized transparent bag, an A4 envelope with "Paperwork" written on the front in Janet's neat spidery handwriting. Picking both of them up, he shows Anne Stekel to a bleak little room containing nothing but a table, two chairs. Indicates they should sit.

"Actually I'm glad you have come," he says. "I know the top governor here, John Simmering, has written formally to the embassy. But I would just like to say myself how incredibly sorry we are for Mr Schild's death. It is a tragedy, and it's one everyone who works here at Hatcham has been deeply affected by. You may not know, but the incident was initially referred to the police ..."

The woman looks up.

"Yes. Just in case there was any evidence that Mr Schild's death was not, in fact, a suicide. However that process is now complete. So, starting very soon, there will now be an independent investigation by The Prisons and Probation Ombudsman."

She expresses relief, the woman. Says the embassy would like very much to see the Ombudsman's investigation once it is complete, share it with Mr Schild's family. Asks what the closing of the police investigation will mean with regard to Mr Schild's cellmate.

"He won't be affected. Or rather, he won't face a murder charge. Although he is in another prison at the moment."

"Yes, I suppose he'd have to be."

Paperwork complete, they stroll back to the Gate Lodge, McKenzie carrying the bag of property. Deftly maintaining her interest as they pass an altercation between a prisoner and an officer, he starts talking about the problems of visitors smuggling in drugs. How, recently, drugs were such a problem, they were threatening to jeopardise the vital rehabilitation work the prison carries out.

"It must be extremely demanding," she says, nodding. "Being a Security governor in a big remand prison, I mean. Especially with all the visitors you must get every day and such a large group of staff. On top of all that, so many prisoners going in and out to court the whole time! Even then, I suppose the hardest aspect must be those things you don't expect. The things that come straight out of the blue ..."

She looks sideways at him as she says this. But only for a second.

They reach the hefty wooden door that leads into the Gate Lodge. Outside it, stop. Apologising for reaching in front of her, McKenzie presses a button on the wall, then stands back and waits. And it is here, now, at this very moment, that Hatcham's Security governor has a crazy idea. His craziest yet. He wonders whether the woman standing right next to him could be the woman who tipped him off about the pigeon. The woman who somehow knew about the drugs coming in. Who - fucking hell! - knew about the bug.

It is only this last possibility that restrains his remarkably strong desire to ask her about the first. And yet he is dying to know. Was it her? And if it was, how on earth does she know so much? In other words, is she MI6?

He turns to look at her. Cannot stop himself. Feels the question boiling up inside. Can only listen as, out of his treacherous mouth, erupt the words: "Er ... Ms Stekel."

"Yes?"

"Talking of things that come out of the blue, I had this phone call the other day ..."

"Oh right ..."

"Yes. It will probably sound very silly, but I ... er ... in the phone call, I got a tip-off about all the drugs coming into the prison. And the same person who rang me somehow knew about all the things I was doing to try and find out about the drugs. Even quite covert things, as it happens. Things that also involved Mr Schild's cellmate ..."

"Gosh ..." says the woman, suddenly taking a few steps away from the door so that McKenzie has to follow her.

Catching up, he looks around him. Waits while staff going off duty bundle into the Gate Lodge, slam shut the heavy door.

Then finally succumbs.

"Are you her?" he blurts out in a hoarse whisper. "Do you work for MI6?"

The woman purses her lips, as if she has just applied some lipstick.

"This cellmate you mention ... I'm guessing you mean Mr Djemil."

"Yes. Yes I do! You see, I think he was working undercover for MI6 and was on a secret mission to protect Matthew Schild. He was definitely not a normal prisoner, I know that. I could tell. And ... well, what with the phone call I got and the information the caller knew, and now you turning up to collect Matthew Schild's belongings ... and then this fight Mr Djemil had with two Israelis ... plus the fact that Mr Schild was also Israeli ... well, I'm sure you can see, it adds up. Every bit of it."

The woman nods thoughtfully.

"I suppose ..." she begins. "I suppose if you got a tip-off in the phone call, then you must have benefitted from the information. Perhaps even taken measures to dramatically improve the drug situation in the prison."

She pauses, but McKenzie does not move a muscle.

"And if that's the case, then you might say that you owe one to whoever made the call. Not that there can be any truth whatsoever to your outlandish theory!" she adds, making the observation sound like a command. But then her voice softens. "Although, I have to say, with your lively mind and your curiosity ... it strikes me the security services would be jolly lucky to have someone like you, Mr McKenzie."

And with that, the woman takes one or two steps back towards the hefty wooden door. Is motionless for a good few seconds before McKenzie sidles back up to her. Sounds awestruck when he speaks.

"Before I forget," he says. "I should probably give you this. It belonged to Mr Schild."

He reaches into his inside suit pocket. From it, produces two pieces of paper folded in four.

"Belonged?"

"Was written by him. It's a letter which we found in another prisoner's cell. But it's signed by a Matthew and ... well, I'm pretty sure it was Matthew Schild. It's addressed to someone called Farideh. She came here to visit him once."

The woman takes the paper. In a noticeably courteous way tells McKenzie she appreciates his remembering. Starts unfolding the quartered sheets right there in front of him.

"The top one's the original," he says, fussing at her side. "It's in Arabic, I think. Then you've got the translation underneath. And if you look at this bit here ..." - a large index finger points to some text near the bottom - "... it tells you how to access some information which Matthew Schild was obviously trying to pass onto her. See?"

Seconds drag while the woman scans the place indicated. End when she slowly looks up. Lets her cool-steel gaze fall on the tall haggard man in front of her: the corners of his shirt collar frayed to reveal tiny tufts of white cotton; the shiny size-twelve shoes splayed wide apart, stance of a silly clown; the bulky radio which won't stop chattering away, holding him hostage to the role of Victor One - a role magnificent in its mundanity.

And at this ridiculous figure, the woman smiles. Says in a calm level voice: "Do you know, Mr McKenzie, I think you might be a hero."

22210782R00135

Printed in Great Britain
by Amazon